Ogygia

Ogygia

Eschatos Diagram Novel

Monty St John

Sultrani LLC

One

Thock!

"Down!" At the sound of the yelled command, I dropped flat into the foliage and then rolled left. The crushed greenery released a sharp minty scent, which on a different day, I might have enjoyed. A line of overgrown trees guarded the vegetation. The eight of us were spread out along the trees to prevent stragglers from escaping the besieged manor. Vice commander Leig didn't want anyone to get free and alert the city lord. He also wanted anyone we found for interrogation.

Command be damned, I would rather be dry, I thought. The attackers had used magic to drop rain on the area for days, and everything was wet. Nothing ever dried out. Just stayed a damp, dismal mess. The Wizards had laid an enchantment on our equipment to deter the moisture and to provide silence. Supposed to make is noiseless. Neither worked out all that well.

Someone might say that the volley of arrows piercing through the overgrown trees sounded like rain. I wouldn't. To me, it sounded like death.

Rolling again to find better cover, I searched the horizon with reddened eyes. I thought I saw movement but wasn't sure. It earned me an arrow, a bare hands breath above my head. I rolled again, and one more time for good measure. Sometimes one roll wasn't enough. You had to go the extra mile or earn an arrow for being lazy.

I jammed the coin between my teeth while I looked through the perforated leaves. Clicking the coin released a metallic taste that coated my mouth. My tongue thought I ate a pile of slag. It quarreled with my throat, which wanted to eject the offending object. I pushed the urge down. Between fighting heaves to vomit, I rapidly clicked on the coin with my teeth, sending the code to the Wizard who commanded us and swore to me it would work.

Seeing it wasn't working, I spit out the coin. I took out a different one, a silver one this time. Under the sound of another volley of arrows piercing the trees, I heaved out the acid in my stomach. It did nothing to counter the metallic taste coating my tongue, so I sucked on one of the minty leaves lying around instead. Probably poisonous, but at least it created a different kind of nausea that was more tolerable. I left it in my mouth and put the silver coin between my teeth, clicking on it to send the code like before.

<<*You idiot. Quit chewing on the coin like it is yesterday's biscuits.*>>

I couldn't help but curse. I'm not an idiot. You are the idiot, Wizard! You are the one that told me to do it this way. Not that I said it out loud. I wanted to have the illusion of surviving. The Wizard would likely turn me into a pig and make me dinner.

<<*Just keep the coin in your teeth and talk as usual.*>>

An arrow impacted the tree I was hiding behind. I couldn't help but stare at it. Watching the fletching of the arrow quiver was somehow soothing. But, unfortunately, talking with a coin and a mint leaf in my mouth wasn't.

"Understood. We have a group escaping on the back path. At least a couple of dozen, with archers tying us down from stopping them. Need reinforcements to hold them back."

It took three tries to get the Wizard to understand.

Meanwhile, the number of arrows in the tree had grown several times. I considered changing position again and crouched to do so when the Wizard came back. It gave me time to count again, figuring we were up against at least three dozen, maybe a few more attackers on top of that.

<<*You'll have to delay them until my summons shows up. Don't let the people escape before the summons arrives.*>>

Eight of us against three dozen? They were better armed, better organized, and in a better position. How was that to work?

"We will be hard placed to do so. The people are aggressively moving on our position to escape."

<<Use your corpses to hold them in place if you have to. I don't care. You are dead if you let them escape.>>

I spat the coin out and didn't bother to listen anymore. If it wasn't for the rain and everything being so wet, I would have set the trees ablaze. Instead, I shifted back, running or moving in a crouch to avoid the arrows. Anyone still alive would know to fall back. Once I used the coin, it would have resonated with the ones they carried too.

Only five of the others were present. The other two that once graced our small team had fallen to the arrows. So now we just had the six of us.

None of them had a good look when I passed on the orders. They knew I had called the Wizards. They just couldn't hear what was said. That was something only I, as their team leader, was blessed to be the recipient. Like knowing the information somehow kept the majesty of the Wizards intact or some such nonsense. Of course, we all thought the Wizards were bleeding sacks of scat, so it didn't make much difference.

"How are we going to do this?" That was Ar, young and scared, barely with the unit for a month.

"We are going to have to distract or take out the archers while we tie down the main force trying to escape."

"How will that work?"

"Bait. One or two of us will have to draw arrows while the others try to kill them. Barrow. You are the best marksmen. You will try and kill them. Me, Ar, and Coln will be bait. The rest of you — Hoyt and Raul — will fall back to the rock slide. If we fail, release the stones and try and trap them in."

"We'll die!"

I have no idea who said it, but it wouldn't matter anyway if I did.

"The Wizards say they are sending a summon. If we don't hold out or run, it kills us. If we fight, we might die, but at least it's a chance."

We lasted a while.

Coln took an arrow first, but Ar died ahead of him. Arrow right into the eye. He had a look of peace when he fell. Three arrows hit all at once, and I couldn't dodge. It sounded different from when the arrows hit the trees. I looked at the sky full of rain-drenched clouds. It looked peaceful, at least until I saw a giant shadow press against the clouds.

"ZZZZZZZzzzzzz"

A dull, off-key buzzing rolled through the sky — and the dampness of the trees was gone, but I felt wet. Sitting up, I smashed the alarm button, one hand probing at my chest and shoulder where I felt the arrows go in.

Another flash. One where I died. I had dreams — except they were too real. All too real. Almost like flashbacks. That's why I called them Flashes. It felt more like remembering than dreaming. Who knows. Maybe it was.

I lurched up from the bed and staggered toward the other room, digging sand from my eyes. I picked up shorts from the floor, dropping my sleeping ones in their place. Food, exercise, and coding would help.

They always did.

Two

"Why is there a puddle of water in my autopsy room?" The question came in over the intercom.

Scott paused the game on his phone and threw it on the desk. He knew there was no point in responding via the intercom. Doc Matson would call him into the next room no matter what.

He grabbed the file folder of intakes that came in last night and badged his way to the autopsy room. Like always, he grumbled when it took three swipes to get in. Who the hell is going to steal a body anyway? Anyone who wants in has to drop a Benjamin on the desk and take what they want. So stupid.

The cold, sterile lights and dry air on the other side of the doors rolled through his nose. Doc Matson wasn't in the autopsy room, so Scott turned around and went out the side exit door next to the freezers. Three layers of badge in and badge out security. Not that it mattered. One emergency exit door propped open with a brick bypassed it all.

Scott followed the spicy scent of cigarette smoke and found the Doc leaning against the rail. The balcony wasn't much, and it was old. Probably older than the facility since it was a converted building. As rickety as it was, Doc was lucky he wasn't a customer of his facility.

"Hey, Doc."

Doc Matson enjoyed his last puff and rubbed it out. He tossed the filter over the rail to join the littered pile of previous days' smoking. He looked at Scott sideways and asked, "So why do I have a big puddle of water in my autopsy room? Soaked my good shoes walking into it, you know."

Scott offered the file folder of intakes, but Doc Matson didn't even flinch. Then, sighing, Scott pulled it back.

"It's simple. Number three that showed up last night is a frozen stiff."

"Don't call them stiffs," Doc Matson said absentmindedly. "Even a frozen body isn't going to create that much water on the floor. Spill, what is up? Come on, where's the leak? Or, did you try some freak sex thing with one of the bodies again?"

Scott recoiled at the horrible attempt at humor and wrinkled his nose.

"Doc! Truly, it's number three. The corpse is not just a frozen body but a real chunk of ice. The corpse is on the heavy-duty metal table because it's too much to put on the normal beds, and they didn't want to put it on the floor."

Doc Matson looked interested for the first time.

"A chunk of ice, huh? How did that happen?"

Another offer of the folder got rejected again. So finally, Scott just gave up and read the file himself.

"Says here that the guy hit a refrigeration truck and managed to rupture the nitrogen tank underneath."

"That's a load of manure. Hitting a truck is not enough to turn someone into a block of ice. Sure, freeze people to death or asphyxiate, but turn them into a chillcicle? Nope."

"I'm not lying, Doc. The stiff was driving a water delivery vehicle. Report comments say the dude not only broke the water tanks but he also ruptured the liquid nitrogen tanks at the same time."

Doc Matson wrinkled his nose and just scoffed. He also reminded Scott not to call them stiffs, ignoring the protest that he had just called one a chillcicle.

Scott went back to reading, frowning and looking intrigued, alternately. "Doc, if I read this right, it's a combination of just terrible luck. It was super cold and sleeting last night. The low temperatures and the way the collision smashed the vehicles in just the right way created an effect where the fire was on one end, and it pulled the heat out from where the water and liquid nitrogen poured on the body, creating the ice."

"Huh. Sounds more interesting than the usual mix of stabs, cuts, and head bashing. Shall we go check it out?"

Three

I stumbled off the treadmill and into the shower. I gargled some water, tossed down my morning pills, and a mouthful of shower water to down it. I had the whole house on filtered water anyway. The thick water streams helped clear away the earlier Flash — my name for it. I refused to call them nightmares or dreams — they were too fucking real. I had called it PTSD for a while but finally got tired of the arguments it caused and just called it a Flash. I had pushed it hard on the treadmill, something I didn't normally do on a Wednesday. But I needed it after the Flash.

A baritone voice cut through the sound of the shower. "You have a meeting with Peregrine in 15 minutes."

"Fuck," I muttered. I forgot the damn meeting was today. I killed the shower and stumbled out, minimally drying off while I shoved my body into whatever clothes were around. They were mainly clean, and I wasn't turning on the camera anyway. I yanked back my hair into a band on my way to the computer.

"You have a meeting with Peregrine in 5 minutes."

"Shut up, Immerlin," I shouted back. It didn't answer, of course. Immerlin was my name for the mix of virtual assistant devices I had hacked and hobbled together. The original was some freak female voice that I killed immediately. The voice creeped me out, so I replaced it. I found the baritone voice online, buying it from a music mix website. I even paid for it. It matched the one in my head from a Flash a few years back and just seemed right.

I settled in the ergonomic chair, adjusting everything into its place. I had a couple of minutes before the meeting started, so I found my smart cup and set the temp on my phone. Water and tea went in. It didn't matter that the water was lukewarm. Cup would heat up to the right setting and stay there for me to enjoy after the meeting.

My eyes drifted to the uneven stack of books, sketches, and pics that littered the other half of the room. While I had downloaded most of the pics, the drawings were mine. I drew the sketches from the Flashes, as well as compiled the books. I'd started writing out Flashes when a shrink told me it would help. Well, it didn't, or at least not quite like the lady shrink said it would, but I did like doing it. So, it became a habit. Making them into books was a spur-of-the-moment thing. No one ever read them besides me. And Alice. She used to like to read them when she was still here. Even then, I kept a few of my notes from her.

Some Flashes — were Hell.

I looked at the time and opened the web conference while simultaneously bringing up the source code for the Peregrine project on another monitor. Ron joined the meeting right on time. Figures. I clicked accept to let him in. At the same time, I told Immerlin to go on mute for the video call. I didn't want him chirping while I was in a meeting.

Ron's video was on. A skinny guy with a round belly. His loose shirt, no matter how classy the material his shirt was made from, did little to detract from the spider feeling you got looking at him, especially with his pinched features and tiny eyes. Even after a couple of months with the two of us conferencing back and forth, it still unnerved me slightly.

"Bret, it's good to see you."

"Hello Ron," I said back. "Did you receive the last code push?"

"I did," he responded. "Good work there. I have to admit that you are one of the best coders I've ever had the pleasure to have on contract. When it comes to delivery, it's ahead of time, and I have to do so little refactoring or make code adjustments from security audits."

"Ron, you know I don't sleep. It helps to get the code done."

He laughed. It creeped me out. The tiny hairs rose on the back of my neck and everything. I've worked with him several times. When he starts flattering me, I know he's about to ask for something, a thing that happens to not be in the contract or try to get work without paying. He got away with it once in the past, before I got savvy to what he was doing.

"I'm aware. I enjoy my eight hours, so I can't imagine it."

Eight hours. Goosebumps rose on my forearms, and I rubbed both arms alternately to make them go away. I made sure not to respond, though. I knew better.

"Anyway. The last code push is with the team to run the audits and then put them in the test harness. Given your track record, I doubt we'll have any issues. That puts us weeks ahead of schedule, something I never thought I would say out loud, but look at us."

I continued to wait but pulled up the hourly logs on the monitor. Out of the corner of my eye, as I smiled and nodded, I could see we still had twenty hours left on the contract. I was about to bring it up, but Ron beat me to it.

"Bret, according to my calculations, that leaves around twenty hours left over. So I want to use that for a small side effort."

"I have the same," I said. "We have twenty hours left. But, Ron, that doesn't give us much time to do anything too detailed. What did you have in mind?"

"I want you to talk to a friend of mine who is building a unified platform for trending material online."

That puzzled me for a moment. I had to ask. "Ron, you want to use your remaining hours to have me talk to someone else?"

"Not quite. I have a small side project in mind that will take the majority of the remaining hours. More than anything, though, I do want you to talk to them. They could use someone of your caliber for the coding, and believe me. They are flush enough to pay your full rate."

Ron, giving me a referral? Did the world end or something?

"Who are these guys, Ron? Trending material ... what does that mean?"

Ron smiled, creeping me out again. "I'll leave it for them to detail their business since I have no chance of doing a good job speaking to it. The company is called Inverse Voices. They have been in business for around four years, and they are in Series B funding. Flush with cash, looking to grow, but need coding talent to transform their platform to match the vision they have hatched. I'll throw the contact details in an email after this."

"Fine," I said. "Thanks for the referral."

"Happy to help my snap coder. I'll have my hands tied up anyway for a few months while I am working on getting this out the door. But I'll want you back, so don't get too comfortable over there."

"I'll do my best," I said. "And, the 'tiny' project ...?"

"Details to come in a separate email."

"Fine. Alright, Ron. That's — wait, who is the contact at Inverse Voices?"

"Sam Escarra. It's short for Samantha, but she hates her full name and uses Sam. VP of Engineering & Product."

"Fine. I'll fire off a contact email. Thanks again for the referral."

"Of course. Like I said, though, don't get comfortable over there. I will have a lot of work coming your way in a few months. And you know I pay on time."

While he does give me the creeps, Ron does pay very on time and does pay the full rates.

"Sure. I'll watch for your email. Thanks."

I checked the water. Just right. Tea needed a few more minutes. So, I walked over to the scattered notes and books and grabbed some clean paper from the stack. I jotted down the Flash in a couple of paragraphs: names, impressions, and similar stuff. I sketched what I thought the trees and foliage looked like in the Flash. Paused, then roughed out a vague map of the terrain from what I could recall.

I threw it down and retrieved my tea.

Flopping in the chair, I said, "Wake up, Immerlin, let's do the morning roll call."

"Of course," came the smooth baritone. "You received 119 emails last night, of which only four require any attention on your part."

"Immerlin, subject line, first email."

"First email, subject line, Annual safety inspection required on —"

"Immerlin, stop. Was a due date noted in the email?"

"Yes. 31 Aug 26."

"Fine. Immerlin, Forward email to Howard Kearns, subject car inspection, body greeting Howie, first paragraph, Howie, please find someone to stop by in the next month or so to pick up my car and have it inspected, standard signature."

"Email forwarded to Howard Kearns with requested text."

"Good. Immerlin, add this email and other registration requests to the forward list for Howie."

"Forwarding keyword list updated.

"Good. Immerlin, continue roll call."

"After re-filter, no emails require immediate attention."

"That's how I like it." I leaned back and finished off the tea. I started another tea to heat up when Immerlin chimed in. "Priority email received from Ron Desantos."

I waved at the air, prompting Immerlin to start the music. The motion sensors only worked when I was at the workstation. But, they proved handy when I was on a video call and needed Immerlin to do something and I didn't want to give that away to whoever I was talking to that I required Immerlin to do something. Or let them hear the sound of me typing.

The tea needed to heat up anyway, so I accessed the email and looked over what he sent. Ron had sent the email to both Ms. Escarra and me with a simple introduction and contact information. I typed a quick thank you and reply and sent my availability times. Finally, I built a short keyword list with the new company's credentials and data for Immerlin. Have to keep that automation rolling to make life simple and all.

I leaned back to decide if I wanted to add more when an email returned. That was fast. I clicked on it and saw a standard response, attached NDA and confidentiality agreement, and a tomorrow afternoon meeting time request. It didn't take long to send everything and set up the meeting.

The tea was gone by the time I finished, so I got up and stretched. Too much tea. One of my earliest docs used to bitch about the caffeine I drank. I had switched to kukicha to shut the doc up. A coffee taste and mild stimulation without the caffeine problems. I still drank tea, though. I just mixed it up a bit more — one day of tea, another day of the kukicha. I occasionally added in coffee.

I moved to the front room and manually opened the shades to the large picture window. Immerlin can do many things, but control over doors, locks, cameras, and blinds is not on that list. Maybe it's too many horror movies or my desire for control. I keep some things manually operated.

Alice used to give me a hard time about the house being so big. So many rooms, she said, and you use maybe half of them. Probably. I worked for it, though, and paid the taxes on time. So perhaps not using a couple of rooms was a waste, but it wasn't hurting anyone. Plus, privacy was a bonus, especially when I worked for clients who had severe privacy concerns.

Immerlin's baritone broke into my thoughts. "Incoming call from Dereck Eisenrohr."

I almost didn't accept it. I let it ring a few times and then sat down. "Immerlin, music off. Accept call."

Dereck's voice was the mix of anger and frustration that I expected. "So, you decided to accept this time."

Yeah, I was already regretting it. "What do you want, Dereck? If I didn't want to talk to you, Immerlin would not have even let you through. You know that."

"Fuck you and fuck your damn talking hardware. Get a real person."

"Probably not," I responded. "I'm working. What the Hell do you want?"

"How about a little humanity? Some concern?" His voice raised an octave. "I'm at the hospital and she looks washed out. You should come and visit once in a while. Maybe she will respond to you."

The idea of leaving the house made the goosebumps return. Panic flashed, and I tensed. Then, to relieve it, I rubbed my arms, saying, "I'll pass."

"Quit rubbing your fucking arms, you prick. I can hear it through the call. That's your mother laying in that hospital bed."

My mind flashed to the matronly stern-faced being that was my parent. It was not a kind thought, and I banished it to Hell, where I expected she would enter once she finally died. "I'm quite aware of who she is. And fuck you. I'm cold. I'll rub my arms when I want to."

"What are you, five? Quit being a fucking man-child and own up to being a half-assed son if you can. If Alice were here, she would be kicking your ass."

"If Alice were here, we wouldn't have this conversation. She would have already handled it, and you would be out of the picture, off jet setting somewhere, making money, like you did before she died. Brother-in-law."

Silence and Dereck's heavy breathing were all that followed. Then, finally, his response came from what felt like the other side of the universe. "Don't even say her name. She's the best of this fucking family, especially compared to you — where were you for the funeral, huh? She loved you to death, but you couldn't even step out of your house to go to the funeral. So now, your mother is worse off, and you can't find a bit of soul to see her before it's too late? You are nothing but a human tumor!"

I didn't say anything. Dereck had hung up already and wouldn't hear it. Who did he think was paying for that hospital stay, anyway? That was the only reason I was working again, as I had to mortgage the house to subsidize her care.

Dereck was wrong, anyway. I was at the funeral, just not by the graveside. The reason I had bought a Tesla was for its autonomous driving ability. I parked and sent a drone, letting it get close for me, streaming pictures through someone's WiFi hub that I hacked for an internet connection. I watched them bury her and cried in private. So many people came, and it was too open. No damn way I was going out there.

I got up. No code today. Especially not when I was upset. I moved from the computer, firing up the gaming console in the gaming room. Monsters, quests, and puzzles await!

"Immerlin, I'm out for all calls except for emergencies. Route all calls from Dereck to voicemail, transcribe and keyword search. Unless they indicate death or similar synonyms, don't alert me anymore."

"Yes. Filtering complete."

Four

It was cold. Bone biting so, with snowbanks swept against trees everywhere. From that alone, I knew I was in a Flash. I didn't have to find a clock, try to read or book or pinch myself. Not that I had a watch or book to try.

My point of view shook and moved, sometimes disappearing as we drove through snowbanks. I say 'we' because I have a lot of different Flashes. Not all of them are in the first person. This one felt like I was 'riding along' instead of 'being.'

Docs say it's my overactive imagination. Shit, I had one priest tell me I was possessed. Had another tell me I was the fucking demon that was possessing other people. Squirrelly bastards, all. That line of continued responses was why I quit trying to find help from any of them. Doctors and priests all ended up making it worse. I sometimes wondered if it was all those things or some mix. I was being possessed and possessing. Though what I feared — on days when it became too quiet or seemed flat — I feared that I was only dreaming while strapped to a gurney in some forgotten hole of a hospital.

The sensation of cold ripped me away from that thought. The feeling also made me sink deeper into the Flash. Senses connected, providing a sudden influx of inputs, smell, hearing, and touch.

We — the thing I was riding along with and me — dug into the snow, and I realized that the being had a huge schnozz — a bit flat one. Once I got past the litany of puerile jokes my mind conjured, I realized it was a snout with a cluster of jutting fangs pushing out of the lower jaw under it.

Am I a fucking pig? It tumbled around in my head over and over. As it moved around, I quickly realized it was true. Hooves, snout, behavior ... it all fit. The creature was less than a pig and more an enormous wild boar.

Not the first time I Flashed into something not a person. In fact, far from it. It had happened several times this year, alone. Last time, before the previous Flash, I was some odd geometric thing that I couldn't even visualize well enough to sketch. I couldn't look in a mirror any time during that Flash or a bit afterward. Seeing myself reflected on a surface somehow made me feel that what I saw back wasn't real. It seemed flat and blurry. Somehow, I presented an image that was a mix of too far, too close, too big, and too small all at once. I either went catatonic or exploded in intense nausea and projectile vomiting.

It was fucking horrible. Just another day in the life of Bret.

The cold feeling transmitted to me again. It pulled my attention back to notice we — the boar and I — pushed through a snowdrift. We were almost totally passed through the snow when we suddenly stopped. The air felt weird. I could sense it too. The boar snorted and shuffled around, sniffing at the air. Something wasn't right, though all I could see was snow and trees. Maybe the boar smelled something because we kept shifting around.

The heavy burden of some creature landed on our back, driving us to our knees. I heard a voice whisper, "Found you," right along with a powerful blow. It stunned us both, and everything swam.

"ZZZZZZZzzzzzz"

A dull, harsh buzzing sound exploded everything into sparks. I fell out of the chair, smacking my head against the TV stand. Stunned, all I could hear was blasting Opera music and Immerlin calling my name from all the speakers in the house. Timers showed up on all the TV screens around me, counting down to calling emergency services, my current doc, Howie, and even Alice.

My fingers trembled as they touched the back of my head and came away wet. I stared off into space for another couple of seconds before canceling the countdown.

"Immerlin, kill countdown. Kill the music."

My voice was shaky, and it took a couple of tries.

His baritone caught my attention. "Restarting emergency services timer. Biometric devices show continued elevated telemetry that indicates an injury."

"Immerlin, kill timer. Cancel the fucking thing. You idiot, I just banged my head."

"Timer canceled. Call initiated to Alice according to stated procedures. Ringing Alice."

Stunned, I stopped touching the bruise on the back of my head. Had I not updated that? It rang several times. Part of me didn't want to stop it. I wanted her to answer. She had held me so many times growing up when this happened and made the bad things disappear. Or, bandaged whatever cut or bruise invariably would occur.

"Immerlin, kill the call. Alice won't pick up. She's dead."

"Call terminated."

"Immerlin, modify emergency procedure."

"Negative. Emergency procedures cannot be modified during emergencies or elevated telemetry."

"Fuck you, Immerlin, Fuck you."

"Command not understood. Repeat."

I didn't bother.

In the bathroom, my face looked hollow and pale. Breathing deeply in front of the mirror, I closed my eyes and repeated the mantra. Feet, legs, pelvis, back, arms ... I rattled them all off and focused on visualizing myself as me.

I needed it.

Otherwise, I couldn't deal with the chaotic jangle of feedback shifting from being a human being to something that isn't. Just standing on two feet felt like a struggle. Any time I went from person to animal and back to person spun me in a loop. Clutching the edge of the bathroom sink kept me from kissing the floor again. My head felt painful enough as it was.

Getting my bearings, I finally got around to looking at the bump on my head. I couldn't see it in the mirror though I could certainly feel it on the back of my head through all the hair, which irritated me. All that damn hair and it couldn't pad my head not to get a bruise? What gives? I suppressed the urge to cut it off and elected to put my head in the sink and let the water run over it instead.

Five

I didn't bother going back to sleep. It was early hours, dark and crisp in the cool air. The treadmill wasn't going to cut it, so I took the cocktail the docs had built for me to help with post Flash events and went to the roof.

While the docs diagnosed part of my condition as Agoraphobia, wide-open spaces aren't one of my triggers. At least, my roof isn't. I owned the building, all three stories, and the roof. It was more a bottom-level garage and two medium-small apartments, one stacked on top of the other, connected by stairs. I'll admit to a bit of luxury when I was flush with cash. I had planned a roof full of solar panels for energy and a pool where the garage was for better exercise. The first got done before Alice died, and Mom went into the hospital.

When I had the solar panels installed, I made sure to plan it, so I had a walking path around the edge. I found it suitable for thinking and pondering, especially on cool early mornings like today. Better than the treadmill, at least. Alice used to tell me I should learn to run, but I liked walking. It reminded me of one of the more awesome Flashes when I was a monk. I was more of a bystander in that Flash, but we — the monk and me — walked for zen and cultivation. At least in the Flash. I learned the sutras and the patterns the monk walked. For the monk, each step built power and purpose. It never really worked for me in real life, though I sure tried. The habit of walking, though, persisted. One of the few ways I've managed to stay sane and functional.

I walked until the sun rose high enough for the solar panels to adjust to track the sunlight. Sweat was pouring in runnels, making the bruise on the back of my head sting, but it still felt good. Better, even. I did some calisthenics on the roof in the morning sun until I saw my neighbors stirring.

I toweled off the sweat as I went downstairs. "Immerlin, roll call."

"No new messages. Email from Ron Desantos, subject: small project. One web meeting, scheduled at 2 PM with Sam Escarra, Inverse Voices."

"Immerlin, start search, IV1. Depth level 3. Keywords: Inverse Voices, Sam Escarra."

"Acknowledged."

Once I got cooled off, cleaned up, and dressed, I looked at Ron's project. It was tiny, not his regular funny business. It took an hour to build the logic, and I kicked the rest over to Immerlin with instructions on how to finish it up. Repetitive, simplified coding like this was well within Immerlin's capability. All I would need to do is parse through it to make sure it met Ron's requirements and was tight.

That gave me time to use. Not a lot of time, but a good couple of hours before the meeting. I used the time to go over the initial material that Immerlin had discovered on Inverse Voices and Sam Escarra.

Miss Samantha was pretty impressive. She held dual doctorates in computer science and data analytics, both from Ivy League colleges. She had been a founder or board member of three other startups, all of them culminating in successful IPO. There was not much on the speaking circuit but a fair number of the necessary publications and patents that matched her doctorates.

Inverse Voices was equally impressive. The company was even more flush than Ron had indicated, with a steady income stream and a pretty strong upwards growth path. The initial investor wasn't one I recognized, but the pivots revealed it had a good track history for picking winners. The series B backers were more in my wheelhouse and were a solid group focused on maximizing capital earning. They weren't charity investors, by any means. Most backers are not, at least until they get closer to dying. Then, I suspect a dump of cash into organizations more oriented to doing social good would follow.

What bothered me was the core offering. Inverse Voices made its initial success by curating hard-to-get exotic writing happening across the world. Ephemeral mediums in social media, especially, were the company's first bucket of assets. Ownership in the transient spaces of the internet was a contested concept, ill-served by any country's laws. Inverse Voices curated content there and made it available to an internet clientele, translating, editing, and cleaning up the work to make it something they could offer as a product. They also generated several scholarly works to support their position and even dabbled in a couple of country's laws to build support and traction for their effort. The authors and lawyers involved had impeccable academic and professional standards. But, from what I could tell, it was typical corporate tactics. Their second run of money via Series B looked completely banked, though estimating corporate financials is blurry. Companies have too many ways to hide and bury actual actions.

"Immerlin, start search, IV2. Depth level 5. Keywords are authors of publications in IV1, layers in IV1. For authors, correlate times of publication and publication topics. For lawyers, the same correlation for lawsuits and client changes. Cross correlate both, especially if called as a witness or provided written support."

"Acknowledged. Reminder: depth five search estimate 77.8 hours to complete for initial results. Correlation estimate indeterminate."

It didn't hurt to check on a few things. Something about the company's situation was tweaking my intuition. More in-depth looks could wait. I was more interested in the codebase used for their online platform. A portion of it was open source, and more was poorly secured, stored haphazardly in online code repositories. While I'm better at writing code than being a pretend security sleuth, it never hurts to point out when a company is not securing the information it should. In doing what I did, I had to point out and fix bad security at times, and some companies would instead shoot the messenger than face the facts. Experience taught me that it didn't help to be too soothing in those situations. Diplomatic, yes, but no hand-holding. That sort of client politics always was a waste of time, pissed them off in the long run, and just ended up wasting their money and my time.

I pulled up this platform on one screen, and on a second one, a host of debugging tools. A couple of different screens had comparison code snippets and other software tools. After I interactively went through client-visible operations, finding a couple of improvement spaces didn't take long. Next, I made logical conclusions to a few server-side ones. Finally, I had Immerlin spin up a couple of virtual machines in cyberspace to test things as I thought of them or found them in code.

I leaned back to think. An eye on the clock told me I had a little time left before the initial meeting. While I didn't have a contract yet, experience had taught me to do a little footwork if I could before going in.

"Immerlin, activate the Argyle cluster. Allocate 200 droplets. Proton Trident search, Inverse Voices content list, starting today and going backward. Variable content template. Pivot on authors, keywords, ephemeral platforms, and tags as starting keywords. Dynamically add keywords.

"Acknowledged. Reminder: Argyle cluster activation raises costs past the monthly threshold. Reminder: estimated delivery uncertain."

"Fine, fine," I said. "I'll make it back with this contract or another one. This contact has me curious."

The web meeting software was one of the more secure ones, and I had gotten the hint from the NDA and confidentiality documents that I should at least pretend they were taking security seriously. So I fired up the computer and joined the meeting. It was one of those with a waiting room. I had one of my better pictures set up for this one so she wouldn't be staring at floating text. The software didn't like my clip-on mic when I did the sound test, so I switched to the desktop bullet mic.

Dr. Escarra looked like her pictures online: statuesque, short-cropped blond hair, delicate features, with piercing ice eyes. That didn't translate in the images as well as it did in the web conference. She was obviously in her office, and I had a good view of an outside skyline through the window over her chair.

"Good morning Dr. Escarra," I said.

"To you as well, Mr. Byrne. Any chance I could have you turn on the video? As much as I admire avatars, nothing replaces seeing an actual human. Video is, of course, as close as we can come at the moment."

Glad I had tidied up and changed offices. Sigh. I was not looking like a good start. "Sure. One moment." I pulled my hair up into something more presentable, and soon, she had a view of my simple office. I kept an excellent code design on the back wall to make it less bland. I could use a digital background, but I have yet to use a web conference software that does it justice, so I avoid them.

"That's better. Ron spoke great volumes about your skillset and capability, and it's nice to put a face to the work he glorified."

Did he now? Was he drunk? He usually doesn't talk about any of our work. "Very kind of him. We have done work for a few years now, across a variety of contracts."

She smiled. It helped light up her face. "Yes, Ron has mentioned your work off and on for a while. Full disclosure, he and I worked together in the past and have kept in contact. He has bragged about you, and I worked on him for a while to get us in touch. He has expressed that your coding skills are topnotch."

"Again, very kind of you, Dr. Escarra," I said.

We exchanged a round of pleasantries and 'do you know...' exchanges for a few minutes. Then, finally, we moved to what Dr. Escarra needed. Unfortunately, this polite talk was not my forte and made me nervous.

"I see we have an executed NDA and agreement. I expect you have looked into us, but in short, Inverse Voices specializes in curating and preserving ephemeral content on social media. Inverse Voices also selects the more unique and hard-to-get story content from key authors whose voices might otherwise be lost or silenced. Then, we bundle that content into our primary offering, which is an interactive space to allow readers, teachers, researchers to take advantage of this otherwise lost content."

Okay. That is pretty much what I had uncovered once you stripped away the corporate marketing speech.

"Before I go into the project that I would like to discuss, let me add a quick reminder of the confidentiality agreement. Anything after this point invokes those clauses. With requisite penalties of immediate redress under the law and or the release of 50 percent of the agreed-upon retainer."

I sat back. That was rather stiff. I had noted a couple of drop zones in the agreement, including that clause. I didn't expect Dr. Escarra to slap it down in the first meeting.

"Ma'am, I appreciate the clarity, but I've never had an issue with client confidentiality and don't expect to have any now or in the future."

She didn't love my close-to-smarty response, and it showed. Frankly, I didn't give a damn. I didn't like her confidentiality clause shit either. So get to it, lady, or let's move on.

After scrutinizing my face for a moment, Dr. Escarra leaned forward slightly. "Mr. Byrne, have you heard of the Ship of Theseus?"

"Can't say I have. Theseus, of course, I know from history classes back in college — the ruler of Athens, and all — but I've not a Greek buff, so I can't say I know his story particularly well."

"I see. The reference is less about the king or man, if you will, and more a thought experiment. Bear with me since it's relevant to our conversation. The reference is born out of what was a philosophical discussion. The problem is about the famous ship sailed by the hero Theseus. Athens kept the ship in a harbor as a museum piece. As time went by, wooden parts rotted. So the Athenians crafted new ones to replace those. And so on, and so on. Finally, after about a century, the Athenians completely replaced each part of the ship. The question then is whether the "restored" ship is still the same object as the original."

"Okay." I was puzzled. How is this relevant?

"You may be questioning my use of this metaphysical conundrum. Allow me to say this: for Inverse Voices, this question is less philosophical. We pull from social networks what we see as content that would otherwise be lost to time. In most instances, many sources contribute content to the stories we fashion. Think crowdsourced versus single-sourced. That becomes an issue for the person who believes they are the originating author. It becomes a question of ownership and authenticity. A story that Inverse Voices changes see numberless amounts of addition, subtraction, and refactoring. Like the ship, wood parts are removed and replaced. In the end, the story may look like the original in basic theme or name, but is far from the original."

I sort of saw where she was coming from but not how I featured in the equation. I said, "Okay. However, perhaps I misunderstand. I am familiar with the threshold of originality concept from working on patents in my life. I brushed against how twisted this can be when working on a contract for a company in the United Kingdom. That contract ran afoul of 'sweat of the brow' copyright laws that differed widely from those in the United States. Regardless, this topic seems like more of a question for the lawyers and the legal systems." Not to mention some serious, moral difficulties that should be considered. The music scene is full of this type of acrimony over actual or alleged theft shaped like this.

"Most certainly. However, the dissatisfaction of man is, without a doubt, endless. When legal measures fail, people have moved to more direct and less than legal, technical means. We have seen attempts from malware to even more intricate intrusions. And, I'm sad to say, successes in damaging our platform. Our platform has served us well, but we have had issues with the backend orchestration moving the data and keeping it secure. This weakness is giving our opposition an edge to disrupt the company. That process needs re-engineering, obviously, and not to mention different resource management. Critically, though, I need an analysis to depict what and where failures in the data transfer and the security occur in the process. You name a product, and I've used it to try and find out this information. Both the products and people who have purported to do the same thing have failed. Ron swears you are a wizard when it comes to this type of code analysis. I've spoken with several others who have used your services, and they swear the same thing. I'm looking for that kind of expertise, and everyone says you have it."

I said, "Obviously, I'll need more details to answer authoritatively for this type of detection. But, just for clarity, I specialize in working from the outside-in, probing and determining issues, before I look from an inside-out perspective."

"I'm aware of your approach. I'm fine with whatever path you take, as long as I can get an answer to this problem. I have no issues with your retainer or hourly rate. The only question I have is whether you are willing to work onsite ...?"

I was already shaking my head. "Sorry, Dr. Escarra. If you have chatted with Ron or any of my past clients, you will know I worked exclusively offsite. Unfortunately, I have several ailments that do not make travel an easy activity."

She looked down at her desk, eyes flicking to show she was reading something. She looked up. "I see. That does make some aspects more difficult. The internal checks will be impossible to perform at a distance."

I smiled and leaned back. "Dr. Escarra, I understand my travel restrictions may seem to limit my capability to help, but I promise you it's not an issue. I'm very familiar with leveraging remote access to perform any check I might need to deliver the analysis."

She remained unconvinced, I could tell. So I waited for her response since saying more wasn't going to change her mind anyway.

"I will consult with my internal staff and touch base with you. You can expect my staff to be in contact with you to talk about necessary details."

"I look forward to working together."

"Same here," she said. "Good day, Mr. Byrne."

I unclipped the mic and left the room.

"Immerlin, random thinking music."

It probably responded, but I wasn't paying attention. I started to make tea but put it down to walk on the treadmill.

I needed to think.

While I was happy with the money, what was Dr. Escarra after with this project? The details would show up soon, and I wasn't worried about the technical work. A couple of testing and search routines followed by the proper analysis would show everything she needed to identify data sync and security issues. Probably not all of them, but more than enough to harden and secure them against the most dedicated cyber attackers. What I didn't want was to be used as an ax to chop employees. Not everyone wants to address their problems. Some want you to be the demolition team to destroy an opposing block in the company. That wasn't what I was interested in doing, so I planned to tread carefully.

Immerlin's mellow baritone broke my train of thought. "Reminder: Catchup call with Howard in 15 minutes."

I'd curse the timing of it, but frankly, no time was a good time. I had canceled the last two catchup calls so that I couldn't put it off another one. Howie would kill me. Given he does so much to make my life livable, I can't alienate him.

Even if he is a lawyer.

Six

The view out the ice-eyed woman's window was pleasing. This world held many pleasures, and looking across the city line from her office in the heights of the clouds was one of them. It reminded her of the whimsy of home. Toggling buttons on her desk shifted the web meeting video to the window, letting her see the other four in ghost shapes on the glass with the beautiful cloud scene behind.

"We have made progress on two of the known bugs. Mainly in identifying the issues and locations of the problems. One we've solved, though the action wasn't very efficient and left behind a right-sided mess to clean up and spin in the media. The other is in process, with an expectation of cleanup finalized sometime next week." The lean, sandy-haired man's voice was measured.

The only woman of the four projections spoke, voice full of the sound of chimes. "Manageable?"

The sandy-haired man snorted. "Nothing is completely certain, and I don't think it is something we should gamble on." He glanced at the icy-eyed woman in the office. The movement lined up with a stir in the clouds around him. "If it were not for your prohibition, I would have finalized these issues myself."

The piercing ice eyes of the woman in the office stared back unflinching. Eyes dueled across virtual space until the sandy-haired man dropped his eyes, looking to the side.

Another voice broke the tension. The speaker was the youngest of them, blond, blue-eyed with Elfin features. "Do you want me to release the hounds? They are good at sniffing out these kinds of problems."

Ice eyes shifted to the Elfin-faced man, making him shift around uncomfortably. "We shall tread cautiously. Our stance will remain that we use those assets only when we must and where we must. While expenditures are necessary to ensure success, Upstairs does mind the books and hates unnecessary costs." She stared out the window at the cloud with a slight smile.

"What about the longstanding bugs? The ones we cannot pinpoint but know are there." The speaker was the last person, a bulky man giving off an ill-fitting atmosphere in his expensive suit.

The ice-eyed woman said, "What about them?"

The bulky man looked uncomfortable under her gave but persevered. "Are they not a core concern? Those bugs have troubled us the longest, and some have been the largest obstacles to growth due to the continued disruption they cause."

The ice-eyed woman traced the glass, fashioning a stick figure in the condensation. "I've found a consultant to help. Think of it as someone to look at things from the outside. But don't worry, it's a local figure with no knowledge of our workings. Their ability to analyze, synthesize and create results is rather unique."

The sandy-haired man frowned. "Is that wise? They could be part of the problem since we haven't isolated everything yet. Besides, we can run down and find bugs without outside help."

She looked at the sandy-haired man's projection and tapped the stick figure she drew on the window. "You won't be unhappy with the results. You might even say I have reasonable suspicion that they can solve one of those longstanding bug issues."

The sandy-haired man sneered. "I see. Nice and clean, then."

Her response was lukewarm. "Exactly."

"I don't like it." Even the look of annoyance came off as ethereal on the Elfin man's features. "We've never allowed an outsider to come in.

I know you have the command here, but I want it clear that I can't entirely agree. We should use our hounds to sniff out bugs, and if we discover one, we should resolve it like normal and not try to be fancy about it."

"I'll keep that in mind," the ice-eyed woman responded coolly. "For now, proceed as I have directed. You can chase any bug you want, but keep the public mess to a minimum. Exposure benefits none of us."

Her eyes met the Elfin featured man's eyes until he looked away.

Seven

The Tesla pulled into the driveway, the soft sound of its tires over gravel gently echoing. Inside was more chaotic. 1980's rock bounced off the interior windows blackened with the deepest tint allowed. It was a vain attempt at distraction but had helped me deal with the car ride. As it was, I was shaking but had managed not to vomit. At least, not in the car.

Motion ended, but I had closed my eyes to focus on calm breathing. Traveling isn't always this bad. It's never good but not constantly this terrible. I had Flashed again after falling asleep accidentally and thought the boar had died. It looked like I was wrong when Flashing sent me into an ocean of blurry, mixed-up sensations. I couldn't sense up from down or anything concrete until it finally dissolved. I spent the next couple of hours as a puddle on the floor. Any movement set off intense nausea that doubled me over. Finally, I managed to scrabble into the bathroom. Trying to take a shower was a disaster. The feel of water on my skin set off the vomiting and disorientation. If it hadn't been for the fact I had already canceled on Howie several times, I would have never attempted to travel.

The knock on the window I expected came, and I didn't bother to look, just pressed the button to unlock the doors and let Howie slide into the driver's seat. He entered with the expected scent of chicory and gently guided the Tesla into the open garage. It swallowed us and seemed to eat some of the anxiety of traveling and motion sickness from the car along with it.

Howie put one of the colored mugs he liked in my hands once we were inside, and neither of us said much as I slowly sipped the chicory coffee. Once my hands stopped shaking, Howie took it as a signal to talk. As always, we talked about how long it took to get here.

"Forty minutes? Wait, no, we had rain yesterday, so forty-three minutes," he said triumphantly. Howie was a big man. Not fat, just wide-boned and muscled. During the hell days of high school, he had been a demon on the football field.

"Forty-seven minutes," I muttered through the coffee. "I had to detour to go around manhole maintenance on 67th street." We exchanged a few other banalities. The entire exchange was for my benefit. We had had this exchange for years, a decade at least, give or take a few years. It helped. Not that I left the house for just anyone. Especially after a bad Flash. Besides Howie, only Alice could pry me free. At least, when she was around. Alive. Now ... I held up the dregs of the coffee in a toast and said, "To Alice."

Howie raised an eyebrow but raised his cup and echoed along. I didn't change the pattern often — next to never, so he said, "That's new."

"It seemed fitting," I said, voice muffled by the cup I didn't want to put down. Reluctantly I did so and met Howie's eyes. They were curious but kind, opposite the sense his muscular frame and profession customarily conveyed.

"I miss her." The statement was gentle. He was asking if I wanted to talk about her. It had been a while since we spoke about Alice. Our last discussion had been about what to do with what she left me.

"I don't want to talk about it." My response was gruff. The same one I had given all year since her death when he brought it up. The car crash was no easier to talk about in person than over video.

"You want to just get right to it?"

I was already digging out the hardware. I plopped down a virtual assistant cube and some headless computing bricks and started the power-up sequences right along with the laptop. Howie had long installed electric plugs for me at the table.

"Immerlin, silent self-diagnostic."

I bashed keys on the laptop to fire off tools to start checking Howie's network while he returned with more chicory coffee. He knew I found the scent of hickory incredibly soothing when I traveled. Howie had been the one to figure it out, anyway, on that long damn trip my mother forced me on when we were kids.

"It never ceases to amaze me that you can carry it around like that. Hey Immerlin, how's it hanging?"

Immerlin didn't answer. I looked at him sideways as I started reading network telemetry.

"You know it's not artificial intelligence, right? That's just Hollywood crap. The real AIs out there is not going to reside in my little virtual assistant's cube." I waved Immerlin's home around for good measure.

He shrugged. "Doesn't look that far off to me. Hell, you talk to Immerlin, and it answers. That's pretty damn cool. Not to mention useful. Why I don't have an Immerlin?"

"Buy an Alexa. It's a virtual assistant."

Hmmm, someone was banging hard on his network recently. Not successfully. While I'm a half-assed security guy, I've plenty of associates who are not. They had made good recommendations for protection. Howie just happened to have the financial figures to afford all of it. My fingers danced to process and sort the data.

Howie protested as he drank his coffee and watched. "I've had a couple of those virtual assistant types. You know it, too. Different brands. Different types. They all have the same issues. Hell, you outright killed a couple of them yourself."

"Yeah," I nodded, remembering. Virtual assistants were invasive, recording all the time and collecting data in ways they not only shouldn't but had no chance of securing. "You deal with too much sensitive client data to use them for work."

"That's my point," he said, voice rising. "I need an Immerlin. It doesn't do any of those things."

"True," I said, poking at more data. "Immerlin may have started like them, but he's far away from them now."

"My point, in one," he said, arms spread wide in triumph. "I bet dimes to dollars that you have him wired into the Tesla, my network, and all these ... things you brought, right?"

I stopped typing and looked at everything Howie indicated. Well, yeah, I guess I do. "Sort of true. It's a cobbled-together mess that works well because it's me. I do a mile of maintenance, tinkering, and constant adjustments that no one would put up with if they had one. If I added a clone of Immerlin to your house, it would break in less than an hour."

Howie just smirked and shook his head. "I get it. I get it. So don't worry about it. However, you need to justify it to yourself. It reminds me of a certain someone and a 'just another rather intelligent system' they were proud of ... and didn't share."

"I despise that comparison, and you know it."

"Doesn't mean it isn't true."

"Bullshit," I said, pausing the data capture. "Immerlin, process PCAPs 1, 4, and 5. Analyze, backtrace and identify top 3 leads. Push to my screen when done."

"Didn't you just prove my point?" Howie's smirk grew to a broad grin, and I rubbed my face in disgust. Why was I having this discussion anyway? At what point had I ever won in an argument with Howie?

"I don't want to talk about this. How about we talk about money?"

He chuckled and grabbed some notes from his briefcase tossed on the counter. "Sure, let's avoid saying I'm right and that you don't want to share."

I waved him off and sipped the coffee, alternating between eyeing the screen and watching him.

"I'll summarize since I know you magically can stare at miles of code but can't be bothered to pay attention to a couple of numbers that mean you can fuel your techno mess. The good news is your last couple of gigs brought in a lot of money, which I kindly turned into more money for you. Of which, I took a small fee."

I rolled my eyes. "We all gotta eat. So, can I ditch the mortgage yet?"

Howie pressed his palm my way to motion me to stop. "Not quite. You spent a fair amount of money servicing those contracts, and this latest contract will go a long way towards filling up the gap that service cost caused. However, unless this contract returns more income than projected, you'll need to take on a couple of more gigs before you can pay off the mortgage on the house. That means I should do my job and warn you."

Howie paused to take a sip of coffee with measured, practiced motions, giving me a moment to process.

"Hospital care isn't cheap. But, unfortunately, that bill doesn't look like it will cease anytime soon. I know you are more than willing to pay for it, but we are not taking advantage of all the resources we could take in to balance it."

I flat refused him. "No."

He paused and tried again. "Bret, I know how you feel about this. But, as much as I know, you would rather fade away from the world and not work again. It's why you busted your ass for years now so that you could have that kind of lifestyle."

"Howie," I cautioned, warning him with my voice.

He proceeded doggedly on.

"Alice made precautions for a situation where she might pass before you. That money is just sitting there. Dereck has tried to access it several times, a right he feels is his as he was her husband, but is specifically counter to Alice's wishes, so I have shut him down. You, however, have full rights to it, as she set the trust up to help you in the event of her demise. It was to help you."

I slumped, forgetting everything for a moment. Then, Alice came into view in my mind. She was a bundle of energy, head height shorter and not shaped to current society's norm, but still managed to convey a sense of strength and compactness, from the short curly brown hair to the deep blue eyes and the restlessness that drove her to pace when thinking. In my mind, Alice danced on the street, talked with random strangers, and fiercely defended me when someone became a bully. Alice was my sister, companion, and friend. A light in my life that was extinguished by someone else's uncaring, poor judgment.

Abruptly I stood and stomped down the hall. "I'm going to the bathroom."

I shoved my whole head under the faucet and let it run.

It was warm.

I watched it pool and swirl into the drain, face inches away. If I were at home, I would walk, but Howie's house is not safe. Not for that. It's too open. The neighborhood overflowed with the scent of too many people. I closed my eyes, muttering to myself the sutras the old monk from my Flash would recite. He would walk and say it, over and over, eating a path in the stone where he lived in solitude, seeking after transcendence. Walk and walk, saying nothing. From bell tower to drum tower in his temple. It had been one of the calmest Flashes when I was growing up, providing the solace, even if imaginary, that I needed. While in my Flash, it gave him powers. It just became comforting in real life. Like I had a little of him with me. Before his last walk in the Flash, the monk had spoken. Perhaps we both needed to hear his voice. The two of us were headed to a glorious walk; me into the courtroom and the monk to fulfill his destiny.

The water seemed to increase pressure and push my head down towards the swirling water. Then, I heard a voice mutter softly in my ear, the words indistinct but venomous. It shook me, and my eyes opened as my face pressed in the water.

I exploded backward, not minding that I dinged my skull on the faucet as I stumbled back into the door, water flying. Looking through my wet hair, I felt like something was in front of me in the mirror. Something horrible and dangerous. I charged without thought, my waist hitting the sink while my head smacked into the mirror, sending it tumbling in shards like a deadly rain.

Howie's shout was a mile away, and the door nothing but paper in front of his muscular physique. It took me a moment to separate and comprehend what was going on. Howie didn't wait for me but took control. When I finally started processing, he was already doctoring the cuts on my face.

"Don't move," he commanded, voice fierce. "I'd insist you go to the emergency room, but we both know you won't, and it wouldn't end well anyway."

I tried to nod, but his hands had my head in an iron grip. I could see his worried eyes looking into mine while his hands moved with practiced care. This time wasn't the first time he had patched me up. Growing up, getting hurt was almost a daily occurrence. He thought my mother was abusive for a while before he figured out it was because of the Flashes. It's hard to operate when you are human for a couple of hours and then something entirely different for the next. The mask of insanity is what my mother called it. She hoped the doctors in the asylum would remove that mask so she could have the child she imagined — but never had.

I could hear the guilt in his voice. "I shouldn't have brought up Alice."

He pushed my head to the side to pick out more glass with tweezers. It made my voice muffled as he pressed my chin into the blanket he had wrapped around me.

"No, it was okay."

The iodine burned as he aggressively applied it. His voice was calm, but his hands betrayed him.

"I appreciate you for forgiving me, but we both know it wasn't. Intense emotion always brings on a Flash. I should have known when you went to the bathroom that something was going to happen."

The way he said 'Flash' reminded me of the muttering whisper.

It wasn't the same.

I've had 'daymares' as one doc called them but not like that. Hearing voices was different, and I said that out loud to try the taste of it.

"Howie, it was different. Not the same."

His hands stilled a moment before continuing to apply iodine. "How so?" He asked.

I opened my mouth to say I heard a voice but closed it instead. Howie continued to wait, hands busy finishing doctoring cuts, turning my head one way and then the next to make sure he had gotten them all.

It was different, wasn't it? I wanted to explain that it was but equally didn't want to say I heard voices. Never good to admit that, especially with a history like mine.

"Hey Bret, how long have we known each other?"

"Since we were five years old."

"Who covered for you when you thought you were a bird and jumped off the roof and broke your arm? Kept your mother from going batshit crazy over it?"

"You did," I whispered, remembering that time. The memory had faded some, but it was clear enough: I had been a brilliant multi-hued avian in the Flash. It felt so good to fly, and I wanted to do it for real.

"How about when you thought you were a swordsman and went around challenging the kendo club? Who bailed your ass out when they beat the tar out of you and helped you get revenge?"

"You."

"How about when you disappeared in the woods? Helped you navigate that mess with Clair? Used their newly minted law degree to get you out of that hospital your mother deposited you in?"

All those times spun in front of my eyes. Each time was horrible, especially that hospital. The time in the asylum was what broke me for people. And made mother and me irreconcilable.

"You, Howie, it was always you."

"So, me. The person you can trust. Every time. Any time. The guy with a shovel and a bag of lime at the ready if you need it. So. What. Happened."

I could almost hear the voice again, playing out of memory, words indistinct but almost in reach. Like a language I had heard before but couldn't translate.

"I died in my latest Flash."

Starting was hard. Words were hard, especially about my inner self.

"Not the first time. Hell, from what I remember, that is the norm for Flashes. So what's special about this one?"

He let my head go, and I broke away from his eyes. "Not much. I was on a battlefield or something. Died when arrows hit me in the chest." Howie was listening like he always did. He motioned for me to continue.

"Another Flash started not long afterward. In this one, I'm some kind of oversized boar."

Howie suppressed a grin. "Normally, I would make a joke, but I don't think you would appreciate it. Having done this with you a few times, I recall that you usually have a bit longer between Flashes than that, but it's not odd to have them back to back. Not like it isn't stressful or anything right now."

I found myself nodding along. "Yeah, I know. It's just ... it's weird. The boar got caught before I woke up. Not sure what or who did it. Not like I can look around and such when I'm a boar."

"Really? I thought you could, you know, look around and even zoom in during a Flash."

Grimacing, I said, "Sometimes. With a few of the Flashes, I can kind of look around. It's just not consistent. Do you remember that one doc said it was part of whatever he called the problem? That it was a reflection of my mental state and emotions. Anyway, I couldn't look around in this one. Whatever it was that attacked the boar said something like 'I found you' or something akin to that phrase when it nabbed it."

He motioned for me to go on. I hesitated, but he was right. If I was going to trust anyone, it was Howie. Looking down, I said, "I won't lie. I was upset. You know when you brought up Alice. Even now, it still messes with me that she's gone. I went to the bathroom to run some water over my head. It helps, especially when I'm not home to walk it off. But, I swear ... dunno ... I thought I heard something like that voice and felt like I was being pushed into the water like I was going to drown or something."

It was quiet. Too quiet. I glanced up and saw Howie was looking at me with concern. That 'I want to wrap you in something for your own good' kind of look.

"Forget it," I said, slamming shut the laptop and shoving it and the other things I brought along with it into my bag.

"Hey, hey!" He said, grabbing my arm but letting me shrug away. The difference in strength between us was ridiculous. If he didn't let me go, there was no way I would have pulled free.

"Don't clam up or pull away from me. This time isn't the first time you have heard voices. Remember when you almost drowned in our swimming pool? If I hadn't pulled you off the bottom of the pool, you wouldn't be here. You swore to me for years afterward that you heard a siren calling you in the water. How about the server room incident when you worked for that data center company? They found you trapped in the server room. It had been two days. I had not only to bail you out but fight them legally when they tried to commit you since you came out talking about hearing voices."

"I know," I yelled back, face flushed. "I lived those moments. Yes, yes, and yes. All and more!"

"Fine!" He yelled back. "Then pay attention. Every time it has led to some kind of bad incident when it starts."

"Nothing is going to happen."

Howie wasn't convinced. He jabbed me in the chest and said, "Swear then. Swear right now, face to face, that you will call me immediately. No, you will program Immerlin to call me immediately if anything happens. Anything! If you don't swear, then I'm moving into your house to make sure nothing does."

Howie and I had shared a place before. My life drove him crazy, though, and I had forced him out for his good. No way was I allowing that to happen again.

Mustering up all the courage I had, I nodded. I turned to leave, and he stopped me, motioning firmly. Sighing, I put the bag down and pulled out everything to update the emergency procedures with Immerlin.

Howie wouldn't let me go until the changes happened, and he knew I wouldn't change them if I did it in front of him.

Eight

The next few days were dreadful. Every drift to sleep sent me into the Flash with a swirling ocean of inchoate emotion. I had tricks to break free. None of them worked. I spent hours biting back nausea over the slightest movement and physical touch.

Even my clothes brought it on. I finally got it under control with a mixture of medication and self-hypnosis. While I hated my time in the hospital, it was one of the tricks I had brought away. The right kind of biofeedback helped. I just had to figure out the approach. In this case, I miss measured the amount of ashwagandha to use. As a result, I ended up in a hazy state of limb paralysis. Luckily, I had just enough brain cells to rub together and started heavy-limb self-hypnosis. It helped me concentrate enough to deal with the sensations. Even when I slipped into the ocean of feelings in the Flash when I did fall asleep, the combination helped me start to manage the overindulgence of sensations.

When I got my head somewhat in order, I found a sizable box waiting for me. I was finally stomaching liquids, so I made a fresh kukicha cup to attack opening the package. It contained the equipment that Inverse Voices required me to use. Their laptop and installed image and a particular router to act as a hardware virtual private network.

I like security. But, I didn't want other people probing my network. Luckily, I keep a separate internet connection for this kind of crap. In fact, I maintain four different lines on any given day — five or six, when clients warrant — not to mention a separate room for unique clients with security or privacy needs. One shielded against signals. When I had it built, it originally was to soundproof the room. Adding extra shielding to prevent signals was trivial. Too many times, I find client hardware is a bit too snoopy for my comfort. It all has to balance. I like my secrets to stay mine. They want to be secure. Remote contractors had to be an easy vector for attackers to penetrate the corporate network.

I plugged the router from Inverse Voices into the one I own, and it did exactly what I expected. It was a router plus plus. Full of a couple of additions that started probing, learning, and setting up shop in my home network. Or, in this case, the client network I built primarily for them. It complained about my router, insisting on a direct connection. And the router was not going to allow any further progress until that was done.

Inverse Voices is either really cautious or one of those evil empire companies. My bet was on the evil empire. Having gone down this road a time or two, I had my own sensors in place, mainly below their ability to detect without some serious effort. That's the beauty of owning the ground. You can control what's there. Some very tailored software disguised as software drivers and attached hardware in my case. A tap on the incoming and outgoing Internet. Pulling my router out of the mix would remove many of those sensors, but I could still monitor via the Internet tap.

Sighing, I warmed up another cup of kukicha and decided to go ahead. The only risks I could really see were their hardware trying to access the biometrics I used. I heavily customized the watch and vest I wore. Like the Tesla, I had long ago altered them to suit my needs. Their protections are not invincible, but I'm confident that access was impossible without throwing an alert.

Inverse Voices' router phoned home with a complete dossier of information about the fake network. It didn't make me happy at all. When I fired up the laptop, it up did something similar. Pretty much anything I did on this hardware was monitored and scrutinized to the Nth degree.

I decided to be cautious since they were so snoopy. I had supported an interesting product on Indiegogo a few years ago. It was a pad that generated white noise waves. The branding on the eye pad marketed it as an efficient way to massage the eyes and face while providing relaxation. It worked, too. But, I also found it was convenient to inject noise into speakers. Most people don't realize the same speaker that can put out sound can also be reversed to record. It just takes the right effort. Gadgets we use daily are built to do it efficiently. It just gets overlooked.

I situated the soft pads of the white noise generator over the speakers and microphone of the laptop. A simple webcam cover completed the controls. I could do more, but it wasn't necessary. A couple of tests made me happy everything was working like expected.

I navigated the tools and software accesses installed. They didn't stint there, at least. I read the directions and warnings the company required. Being busy pushed the last few days of nausea away some. Squinting at the information, I fired up a few chats to connect with Inverse Voices engineers.

It didn't take long before I ran into the first roadblock. Typing in the chat, I asked, "So, I need to connect with someone from the Back End Engineering Team? I thought you were the man, Stefani."

I could feel his shrug through the chat. "Aiioo, I am — if you need something from the Back End Engineering Group. I know the names are close, but we are different departments in IV. So you gotta connect to Nandini at BEET to get the access you want."

The right emojis ended that chat. I turned to the one where I was chatting in Russian to Nogol from the Back End Engineering Team. "Nogol, so I have to talk to the Back End Engineering Group guys?"

His response was a thumbs up.

Sighing, I closed that chat up and rejoined the Second Technical Group chat. Idly, I wondered where the First Technical Group was in the labyrinthine mix of teams, groups, and departments.

Inverse Voices had a naming issue. No one seemed to have a detailed org chart. The people I met worked for other contract companies or service agencies.

I found a place to edge in. "Linda, who is the contact that you go to when you run into roadblocks?"

Linda had helped navigate some of the messy org charts already, so it was worth a shot.

She sent back a smiley face and a name.

Elise Carpenter.

"What's her role in the company?"

Linda typed, "Vice President of Architecture. Not sure what that means, necessarily, but she had been the one to cut through red tape for me when I needed it."

I thanked her and asked for the email and contact information for Elise. When she sent it over, I closed up the chat.

Maybe she could cut through some of this red tape for me.

Moving carefully out to the front, I decided to brave the treadmill. Walking hadn't been too bad today, and I wanted to get back to my normal swing of things. On the way, I called out to Immerlin.

"Immerlin, text Howie. Feeling better. Finally, be able to eat. Will check in again in a few hours."

"Text message to Howard Kearns sent."

That should put Howie off for a bit. He had been all over me to make sure I was okay the last couple of days. So I got on the treadmill and cranked up the music.

Activity helped.

Always did.

Nine

A few days later, I was elbow deep in code and typing in several chat tools to various engineers for Inverse Voices. Contractors, too. Unsurprisingly, most of them were foreign, not that it bothered me. I spoke Russian, Italian, and Afrikaans reasonably well. After several consultant gigs that worked in machine-translated language, I had picked up a smattering of just about all the major business languages to supplement those three. It was enough to make the right jokes and gist the general atmosphere. When that fell flat, Immerlin interjected to help me save face.

The video call — sans video, of course — was with a very sunny Elise. As advertised, she had cut through the red tape and connected me to what I needed to get started finally. She was not only bubbly and easy to get along with but equally used a stylized sun for her avatar. It flickered when she spoke, making it look like the sun kept shimmering.

It was a nice touch.

"Sooooo, let me get this straight," she said between smashing the gum in her teeth. I couldn't see it, but it was a pretty distinct sound that I had picked up over the last couple of days working with her. "We had someone throw a missile at us?"

"Not quite," I said with a chuckle. "I was just using an analogy, so don't take it literally. Your data is a moving target, and someone used some crafted software to intercept it. Unfortunately, the attackers didn't quite fail, which is the problem, since while your security stopped it, the fix re-routed things in a way that let them take advantage of the change."

"I don't get it. That just seems absurd. Can we not talk about missiles and moving things and be more specific?"

I laughed as a cover for the typing I rapidly fired into a chat. I had coded a bot that was a mini version of Immerlin earlier. Thankfully, chatbots are simple to code, and I needed the bot to juggle all the conversations. So I had it take over temporarily while I focused on Elise. We had started down the road of missiles because she hadn't gotten the more technical explanation in the first place.

"Allow me to try again. Your front-end software aggressively sweeps ephemeral space — chats in social media, alternative reality platforms, and numerous other locations — and brings it back to your aggregator servers. Most of that activity is done by APIs — application programming interfaces you access. Data you pull into your platform. Because of the sheer amount of data in motion, you can't do it all at once. Think of it as a relay race. The baton is the data, and it has to be handed off several times to win the race. Are you with me so far?"

"I gotcha," she replied, smacking her gum. "The servers you are saying have a problem are some of those relay runners."

Nodding, not that she could see it, I said, "Yes, the servers are part of the issue at hand. Pulling data back and staging like this keeps out a lot of issues, but you also push data laterally at times as well. Mostly, when a server is overloaded, having issues, or needs to be taken offline for maintenance. Again, you are moving a lot of data. Servers don't have a lot of time to perform their processing, so you can say they get impatient if they don't receive an expected response. When that situation happens, they look for a replacement to continue to stage and pipeline data as directed. All this happens automatically as part of the engineering in your platform."

"Okay," she said, popping her gum. "So, what's the problem?"

"When a server feels 'impatient,' it asks every server it knows to see if it can take on the data it's trying to move. If a server says 'no', the requesting server ignores that server and lists it to not ask again for a while. If a server says 'yes', it moves the data and then lists it to ask again as a priority option. That means if any server says 'yes', it gets short-listed to be asked again if the situation repeats. The issue is our cyber actors. They tried to create a slow down in this process to see what would break."

"Which it didn't," she injected.

"True, the system did not break. However, it did react, and the cyber attackers caught on to your process. They traced some of the data centers you use to move data, built replicas of what those servers look like, and have been 'lobbing missiles,' if you will, to get your system to re-route data to their servers. From what I have been able to gather, they have succeeded more than a few times and are siphoning away a tiny amount of your data."

"That's insane," she protested. "How can they do that? We check and re-check the servers before we allow data to be sent to them. It's one of the dashboards I pay attention to every day."

Elise somehow managed to make her upset feeling still seem cheer-ful. I wish I could communicate with her technician versus her, but whatever. My job is to point out and educate, not handhold. If they only connect me with folks who have surface-level understanding ... well, they get the best I can give them to have it make sense.

"The answer to that is in your authentication checks. You expect certain responses when you interrogate the server before sending data. If those responses match what you expect, you consider it valid, whether that server is your server or someone else's server. That's what is happen-ing here. You don't disguise what you are looking for as an answer at all, so the attackers used that to build responses to get you to send data to them."

"What do you mean we don't cover up or mask what we ask for?"

"When you send a request for authentication, and the server provides something that doesn't match, you return an error message. The prob-lem is that the error message is too helpful. It outlines what you expect to have returned, data-wise, which makes it easy to spoof and allows the attackers to pretend to be the correct server."

"Oh shit," she said.

"Quite well put," I said back.

We both laughed. We had moved well past politeness into a more casual atmosphere. While Elise had egged me a few times for not using video, we worked together well enough. She didn't have the technical bench I would like, but the relationship worked.

"When can I expect to have your analysis of this to pass on to the executives? I don't want to spin up the powers-that-be until I have that, a timeline of how long it's been going on, and some idea how to fix it."

"Yup. Smart move." I sighed.

"I'll push and get it laid out tonight. I'll include a few other suggestions to help secure against this activity, like making sure you are interacting with a server in the right data center. You collect that info and have it handy, so you might as well incorporate it in the security anyway."

"Sweet! Um, damn, looks like you will wriggle out of the virtual coffee get-together I was planning for this evening."

I shook my head. She was persistent; I'll give her that. It wasn't some geekiness or charisma on my part, that was for sure. She just was that kind of person, always trying to suck you into her social circle.

"I'll take a rain check."

She exited with a cheerful goodbye. I killed the conference, muted everything, and leaned back to rub my eyes. The motion pulled a little on the cuts, making them sting. I still had a few of the deeper ones bandaged up. Speaking of ... I checked the time. Of course. No rest for the wicked.

"Immerlin, video call Howie."

"Connecting."

Howie picked up after the second ring. He looked fresh, like he just woke up, even though he probably had been up for hours already. "How are the cuts, partner?"

"Passable," I responded. "When will you quit asking about them?"

"Let's see," he said. "You came to my house, banged your face on the mirror in my front bathroom — fixed by the way — cutting it all up, and didn't go to the emergency room for a check. You then spent the next couple of days barfing all over the place. So I should get another three or four more calls asking about it at least."

"I surrender," I said, raising my arms.

"That's more like," he said, chin raised high. It highlighted the scar along his jawline. Unless you had the right angle, you couldn't even see it.

"Speaking of scars, whatever happened to the girl who gave that scar? Not often a beauty shows up at a party, throws her arms around you, plants a kiss and a cut on your neck at the same time."

Howie laughed, tracing his thumb down it. "She got five years for attempted murder. You know she was looking for you. It was all a case of mistaken identity. I took that scar for you, partner."

"Maybe in my dreams," I retorted, chuckling. "I've had no beauties hugging me for ages now, and surely not back then, as gangly and pimple-covered as I was. Anyone who can't tell the difference between us is blind or insane. Maybe both."

"More seriously," he asked, voice lowered slightly. "Have you had any other Flashes or events?"

Howie, if you were a woman, I would have married you. Well, wait, the idea of a girl with your muscles — pass. Not my style. I'll have to stay single, I guess.

"Nothing. I stayed up the whole night after your house but followed the medicine regimen the doc ordered after that. I forced myself to sleep with the usual help. It's been a dead zone since I came back. I've had nothing but that ocean of overwhelming sensations. I've got that in hand, however. Managed to walk and keep food down now for a bit."

His eyes searched mine to see if I was lying or hiding something. He must have been satisfied with what he saw since he didn't say anything else about it. It had been a bit unbearable, especially the first day. No one likes to think they are crazy or going down that road, even if my current doc says if I can contemplate the idea of being crazy that much, then I wasn't. It sounded more like platitude than medical advice to me, but he and I didn't love each other, so I suspect we would part ways soon. Too different of personalities.

Howie and I traded some usual banter about games before he signed off. He and I had been lifelong gaming buddies, though I suspect where I used it as a refuge, he enjoyed it for the way it was meant. Speaking of ...

"Immerlin, query IV report 9 status."

"Pending final. Waiting for instructions to PDF and send."

Hehe. One of the top rules of good consulting was building padding to have the time to deliver correctly and well to the customer. In this case, everything I told Elise was already written. I pulled it up and scrolled through it.

"Immerlin, IV report 9. Update section 4, 5, and 9 with data in IV9 folder, IV9a-finds, all documents."

"Yes. Format?"

Hmmm, table or embed the spreadsheets? It is easier to embed in the PDF, but it might not look as lovely if printed or pulled out to be put in the slide deck. So let's do the table. It's only three columns wide and shouldn't break the formatting.

"Immerlin, table format exact."

I might as well set it all up.

"Immerlin, queue IV report 9. Spellcheck. PDF. Save IV9 folder. Archive IV9 folder, title Inverse Voices Interim Reporting, today's date. Schedule share file upload, 2130 hours, target archive."

I ignored his response.

It gave me some time to stretch, work out and play some games before I had to try to sleep.

Ten

The beautiful plan to relax and slip in a few games while I leaned on Immerlin to do work for me went up in smoke. I had just started on a tower defense game with a generous mix of city building on my console and didn't get ten turns past the tutorial before reality broke into my gameplay.

Immerlin's baritone cut across the game music blaring on the speakers. "Incoming call from Justin Acquaro, EVP, AnStol One Ventures."

Justin, huh? He and I had a few decent engagements, mainly me poking holes in his technology and pointing out ways to do it better. The last meeting had been a few months ago. Since then, we had a few emails starting an annoying back and forth exchange that went a couple of rounds. When that died out, I figured the deal had stalled since we never reconnected. Immerlin reminded me again as it rang a few times. I threw down the controller and leaned back. "Immerlin, console volume mute. Accept."

Justin's voice was exactly how I remembered it, though a bit distorted from the background noise.

"May I help you?"

"Bret. Sorry for —" Whatever else he said got eaten by what sounded like a passing car or something. Justin's voice came back in fits and starts, saying something incomprehensible before he ultimately dropped out.

I waited a few minutes before picking up the controller. Then, I put it down. I waited another few minutes. Then, figuring I was safe, I turned the volume back up and started the game again. But, of course, it wasn't in the cards.

"Incoming call from Justin Acquaro, EVP, AnStol One Ventures."

Sighing, I threw down the controller again, turning the volume down myself this time.

"Immerlin, accept."

Justin didn't wait for a greeting this time. "Bret, sorry about that. I should have waited to get off the street before I called."

I shook my head. "Don't worry about it, Justin. I know you are a busy man. What can I do for you, sir?"

"Busy doesn't cover it. Let me tell you ..."

Justin started filling me in on his woes as a new information security officer for his company. I mostly tuned it out, thinking about the game I wanted to play. I had little hope for this to turn to work, but Justin had sent me quite a few referrals over the years, and I felt I owed it to him to at least listen to him vent.

"... where you in. I want to chat and see if I can leverage a bit of your ten-pound brain to give me some help."

That caught my attention. "In what way? You are not going to try and twist my arm to work for you full time, are you?"

Justin gave a gruff laugh. "Nope. I know better than to ask that. Anyone else would have messed themselves over the compensation package I offered you, but you were like iron. So, no, I need something else. Remember A1V's Final Sentinel service?"

I pinched my chin, pondering. "I do. If I remember correctly, you guys built a lightweight agent that can fit on endpoints and servers. Something like a next-generation replacement for current endpoint detection and response."

"We like to feel we are a bit more innovative than just a replacement, but essentially, yes. Don't forget, we not only load as a service to monitor the endpoint with our agent and make that data available to security analysts but also keep a shadow installation at a driver level. That lets us gather the information that otherwise can't easily be accessed and prevent malicious software from shutting us down without throwing an orchestra of alerts."

I rolled my eyes. Every security company had some line or another that set them apart from each other. Some cunning trick or approach made them different. Some of the marketing was even mildly true. But, mostly, it was a new spin on an old idea.

"Sure. Final Sentinel, then? What did you have in mind?"

"Bret, you have a head for this kind of stuff. Final Sentinel is doing well. It's fair to say Final Sentinel is the majority of our stable revenue growth in the last couple of years. I like looking ahead. It's obvious to me, though not necessarily the rest of the C-suite that Final Sentinel will not be enough to get us to the target our investors want us to reach. It's doing well and on a good growth path, don't get me wrong, but it's not going to build the $20 to $30 million the company needs over the next couple of years. It will flatline. It's already starting to flatten out."

"Sounds like you have something in mind," I said, wondering where I came in. None of this was new. A while back, I had told Justin that the company was working in a limited market unless they could expand the product's capability or find a niche in the market it could serve. The endpoint detection and response market was already full of many players who did the work well. It is tough to topple and replace giants unless you have something truly unique. That usually translates to crafting and showcasing a can't-live-without product. Otherwise, it would do okay but probably stall.

It sounds like I was right.

"I do, indeed. I've encouraged engineering to add to the shadow installation mainly around some features. I don't think we are using all the horsepower we could when it comes to that. A fact you pointed out a while back. So, I'm working on winning hearts and minds over here. I want help from you on some analysis showing that this sector would be a good place to grow. Suppose I can expand Final Sentinel or even rebrand or craft a new product, especially if the numbers you find support that it would be reasonable to see good revenue opportunities.

In that case, we have a chance to achieve our goals. Don't want to get fired, you know, on my first gig as an executive."

"Sounds like you need a mixture of business analysis here: part brand analysis, part product profitability, and incorporating support for an expansion or new product creation."

"That's it. Or, something like that. I don't have a lot of time at the moment, but are you open to a call later this week to talk about it? I will shoot you the numbers, stats, and some information around the changes I'm thinking of as well over email."

Later this week doesn't mean right now, which cheered me up. "Yes. Any particular day or time?"

"Remember Angela? I'll have her organize the time and set up a web meeting. Then, you two can hash out the best time between our calendars."

"Okay. Looking forward to our talk."

"Thanks, Bret. Will touch base later."

I made a few notes and added a reminder to Immerlin so I wouldn't forget. I wasn't putting too much stock into it yet. Justin liked to talk a lot. I had wasted too many hours with him on pointless talks that did not lead to work. I had a bit of a lull at the moment, so I wasn't going to turn him down. At least not yet.

I picked the controller. It was time to get back to more important things.

Eleven

It was colder than before. That was the first thing that struck me. We were in a cage — or, more clearly, I felt like I was in a cell. I rapidly tried the techniques that might wake me up, but none worked. Finally, I sighed internally and just leaned into it. Maybe relaxing helped, since where I felt disconnected before, I felt more in tune with the boar than I did the first time.

Flashes had progression to them. Animals were more manageable in some ways to adapt to than people. It's just ... hard sometimes. I already had body image issues. Not because I felt too fat or short or thin. No, my body image issues were wrapped around not feeling like I was always human. That shit had almost killed me several times growing up. Nothing like breaking bones and nearly dying because you think you can fly. Or you were having issues walking because you lived in something with no legs for months when you slept. Or, in more softer ways, like the intense nausea of the last few days.

I wanted to look left, but nothing happened. No surprise there. The boar did get itchy, though a little later, and moved to rub on the bars.

That let me see it wasn't a big cage, and I couldn't see much besides snow blown by the wind on cold stone past the cage. Even that was in varying shades of grays with hints of other colors. Last time, it had not struck me that the boar had such limited color perception.

I suspected the boar was imprisoned in a cave or something open to the weather. A food bucket was at the end, and the bucket had food or something in it, but the boar was repulsed by it. I could vaguely sense it was rotten or poisonous, though I could not smell it. The boar obviously could tell. No surprise, given its nose is typically regarded as its strength. That kind of excited me. A sense of smell was a rarity in Flashes, though it had happened off and on in the past.

What intrigued me was the fact that the boar hadn't eaten the food anyway. Boars think with their gut. It's by no means an exaggeration, and the whole reason the insult existed in the first place is to describe someone who did the same. That indicated this boar was intelligent or had some means of discernment. Of course, it wouldn't be the first Flash like that, but I had experienced a few where my 'other' half was pretty much a rock when it came to being intelligent.

I tried my entire bucket of tricks that I had built over the years to see what I could feel/sense/do. Sadly, aside from seeing and some vague sense of smell, not a lot. I was getting a few things. I could tell it was cold and had a faint perception that the boar was thinner and laying down. Not much else. The boar squealed from time to time, and there was a hint of how hungry it was. It was disappointing in some ways. The Flashes with a lot of magic were the best, and being caged and bored was shit. I had hoped for something different than the usual short-term ride before I died. Death frequently knocked in Flashes. Aside from a few, the majority of Flashes ended after a couple of times. Some of those Flashes were awesome, and it was disappointing. It happened so regularly that I had thought it was purposeful for years. Then, I just figured it was my brain and bad luck.

Time is fuzzy.

Hell, in real life, I struggled to keep track of it. Coding could make a whole day and night disappear if I didn't set alarms. I went into a fugue that I had evolved after so many times. It was a sort of a half state where I didn't pay attention to much unless relevant. I crafted the fugue out of self-defense after I entered one Flash after another that was just overwhelming or fucking horrible to endure. It helped to fade back, which always got me the crazy label from the docs when I talked about retreating from what was happening in my 'dreams' while I was dreaming.

They didn't understand how overwhelming or fucking terrible it could sometimes be. The docs said it was my thoughts and brain.

I laughed.

Even I wasn't that fucked up, and with many Flashes, I had no concept or awareness of the subject. Not a lot of time to read about fantasy worlds when you are strapped to a gurney and drugged up.

The fugue saved me from real insanity. Most of the time, it worked as I wanted. Sometimes it didn't. Saying I didn't have complete control over the fugue I claimed to have built to escape the dream I was running from reality for went over about as well as you can imagine with the docs. I learned two important things during that time that stuck with me. One, nobody understands reality. Everyone pretends we share the same space. Two, enough drugs pumped into your body can even make the Flashes fade away.

I came out of the haze gray of the fugue when I realized the boar was very upset, squcaling and calling. The fugue had a good hold on me, so it took a bit of effort. I ended up in someplace dark before the pain transmitted by the boar pulled me back into focus.

The boar hit the top of the cage and rebounded on the cold stone. It jumped around, and I figured out that there was someone in the cave with us. Found it. From what I could make out, the figure looked like a giant yeti as the boar jumped around trying to charge at it or gore the creature through the cage. The person, a hunter, I guess, seemed to enjoy the torment. I tried to calm the boar, and eventually, it got tired or maybe listened. I don't know which.

The hunter crouched down a bit away from the cage and looked at it. From the way it folded when it crouched, the creature's legs were all wrong to be human. Its torso was very long, I suspect, and some kind of wood mask obscured the face. Hard to tell, given the boar wouldn't look at it directly. Now that I had time to observe, its features were nothing remotely human-shaped, more like a gator or croc the way the jaw jutted out under the mask. The thing did talk, though. I knew that voice. It was the one that whispered the first time when it landed on the boar's back. The words were surprisingly clear.

"Look at those eyes. So pretty. It makes me want to gouge them out, yes, but not yet, no, not yet. A skimmer, yes, it looks like a skimmer. They will be so happy, yes, a rare skimmer, one with power in its gut. Weak, so weak. I want to eat it."

If I had a head, I would shake it, wondering what the hell it was saying. The language sounded like something I had heard before, but hell, I had scraps of shit from all over the world. Somewhat Farsi or Egyptian sounding with a lot of different sibilant combinations. That I could understand had me baffled. The language was always a puzzle in Flashes. If I Flashed into something human or human-like, it wasn't too bad. Animals, though? I never could understand when people spoke around them before.

The boar's screaming and squeals jerked me out of my contemplation, and I realized the hunter had moved closer, almost to the bars of the cage. It had trapped the boar. Literally, the stone had melted like water and fused around its hooves. It couldn't jump, move or dodge. What caught my attention the most was the hunter's eyes. They were like a pair of deep abysses from the gaps in the mask, sucking at my very soul.

I don't want to be here. It was my first instinct. I started mentally screaming and thrashing, trying to run, flee, anything to get away from the soul-sucking feeling. Its eyes were like a hunter, and I was the prey, and it was one second away from killing me.

"ZZZZZZZzzzzzz"

A siren cut through the hunter's eyes like a saw. I surged up from the giant bean bag that acts as my bed. Heart pounding, it took a second to comprehend. I could hear blasting Opera music and Immerlin calling my name from all the speakers in the house. Timers showed up on all the TV screens around me, counting down to calling emergency services and Howard.

I trembled head to foot. I couldn't see anything but those fucking eyes almost about to devour me.

"Immerlin, kill countdown. Kill the music." I had to cancel it twice so he wouldn't call Howie

His baritone caught my attention. "Restarting Howard contact procedures. Biometric devices show continued elevated telemetry that indicates distress."

"Immerlin, kill timer. Cancel the fucking thing!"

"Timer canceled. Call initiated to Howard according to stated procedures. Ringing Howard."

Great. Damn you, Immerlin.

"Hello, Bret, you okay?" I could hear the concern oozing from Howie's voice. I also listened to the sleepy low tone of a woman in the background. Shit. Great. I had woken up Howie, and he had a date night. Lovely.

"Dude, it's fine. I just had a short episode, and Immerlin called you. Sorry I bothered you."

"No, not at all. Do you need me to come over?" Howie muted the phone, but I could imagine him telling his current date about his crazy friend who had faced up nightmares. Not that Howie really would or did. It just made me feel better to cast myself as a fucking shit.

I called Howie's name a couple of times before he came back off mute. "Look, don't come over. Let's video conference in a couple of hours when it's a decent time. Then, you can stare at me face to face then and see everything is fine."

He didn't give in, but I pushed, and Howie finally relented after warning me not to forget or say work got in the way conveniently. I promised and hung up. I dug myself out of the bean bag and set Immerlin to turn on the music, lights, and so on. I found some semi-clean clothes on the floor and made my way to the treadmill.

Everything would be better with exercise, tea, and maybe some food.

Twelve

She was displeased and had made no attempts to hide it.

"Have I not warned you to take the Homegrown ones seriously? Did I speak only to hear my own voice? As you can see, the result of not listening is we are one short now due to negligence."

The three ghostly projections on her office window glass looked at one another. The bulky man in the ill-fitting suit was missing.

The ghostly projection of the woman said, "Who would have thought the hacker in Germany was so adept? They seemed primitive, a weak threat at best. Who would imagine that they could rally so many allies or be able to bring something back? Nevertheless, we had to act, especially once they fought back."

The ice-eyed woman tapped the woman's ghostly image on the window, making it tremble. "And it led to his death."

"Dammit," the Elfin featured man exclaimed. "No way this should have happened without a leak or someone plotting against us. Let me release the hounds to sniff this bug-like bastard down."

The sandy-haired man grunted in disgust. "Again? How do you expect to keep that under wraps? The hounds are like behemoths smashing into everything. Hiding them from view is possible but not with events so close together."

"Be quiet." The ice-eyed woman's command shut them all up. They watched as the woman contemplated something outside her window past their ghostly images.

"Let me remind you that every failure erodes trust from Upstairs. I will speak to them about this, to explain our losses and failures. But mind you, I expect better performance than this. So put the right teams on this and chase it down."

The Elfin featured man echoed, "All teams?"

It got him a glance from the ice-eyed woman. "All the 'normal' teams. Don't engage anything else, especially the special ones. It's too expensive to use them. Unless you want to bear that cost?"

That made the Elfin-featured man look away.

"I didn't think so," she said.

Thirteen

Some days you can't get ahead. I had barely turned the shower on when a baritone voice cut through the sound of the shower. "You have a meeting with AnStol One Ventures in 15 minutes."

I cursed into the water that was splashing on my face. I forgot that I set up a meeting with Justin. It had taken his assistant Angela and me a couple of attempts, but we found a time that worked. I had just forgotten about it.

By the time I made it to my workstation, Immerlin had alerted me.

"You have a meeting with AnStol One Ventures in 5 minutes."

I said, "Yeah, I got it, Immerlin."

It gave me time to put my hair into something presentable that didn't make me look like a wet dog. Long hair is incredible; long hair sucks. I grew it partly out of a response to the hospital cutting my hair down to the skin while in the asylum. I kept it because of Alice. She talked me into it for Locks of Love. Donating my hair felt odd, but Alice could talk me into anything.

Thinking about Alice made me slump. Immerlin starting the web conference made me shake it off.

I shook my head hard, hoping it would send the thoughts flying. But, instead, Justin's face came into view, and I put it behind me.

"Bret, glad we could find a time to get in touch so soon."

I turned the video on, hoping I didn't look too worn. "Hello, Justin. Yes, Angela and I were able to find a couple of appointments on your calendar."

Justin laughed. "Yeah, it's best to set up more than one. Did you get the new NDA?"

I nodded. "Signed and sent back already. I also attached a basic state of work to define a couple of hours for our conversation."

Justin nodded, a small smile touching his lips. "I can hear your point loud and clear. A man has got to eat, right? So I authorized at least ten hours of work to cover our conversations and some basic footwork. I hope that you give me a more detailed outline of how much time you will need once I get numbers in your hands."

"I'm glad." I was, too. Justin had an annoying habit of burning my time without paying me. So I decided on being blunt by attaching an SOW to convey the point.

Justin started to say something, but I heard his phone ring through the video call. "Hey, Bret. Could you hold on for a second?"

I nodded, and he muted the conference to take the call. Justin had a harried look that didn't look feigned, so I expect it wasn't great news. I could see him get animated before he shut off the video. I muted my side.

"Immerlin, start search, A1V. Depth level 3. Keywords: AnStol One Ventures, breach, intrusion, malware, data loss."

"Acknowledged." Justin came back on the video, his brow chiseled into a valley. I unmuted at the same time he did.

"Bret, I have to get back to you. I have a small emergency on this end. Let's get in touch at the next appointment or faster if it makes sense."

"Sure. Need a hand?"

Justin shook his head and shut down the call.

I stared at the screen until Immerlin let me know the results were available. I pulled them up on the computer screen. I couldn't see anything directly tied to A1V, but a lateral link to Amazon Web Services outage in an East Coast data center. The same kind of lateral link to a Jenkins vulnerability. A proof of concept that was reported yesterday. Not my favorite automation server technology, but I liked the butler avatar. It helped me remember it more than some of the more esoteric avatars for automation technology. Some crossover links between the two. Given what I remembered about A1V's automation setup, they could have an issue related to it. After some pondering, I made some notes, primarily speculations, and queued up another, deeper search to spin on it.

"Immerlin, morning roll call, end queue, add results of A1V2 search."

"Acknowledged."

That left me a gap of about two hours. I could get an early start on the Inverse Voices work, but I pushed that thought aside. Instead, my eyes drifted to the uneven stack of books, sketches, and pics that littered the other half of the room. I had added a few new pictures that I downloaded to the mix.

Getting up, I went over to the wall, where I had the new cluster pinned. It mostly showed different kinds of boars. I was torn between what type of boar most identified with the one in the Flash. I had it down to a small handful. Hopefully, the Flash would last long enough to find out. Too many times, I didn't even get that far to figure out what I was in the Flash before it ended. Usually with my demise.

For the alligator-faced hunter, I found plenty of parallels. I settled on a picture from a roleplaying game. A bit of Photoshop on my end added the requisite garments it had wrapped around its form. It didn't quite match perfectly, but that was the norm. Usually, I would try to pronounce and then store the language I heard, but I couldn't this time. I had just understood the damn thing, which was baffling me. That ... just didn't happen, and I didn't know what was different this go around.

I shuffled through the pile of notes and sketches until I found what I was looking for in the mess. It had the words the hunter said in English. I had crossed out the unnecessary words to focus on keywords.

Eyes. Skimmer. Power in its gut. Eat.

The first could be a metaphor. I didn't know enough yet to be sure. Power is in its gut. The desire to eat the boar. Those I could see as clear correlations to the boar.

What bothered me was the reference to skimmer. What had tripped me the most in the Flash was the crawling feeling the damn thing was looking at me when it looked into the boar's eyes. That freaked me out a bit in combination with the reference to a skimmer. It might as well have said, I see you.

My skin was crawling thinking about it.

Fourteen

I had to work with Elise the next couple of days, and she finally pinned me down. That's why I was standing in the gaming room about to join a virtual reality chat room. Thankfully, it was a closed virtual room, but sometimes it invoked the same stifling, unsettling feeling that meeting people in reality did. I had Immerlin ready and armed with half a dozen ways to interrupt and pull me out if I needed it. He would record my speech and monitor it for the keywords to kick those off if I needed them. I took a deep breath. We'll just have to see how it goes.

I joined the chat room.

A scene familiar to the screens of many Hong Kong cinema movies greeted me. The setting was a Chinese tea house. Well rendered, it was three floors tall, with a few fantasy elements strategically interwoven. Not something I had seen, so maybe a custom build.

Someone had set up a couple of bots to act as NPCs, dressed to match the setting. I followed one into a room on the second floor, greeting a mess of people who couldn't be more out of place in the background. My current avatar was Zhang Wuji from the book Heaven Sword and Dragon Saber. I figured any fan of the Condor Heroes would recognize the look, mainly since I chose to carry the Dragon Saber today. In front of me was a mixture I didn't quite expect: about a half dozen people, mainly in Disney or Legend of Zelda avatars. A Sleeping Beauty, Mara Jade, Zelda and Link, and two others, one in some generic mech in gray and white; the last avatar something that would fit into the Scorpion

King or a similar film. We had names off, and I hadn't bothered to look at the VR name list.

Sleeping Beauty zoomed over to me first. "Bret, you made it!"

Well, that answered that question. Elise's VR handle was ELSB, so I guess it made sense. "Hello, Elise. Thanks for inviting me."

She motioned me over to the others at the table. I suspect that if VR let her, she would have snatched me, and I would have been pulled along whether I wanted to go or not. But, thankfully, it had not grown to that point yet.

"Everyone, this is Bret. Let me introduce everyone. This is —"

Mara Jade interrupted her. "SB, it's kind of pointless to have avatars and a different identity online if you are going to spam our names every time we meet someone new." She looked at me and waved. "Wassup? I'm running Mara Jade. Call me Mara, MJ, or something like that, and you'll get my attention."

In order, they all fired off their handles. The mech was called Cyclone. The guy running it indicated it came from a story called Lancer Horizon. I had never heard of it, but there are a lot of stories out there. The last guy was called Dominating King from Overlord of the Cosmos but went by King. I had never heard of it either.

"Zhang Wuji. From Heaven Sword and Dragon Saber. You can call me that or Bret since SB has already leaked out my name."

After some small talk, I found myself in a small group with Mara Jade and Cyclone. It didn't take long to get down to one of the questions I dreaded, mainly what do you do, and all that.

"I'm an artist and web writer, how about you? ZW, what do you do?" Cyclone's voice sounded young, though, with filters, you could sound like anything you damn well pleased these days.

Mara Jade snorted, and I figured there had to be a joke there, so I went out on a limb. "Something similar. Writer, huh? Would that be a writer of a story called Lancer Horizon?"

If avatars could blush, I suspect he would have. Instead, Mara Jade burst out laughing. "He got you, dude. Right off the bat. You owe me five bucks."

That started a bit of banter that was somewhat refreshing. Really, as long as it wasn't face to face, I could handle most people just fine. On-line — piece of cake. Eventually, they cornered me, and I confessed to being a code writer. It was Cyclone, as usual, who asked the question.

"Do you work for IV too?"

I caught the 'too' reference but chose not to dive on that grenade immediately. "I'm not an employee if that's what you are asking. That would be SB."

Mara Jade giggled, something entirely not in line with the avatar in my mind but matched with what I was piecing together as her. I had already keyed in all of them for Immerlin to search on. I had a tiny window scrolling with interesting tidbits Immerlin had gathered already. In reality, all of them worked for IV directly. Even Cyclone. It looks like he was indeed the author of Lancer Horizon, or at least he had the same name, but he also worked for IV in their Innovations department.

"Dude, all those folks over there, they all work for IV. It's only you, me, and Cyclone that doesn't."

Well, well, Mara, why would you say that? Why lie? Is it because everyone on the internet lies? Bad habit? Or something else?

Eventually, our little clique broke apart after I fended off various interactions and questions that had me wondering what was going on. Mara Jade and Cyclone worked well together, playing the foil for each other in their roles. However, they seemed a bit too focused on digging for information to make me comfortable. Eventually, I found a good reason to exit without being too rude. Immerlin had messaged me that I had an important call from Michael Varen, VP of Engineering for Wing7. I had done work for them a couple of years back, but nothing since then.

I pulled off the VR goggles and gear, setting the equipment back on its rack.

Elise was part of the crowd paying me, but I'll have to be a lot more forward in rejecting future invitations.

"Immerlin, accept call."

A pleasant tenor came through the speakers. "Mr. Byrne?"

"That's me. What can I do for you?"

"I'm the chief engineer for Wing7, the project head ...."

I really disliked people who explained what I already knew, especially when they did it condescendingly, when, if they thought about it, would realize that I knew who they were since we had worked together for almost nine months.

"... and I understand that you had done some work for us on natural language processing three years ago.

"That's correct. I helped re-engineer your computing cluster into a configuration to support your expected intake. I also wrote some custom logic for you to make the language identification process more efficient. You and I, we actually worked together several times that year."

"Ah ... yes, now that I recall, we did work together a few times. There is, however, a problem. Not with you or your work. The code repository ... we had a ransomware event, and it was sadly encrypted. You probably saw the news."

"I'm sorry to hear that. Never a great thing to have to happen."

"Indeed. There have been difficulties, and original copies of the codebase are no longer available. We are in the middle of a merger — it's public, so no worry about disclosure — and we have conflicting versions of the codebase. The auditing agency's review says the codebase was altered from the versions we employ. Our engineering team disputes that."

I would feel bad for them, but I didn't. Without a change control process — which Wing7 didn't have implemented when I worked with them — it would be difficult to determine. Whatever. No point in burning bridges.

"By the terms of our agreement, I did not retain any copies of the custom code that I developed on your behalf."

He was quick to rush in. "By no means am I indicating you retained code you shouldn't have. We also acquired rights from you for exclusive access to private code you developed independently of us. Namely your NLP-DICE, NOP-YANG, and IPROS code packages. You provided a signed, secure transfer of that code. Unfortunately, that's part of the ransomware impacted codebase. If possible, we would like you to resend those code packages to our engineering team."

"I can do that. Do you have a secure portal you want that code uploaded to?"

"We do. I can transmit that link and credentials to access it after our call. If you would upload the data and respond to my email with your time expenditures and billing rates, as well, I'll see you are compensated."

"Thank you."

After the call, I sat there for a moment. It wasn't the first client that had ransomware. It was a damn plague for anyone on the Internet. I just had never had a client contact me to resend the code before. On the heels of the semi-skilled elicitation going on in the VR chat, it raised my hackles. I would be slow-rolling the response. I wanted to take a few moments to contact Wing7 independently and put out a few queries. Speaking of, I reviewed the data that Immerlin had pulled for me while I was in the VR chat room.

Mara Jade. Her text and behavior patterns in her profile and words led Immerlin to dig up ninety, no ninety-one profiles with identical or similar patterns. People have lapses in security, no matter how careful they are. Few people have spent as long as I have to build a custom search and reconnaissance combination. In some ways, Immerlin is better than a dozen analysts.

Just like his namesake from one of my earliest Flashes. Nothing escaped his eye, not even the tiniest mites.

Fifteen

The last slog through code had me beat. I was beyond tired, but sleep was a shit option on a great day. So I opted for a bath instead. While I had run out of money to convert the garage into a pool and hot tub, I did buy a bitching whirlpool tub. I stumbled there, leaving behind a trail of clothing. It met and joined the other clothes I abandoned regularly. Sadly, one of those things Immerlin couldn't do was pick up clothes. I tried to integrate him with an auto-vac, but it never worked out. It would have been awesome if it worked, but alas, it ate clothes instead of picking them. So I finally just sucked it up and went for a dreaded pick-up once a week, so I didn't break my neck tripping over my clothes.

I dumped a few soothing powder mixes into the tub while it filled. Then, finally, it was ready. I stripped off the biometrics I wear, told Immerlin to monitor by speaker, and slipped in. Few things are heaven like a warm bath filled with salts. It reminded me of herbal baths that so many people in my Flashes would take. I had no idea what was in theirs, but mine was Epsom salts with activated charcoal and rose. I was not too fond of the other scents, and I've never seen a hickory scented version.

The soothing feeling sunk into my bones, sending me into a comfortable fugue.

I must have fallen into sleep.

I have a hard time with rest. It sneaks up on me like an assassin when I least expect it. I usually don't drop while in the bath, which caused me a momentary panic. I struggled through the fog and finally regained some clarity. Breaking open my eyelids felt like lifting a mountain, but I succeeded. Seeing snow in the cave startled me. It took a second to compute, and then I was frightened.

It didn't recede until I realized the hunter wasn't around.

The boar didn't leave its eyes open. But, even while the boar's eyes were closed, I could pull in a medley of scents that felt almost as good as seeing. While I wouldn't call it radar, I could smell the snow, stone, woods, and the faintly reptilian scent of the hunter.

The boar felt weak.

I could sense its energy was at a very low ebb, and it felt super thin, like it hadn't eaten in forever. I couldn't tell how much time had gone by, but I would venture days, maybe a week at least. Time never matched up well in the Flashes. It was always a crapshoot of how much or how little time would go by between Flashes.

The smell of the hunter grew stronger, combining with an odd astringent odor I did not recognize. Maybe the boar did since it staggered to its feet. Eyes open, I could see that not much had changed, though the stone under the caged floor had been ripped and torn into spikes several times. I had the feeling it had been tortured or had struggled with the hunter on many occasions while I was away.

The smell grew stronger and the boar more agitated. A strong woody scent overpowered my senses, mixed with the hunter's scent. The boar slammed into the cage several times in reaction to something I could not perceive.

Both of us were shocked when the hunter came rolling into the cave to slam against the wall. The hunter was wrapped up in a battle with what looked like a small tree with heavy, green leaves. Whatever it was, the hunter was fighting with it. Their struggle revealed he was indeed reptilian, covered in skin that looked very alligator-like. He also had several protruding stems that I recognized as arrows, having fired and been pierced by them many times over the years of having Flashes.

The tree flexed and flung the hunter into the wall. It had a definite face and vaguely humanoid structure, though it definitely was a tree. The thick leaves were either some armor or something it grew. The tree bled sap, the source of the woody smell.

The other scent must be the hunter's blood.

Their rolling battle came close to the cage several times, enough that I got a straight glimpse of the tree's face. It looked feminine to me, which is probably wrong on some level, but I decided in my head that it was female.

The boar tried to smash the cage again to little avail.

I lost sight of them for a short period. Then, the hunter conjured spikes of stone that grew from all sides. The tree woman retaliated with a shower of leaves, pulling them from her body, which sliced through the stone spikes like a saw. The fight devolved into a brawl again after that. I suspected they had both exhausted their powers earlier, though I had nothing to base it on.

Something made me want to help.

Maybe it was the expression on the tree's feminine face or the distaste I had for the hunter. It was one thing if the hunter was going to hunt and kill the boar. It's the cycle of life. But torturing him? What he had done was beyond that and definitely in the realm of the twisted. Given I thought the boar was aware and possibly even intelligent, that made the hunter's actions more criminal to me.

I started talking to the boar, urging it to watch, to wait for the right moment. I had done this before in different Flashes, and nothing had changed, but I so wanted it to this time. I like to think I can influence them, the people and things in my Flashes, that they are more than my feverish back brain conjuring up imagery to deal with reality. One doc told me I was repressing memories, that I had been abused. If I had one surety in life, it was that Alice would have gutted anyone who had tried to do that to me as a child.

No one was stronger or more protective than my sister.

Even if my mother despised me, it was utterly outside her wheelhouse to be abusive.

PTSD, ADHD, you name it, I've probably had the diagnosis.

At this point, I could care less. I wanted this fucker dead, even if all of this was just a fever dream or fantasy. I wanted the satisfaction. If we couldn't charge and smash, then we would bite or slash the hunter.

The bars of the cage were vertical with only a couple of cross-hatch supports. I could see where the hunter had softened the stone with its magic and just thrust poles in the rock. It didn't bother to make a lot of cross support bars. Probably because it had secured the stakes in stone, that gave us a good two feet or so of vertical space to slash upward with a tusk. I'd love to bite, but its nose was too damn big to fit through the gap.

So, we had to slash it.

The hunter just had to fall close enough.

I urged it over and over to get close to the edge of the cage. Not to charge but to wait for the right moment. Over and over, like a mantra, I was uttering. Maybe it listened, or perhaps it was engrossed in the fight, but it didn't go back to where it slept and charged aimlessly against the bars. Instead, the boar stayed in place after the last charge.

Waited next to the bars.

Don't move until the hunter is next to the bars.

Wait for it.

I repeated those sentences over and over. Begged the boar to wait for the right moment. Wait for when it comes close enough to the bars. Then slash upward as hard as you can to cut it open.

Over and over. Again and again. I was holding a figurative breath when the tree woman and the hunter got close, but not close enough — waiting until the right moment.

Finally, we had a shot.

The hunter bit down on one of her foot-root supports, but the tree woman used the move to roll the two of them right against the cage. The hunter's mouth biting on the tree woman's roots was almost in the boards. I felt the boar's stubby legs tremble as it charged and slashed upward, digging one of its bottom canines right through the hunter's jaw and into the roof of its mouth.

The hunter went insane, jerking and throwing its body all over, smashing the boar into the cage in a frenzy. The boar fought back, and the tree woman took advantage of the attack as well.

Finally, between the two of them, the hunter died.

In a way, it was a terrifying feeling to watch it struggle less and less until it finally just quit moving altogether.

The tree woman was wounded. The boar wasn't much better. The attack took what tiny amount of energy it had left in its body, and the thrashing against the cage at the end had broken something inside. I suspected its ribs based on the feeling of the breathing but had no way to be sure.

Slowly the cage was broken enough for the boar to stagger out. The tree woman laid a branch on its back gently. It spoke in a beautiful fluting language that the boar understood. Perhaps I did too, on some level, since the tree woman seemed to indicate the boar would be safe with it.

Exhaustion had my name, however, and I faded into the fugue.

Then, I woke up coughing out the bathwater.

I had fallen asleep in the tub.

No alarms, though.

For the first time in ages, I woke up not screaming, falling, or heart raging. I dried off enough to not break my neck or slip on the water layering the floor and rushed to document the Flash.

And to sketch the tree woman.

She looked magnificent in my mind's eye, and I didn't want it to fade.

Sixteen

Immerlin startled the hell out of me.

"Reminder: costs for research and investigation virtual machines have exceeded the threshold by 147% monthly cap. Current authorization at 150%. Estimated to exceed 150% in 23 minutes based on current data inflow."

"Reminder: authorization required to expand elastic cloud storage to handle projected incoming data from research. Data loss expected in 3 minutes based on projections."

Crap. I gave Immerlin the finger, not that he paid attention. Then, I rolled back my chair from the desk with a gentle laugh. I had to get my hands off the keyboard, or I would never stop. I stared at my hands so I would quit looking at the screens around me piled with data.

"Immerlin, authorize virtual machine costs at 200% this month."

"Immerlin, authorize elastic cloud storage to 200%."

"Acknowledged. Both values are now set to 200% monthly cap. Reminder: Projections for contact, 'IV you ice cold bitch' ratio of expenditures to income show loss of profit if research reaches 200%."

I coughed and stared into my sad and empty teacup: Yup, the dangers of getting interested in something. But, I had found something entertaining in the data transfers and interactions and followed that white bunny right down the rabbit hole.

My bladder began clamoring for attention, so I handled that and then jumped on the treadmill to clear my head and think through what I was doing. I was ahead on deliveries, so I wasn't too worried about not meeting deadlines. This wouldn't be an issue if I just stuck to the work, but something about IV and its employees was bothering me. The employees' unintentional or maybe intentional nosiness into my personal life got on my nerves. Not to mention that weird VR chat and some of the ones that followed between Elise and me. What got me digging was how no one in the company seemed normal.

What's normal? Believe it or not, normal has a range. Most people float to one or more ends of the spectrum with a few plots towards the center. When I dig into a company, charting how people align to the normal creates a nice scatterplot. When you combine people's behaviors and accounts inside a company network, the extra dimensions can help you rapidly pick out any errant or unusual activity. And when plots cluster, it indicates a nexus of action exists. That clustering is what caught my attention. Chasing that down led to the realization that many people inside of IV were too close to normal. Way too close to make sense for the work they performed. If I hadn't forcibly split the plots on the chart, they would have been right on top of each other.

That just didn't happen.

I adjusted the pace of the treadmill down so I wouldn't start sweating too much.

If it had just been that, I wouldn't have cared. It's odd but not weird enough to dig in, especially since it wasn't in my wheel well for this contact anyway. What caught my interest was that those same people had excessive amounts of external accounts using pinholes in IV's security to take data in — and out. I thought it was a quirk of their collection team but realized after analysis that their permissions didn't match up in most cases to their positions, and most of them were in other sections.

It had me thinking that an insider threat might be present, but the data spread didn't match any pattern I had seen in the past for that kind of activity. It made me wonder if IV had an incident brewing or already had one in motion. That's why I started diving into the outside accounts. Once the picture that something internal was happening, I backed off, asking their internal network and security folks for more information.

I had no desire to tip anyone off.

Hitting it from the outside meant I could work out of band from their security and not give away I was digging into their activity.

That's when the situation started getting juicy. Those outside accounts led to multiple identities that were obvious bots — and many that were not. At least one of them had a dozen-plus real-world identities that I could match. It made me feel all cloak and dagger-like. And slightly worried. Nothing synced with any government links that I could see. Nothing aligned with a criminal source from my viewpoint.

Too many people believe Hollywood.

It's tough to clear your trail online when you are creating things. Very hard. The internet is built to leave breadcrumbs and backlinks by virtue of its existence. Primarily, it's knowing how to look and having the ability to look where you need to.

Immerlin disrupted my thinking again.

Thankfully, I didn't go sliding off the treadmill in disgrace.

I shut down the treadmill and said, "Immerlin, accept the call on speakers."

Howie sounded breathless. "Heyas, buddy. Sorry I canceled our morning call."

I shrugged, not that he could see it. "No problem. While I appreciate the gesture, you know I'm fine, right? It's okay if we don't meet face to face every morning. That girl — what's her name — ah, Anna, right Anna, she's gonna get jealous."

He grumbled and said, "Anna is a nice girl, but ...."

"She's not your type," I finished for him. "Yeah, yeah, I know. But, dude, I might be hopeless, but you are the catch of the century. You should realize that."

Howard laughed, but it was garbled by something moving past him. "I can't believe you — you of all people — are giving me dating advice. I might have a tough time finding a girl, but you — is anyone your type? I'd imply something but —"

"You just stop there! I am not going to hear another one of your busted ass siscon jokes. I like the opposite sex, and those not related to me just fine. It's not the issue, and you know it. Who the hell would want to put up with the hot mess that I represent? Answer? No one. And I'm lazy. And confident. Some day the right girl is going to walk right into my life, and I'll know it balls to bones."

"...missed about half of that."

Not surprised given the background noise around him. Luckily it cleared up, and Howie continued. "Best of luck, though, since you must be talking about girls. If she didn't walk into your house, I doubt you would meet Miss Right anyway."

"Ha, ha," I replied. "Look who is today's standup comedian: Howie!"

His reply was garbled again to background noise and a horrible burst of static. "Howie, where in the blazes are you, anyway? The noise around you is shit. Want to call back later?"

"...clear up in a minute. There," Howie said. Not sure what he did or where he went, but it was nothing but beautiful silence. "Stepped into the office foyer. It was raucous out there. So, before you forget, tell Immerlin to set a reminder for you. First, tonight is game night, 6 pm, and I need you to win. Secondly, I've got a referral for you."

Referral?

"I want to beat those play-to-win bitches just like you do, so I'll be there with bells on. Who's the referral? I like it when you send me business. Usually, it's high pay, low effort, and not a lot of nonsense."

"I can't guarantee you that, but I do want to connect you two. So let me trudge the stairs, and I'll call you back so we can do a quick conference."

"Now?"

"Yes, well, in about 10 minutes."

"Do you think I can readjust my whole calendar for you at the drop of a hat?"

"Can't you? Isn't that your schedule — whatever you want it to be?"

I hummed and hawed, but damn, he was right. "Fine. Call me back. I'll be ready, but no video calls."

"I know better," he replied. "I'll see you in ten."

I jumped off the treadmill and moved to the alternate office. It's one of the benefits of having multiple rooms I didn't use except when I needed them. I didn't want to reset what I had going on IV to take a call on that rig. But, of course, as I was powering everything up, it struck me that Howie had once again got me to take a call with a prospective client and, in typical lawyer fashion, told me nothing about it. I think he just likes watching me tap-dance when I go in blind and have to think fast on my feet.

He rang in on time and said, "Let me get us connected."

Two voices entered after a moment of silence: Howie's voice and another soft-spoken one. I leaned forward slightly, not that it helped me hear them any clearer. I tapped the keyword to adjust the volume up. Howie came in a little loud, but the other voice was finally something I could hear.

"Mr. An, please meet my friend Bret Byrne, who is the master of analysis I had previously mentioned. Saying he has developed one of the most sophisticated analysis and discovery engines that exists is an understatement."

I made the obligatory laugh appropriate to the situation. Then I said, "I would like to think that is very true. Hello, Mr. An. It's nice to meet you. What can I do for you today?"

"Hello, Mr. Byrne. My name is Marcus An. I am one of the engineers on the Oniga Kai project chartered by SVU industries in partnership with the U.S. government."

"I see."

According to my fuzzy memory, I had a vague recollection of Oniga Kai. Then, it hit me. A few years back, I worked for a private equity firm to help them handle point of sale fraud at payment processor nexuses.

"We have done a bit of research, and your name has come up numerous times as the authority in analyzing and tracing fraud, especially at the payment processor tier where transactions are in the billions per minute."

"I wouldn't say I'm 'the' authority, but I do like to think I'm that accurate." I laughed. "What I do is as much art as it is science, so it doesn't always translate well to automation. Intuition is hard to code into software, and there are other experts in the field that are better than I am, especially for this kind of fraud."

"If they exist, I haven't been able to find them," An replied. "Oniga Kai would like to engage you in a project that is a little different from what I understand is your standard set of services. It's well within your experience, especially with the good things that Mr. Kearns has said about your expertise. Because it's a bit out of your normal range of work you undertake, Mr. Kearns made it clear it would require the premium rate outlined on your rate sheet, which we are more than willing to meet."

Well, well. I didn't even know I had a premium rate, but Howie had never done me wrong, so I'm sure it's bigger than anything I would ever bother to ask for from a client. If he hadn't done my beginning rate sheet, I'd probably never moved away from working for pocket change and free muffins. Never turn down good money, especially if it's more money for the same amount of time you would have invested anyway. Still ...

"Out of my normal services in what way?"

"I won't bore you with things you already know, but fraud at this nexus has done nothing but increase. We believe a new approach is necessary. You can only go so far with basic matching, inline abuse detection, and behavioral patterns. Computers and software are fast enough, but we, as analysts, are not. Innovation by cyber crooks is always ahead at a pace that defensively is difficult to match."

Hmmm. Singing my song but... "I see," I said politely. "Just to be upfront, it almost sounds like you need an intelligence analyst versus my normal services."

"They are part of the process as the data, insight, and analysis that intelligence analysis provides is crucial. However, at Oniga Kai, we believe that applying A.I. virtual assistants to fraud is a game-changer. We've piloted some improvements that expand language processing to a more complex, multi-topic, and behavioral approach. Applied to fraud, it has the potential to detect and curtail fraud earlier than the norm of 196 days after the fact. Where we want your help is to assist us in building continuous and active learning modalities into the virtual assistants."

"That does sound like an innovative use of virtual assistants, indeed." Howie must have told them some about Immerlin. Or, they looked in my Github repository. I had hundreds of projects. Some of them dealt with a variety of bots, AI chatbots, and similar things. "Where or I guess, what would you need me to do? I'll be clear and mention that training AI with data is not my specialty."

"No? Well, I mean, I understand. It would be a waste of your talent. No, what we are looking for is something akin to your NorAm10 and FiAM3 projects you have on Github. These projects focused on system analysis and how previous events in a closed system were successfully resolved. NorAm10 demonstrated a clear but primitive learning system tied to more complex multi-step procedures and workflows. I'm not ashamed to say that we derived some inspiration from this project in our beginning. FiAM3 sampled conversation streams to pick out intents, entities, and synonymous phrasal slangs and ways to resolve complex requests. Both of these projects and I suspect many others you have built or are involved in are exactly what we want to engage you to do."

I couldn't decide if I should be tickled or annoyed that they had 'taken inspiration' from my projects or not. Part of me wants to see if they had tried to use it and failed because I purposely left out some concepts or they were looking to develop something innovative.

"I don't quite have a full picture of what you might need to provide an estimate of the hours involved."

Mr. An gave a low laugh. "I'm not sure we even know, though I probably shouldn't say that out loud. I'm happy to authorize 50 hours at your premium rate to start. I understand you have a non-refundable $30,000 retainer, which we are happy to provide as long as you are willing to begin this week. We have a project meeting coming up where your inclusion would be stellar."

I was not one to turn down money, especially for something that I could probably do from memory and make good contacts simultaneously. It couldn't have come at a better time, given my burn rate on IV at the moment.

"I'm fine with that. We can hash out the final details over email. What day did you say was the meeting?"

"Friday, 9 am EST."

I'm interested, but damn that's an early morning meeting. I'm typically awake but not client-worthy at that hour of the morning. Fine, screw it.

"I can make that."

"Excellent. Ah, Mr. Kearns indicated you have a dislike for video conferencing. However, if possible, at least for this first meeting, it would be crucial if you could do so."

Grrrrr. Fine. "Yes, that's agreeable. But only as an exception. I understand the trope and all with remote work, but I have never had an issue with professionalism in my work. I have a medical condition that does not affect my work but makes visual conferences challenging at times. That's why I normally avoid them where possible."

"Completely understood. It's truly this first meeting where it is critical. Okay. I'll have a contract and some material over to you this afternoon if that's acceptable. If you have questions, I'll be available all week."

And that was that. Mr. An left, and Howie jumped off to his next appointment. In less than 30 minutes, I resolved an upcoming money crisis and got the pause I needed to realize I needed to back off chasing ghosts at IV. As interesting as it might be, it's not worth blowing all the profits on it. Plus, I had work from Justin incoming. Our last appointment had not been any better than the one before it. He got interrupted, which I suspected was because of an ongoing incident. Sucks. Still, he updated the SOW to allow for another bucket of hours and sent over the data for me to use.

The work was solid, even if it was somewhat dull. The work from Oniga Kai, however, sounded like an exciting gig. I just had to keep from bragging about Immerlin by accident. Still ... no matter how I turned it, things were looking up.

"Doc Matson, you have to see this."

Scott led with that when he walked into the autopsy room. The aforementioned doctor dropped the liver he held in both hands on the scale, watching it sink.

"I'm up to my elbows in work at the moment. So I don't have time to see your Hentai girls or whatever you are into this week."

Scott waved his hand excitedly, almost dropping the laptop in the process. "No, no — wait, what are you talking about now? Whatever. No, not about that," he said, annoyed. "No, about the chillcicle the other day."

Doc Matson returned the liver to a pan and turned off the recorder with practiced ease. "Okay, Scott, what you have to say is obviously more important than my autopsy. So why don't you tell me?"

Scott grinned. "Come on, Doc. It's not like the stiff is going to go somewhere."

"Your humor does not excite me," Doc Matson said, wishing he wasn't painted in fluids so he could burn one. He calculated the time it would take in his head to change and fire up a cigarette while Scott slapped the laptop down and turned it toward him expectantly. Reluctantly, he figured he didn't have enough time and looked at whatever the latest 'must-read' item Scott had to show him.

Sometimes it was actually good.

Mostly it was female and unclothed like we didn't have enough of that around here in the morgue already.

"Doc, check this out," Scott said, tapping on the screen. "That guy lodged in the ice, the chillcicle. I thought it was just an oddball occurrence. I got bored and started looking at the other morgues in the state and found another one! Then, inspired, I looked even wider and found we have had five — five! — almost identical cases!"

Staring at the mishmash of numbers, pictures, and webpages — yep, he had porn open in another tab, why was that not a surprise — Doc Matson snorted and turned to go back to the autopsy that needed finishing.

Scott was surprised, and he stuttered, "Doc, what are you doing? Don't you think it's tre' interesting? I mean, what's the odds of five people dying the same way? Did you see it was in the last twelve months, too?"

"Scott, I've got an autopsy to finish. They are not the same, they just look that way, and I don't have time for this."

"Doc, please, just look at the pictures."

Doc stared at the unfinished procedure he was in the middle of and gusted out a heavy sigh. Already blew my tempo anyway, he thought, stripping off his gloves and gear. He stomped past Scott and kicked open the fire escape door. Scott happily trailed along in Doc's shadow, patiently waiting until he fired up a cigarette. When he looked up, Scott rotated the laptop once again for him to see, this time with just the images side by side.

It caught his attention.

It seems like Scott wasn't wrong. The images, especially when lined up like that, did look weirdly alike. Doc Matson handed his cigarette to Scott and took the laptop. He zoomed in and looked at the pictures from different angles. He took a second and looked at the coroner's report.

Looking up, he saw the glee on Scott's face. Annoyed, he snatched the cigarette that Scott had puffed on, looked at it, and threw it off the side to join the heap down below. He lit another one, keeping the laptop from falling off the rail with his knee. Then, after taking in a deep breath, he nodded, making Scott crow.

Exactly the same.

Not the lead-up to the death. Not the incident or the details of that but the manner of death and how they died. That — no way it was a coincidence.

Serial murderer?

Given the ridiculous facts around the deaths, it seemed far-fetched, but what was the quote? When you have eliminated the impossible, whatever remains is the truth? Even if it's improbable or oddball.

The five of these deaths being linked didn't make sense. They were in different places and happened in widely different ways. But they died the same, and that was a quirk, especially since it was in a relatively short time of a year.

Doc Matson rubbed out the cigarette and shoved the laptop back at Scott. "Find out more."

He stomped back in, wondering if he could speed up the autopsy report so he could dig into it more tonight.

Eighteen

"I'm glad I've been helpful," I said, in response to Dr. Escarra's analysis of the work I had done for them to date. It was the last scheduled briefing, and she had attended, taking over the virtual roomful of eight people with deft ease. At the end of the briefing, she asked me to stay online and talk, just her and me.

"Indeed. Most helpful. I think the engineering team would agree as well though the team might be cursing a bit too given the amount of work this has and will generate for some time to come."

We all laughed appropriately. I admired the view through Dr. Escarra's windows again. I don't know where her office was, but the clouds and hints of buildings piercing them from below were gorgeous. It made me think of Dubai with its tall skyscrapers.

Dr. Escarra shuffled some paper on her desk, pulling my attention back to the meeting. "Mr. Byrne, the last report you sent indicates that we only have three more hours of your time. I find that unfortunate, given the good relationship we have built."

"I do as well, Dr. Escarra. It has been a pleasure to work with such a quality group," I kindly responded, wondering in the back of my head which way this would turn. This kind of lead meant a 'thanks for your time' or 'can we have more' usually with some 'buts' and 'caveats' ratcheted on the work. I wasn't sure I wanted to do more work with them, given the mild discomfort that just hadn't faded.

"Excellent," she said dryly, tapping her fingers on the desk. "I would like to retain your services for a bit longer and extend the contract.

Perhaps even something more open-ended if you are in mind to consider it."

It took everything I had not to have my eyebrows shoot into my hairline. That's a golden line every consultant loves to hear, right along with, 'we'll pay your retainer immediately' and 'can I prepay for a bucket of hours?'. I just wasn't sure if I wanted to continue working with them. I didn't have a single thing on which I could put a finger, but it gave me a creepy feeling.

The money, though, that would be welcome, I had to admit.

"I see," I said, tapping the edge of the computer in front of me. "Full disclosure, I am working on other contracts and contemplating another one."

"That's understood," she said, cocking her head to the side slightly. "Given the nature of the business we work in. If you need, we can make an accommodation to ensure you do not suffer any financial interactions by working with us longer. I'm sure the new work is interesting, but I'm positive you will find what I propose equally intriguing."

Rule number something or other about consulting. Never, ever say 'No'. Instead, lead the customer to say it for you. That way, you don't look bad or create a hostile atmosphere. Even though she was obliquely offering more money as a carrot, I hadn't fallen for it yet.

I made a polite listening gesture, and she smiled slightly. I'm positive she thought that meant she had my interest.

"As a short gist of the work, I would like you to help us evaluate the integration of another company into our current efforts. It would require a significant amount of analysis and code review, not to mention an inspection of specific applications of a licensing agreement the previous company leveraged."

"I see. When it comes to analysis and code, I can ferret out issues and questions you might want to ask. For example, is the acquisition already done or proposed as a purchase ...?"

"Completed around a year ago. Some obstacles have delayed the integration for some time. The usual problems that arise when acquiring a company and its employee base decide to exit en masse. It was unfortunate, but luckily the investors understood that it was out of our hands."

"I see. Is the evaluation of how technically difficult it will be to integrate into your existing infrastructure? That seems something more in tune with your Engineering team, if I might say."

"Yes and no," she said. "From a pure technology standpoint, that's correct, and I would expect you to continue to work with them the way you have these last few weeks. However, I am concerned about the security and, frankly, big picture review of that assimilation into our infrastructure. It needs to be appraised, and I have never been impressed with the usual suspects of penetration testers, software analysts, and systems analysis gurus out there. But, on the other hand, your work has been spot on, very directed at our problems, and frankly, discreet, both in writing and with your efforts to educate some of the more 'skilled' members of my team."

"I'm glad you feel my work is more than beyond standards. I feel ... I could help you partially, definitely, though, if I may, I'm uncertain of the patent agreement evaluation and how that would work."

Dr. Escarra nodded. "Understood. It's a bit of a gray area for me, though I shouldn't admit that. I have acquired the services of a legal representative with significant patent experience and have our internal team of lawyers available if needed for context or legalities. I also know and hope you will pardon that you created several patents of your own. Dozens from what my research dug up. I was pleasantly surprised ...."

She wasn't wrong. I had stumbled into the fun of applying for patents years ago, though it was a friend of Howie's that did the hard work. I had sold one of the first ones outright to fund my first steps towards independence from my mom. Taking away the control of money from her was my first step towards taking control of my destiny.

"... to find that you had participated in several licensing agreements. That was the key that convinced me you were the right person to assist. That and the technical bench of knowledge you have, of course."

"I have extended a couple of licensing agreements on patents I own, that's true, but the lawyers did the heavy lifting on that endeavor."

"True, I suspect that would always be the situation. However, my understanding of the patent you extended to Bildas corporation was one you ended contesting, even to the point of producing the evidence to prove. Equally, that on numerous other occasions you have disputed patents that infringed on your or countered others' attempts to prove your patents infringed on theirs."

"Ma'am, I must say that you have done your homework. Yes, all those things are true and public record, I guess."

"Do you feel I was excessive in my research? I wanted to make sure I was engaging with the right person."

Yes, I wanted to say, but I answered differently.

"It's understandable. I can see how this might be or become sensitive. Would you please send me what materials and information you can? I'll review and respond with what I think I can do, an estimate of hours involved, and other details that can be spelled out in an email."

"Excellent," she said. "I look forward to working with you more."

She wasn't much on goodbyes, so I ended up staring at a black screen before I knew it. Somehow I could see that I would get sucked into doing more work for Inverse Voices even though that little voice inside said I shouldn't.

It's just hard to turn down money when it's offered to you.

"Immerlin, monthly expenditures to date, percentage, all contracts."

"Currently 313% over budget."

Well, that answered that. While I had the premium rate contract fall into my lap, I would go backward monetarily if I didn't take this. Justin's work helped a little but not near enough to balance expenditures as I needed.

I have to take it.

Immerlin would let me know when the email came in so I could respond. Until then, everything else was wrapped up, mostly, and I could focus on my pet project.

I scrambled over to my creation station, where I noted down all the Flashes.

Grabbing a handful of paper, I spread out the latest.

I had Flashed for a bit now with the boar. Several times, at that. It had been a nice change of pace. The tree woman had taken the boar far away from the part of the woods where the hunter had dwelled. The boar and the tree woman went up the wooded slopes of a nearby mountain into a gentle valley. In the Flashes, it felt like months had gone by, maybe longer, though the snowy landscape didn't change much.

The valley area was obviously a place of dwelling, perhaps hers, though, in one Flash to the boar, I had seen another of her kind in the valley. They communicated via pollen, of all things, which drove the boar nuts. They had tried to move away, but the boar had wanted to follow them, so eventually, they gave up and spoke in the musical tones she had used in the beginning. Realizing the boar seemed interested after that conversation, the tree woman talked to the boar constantly, pointing out things and just talking to it.

Maybe it comprehended what was going on, but I sure didn't. That didn't stop me from writing down what I thought the words sounded like phonetically and recording everything I could. Languages had always been my gift, though it was more right to say that I had just heard/learned so many in Flashes that it felt almost second nature. This language felt familiar, like I had heard or read it before. There was a written language, though it looked like highly complex tree rings that overlapped.

I had Immerlin searching everywhere and trying to organize the bits of the language into something I could maybe understand. It's part of why my bill was through the roof this month and last month.

"Incoming video call from Howard Kearns."

"Accept."

It popped up on the screen above my desk. Howie looked calm, which meant something was up. Otherwise, he would be cheerful.

"Bret, Dereck called me just a bit ago. He called me earlier, but I was in a client call."

What did that jerk want? Money? More of her stuff? He was always trying to take whatever Alice owned or pry into the money she had left behind in a trust.

"What shenanigans is he up to this time?"

Howie projected calmness. "It's your mother. He called to tell me that she had taken a turn for the worse. He also, quite loudly, I might add, indicated that you were screening his calls."

I snorted, upset. "Of course, I'm screening Dereck's calls. I do it every time he becomes an ass and then take him back off. And my mother is always 'taking a turn for the worse'. How much did he ask for this time? Or was it Alice's sedan? I still have it stored in the parking garage and see no reason to give it to him."

Howie slowly breathed out. "I spoke to the doctor. Your mother has worsened. I know he says it often, but it's true this time. They have changed her rooms. He also asked you to examine her medical directives, especially palliative care. Also, Dereck has engaged a legal agency to contest the current medical power of attorney."

I thought I was past the hurt she could inflict, but there she was, hurting me again, even on her deathbed. But what riled me up was Dereck. Breathing harshly to stay calm, I asked, "What's his game, Howie? How did he turn from this wonderful person that Alice loved into a grasping, greedy scumbag who is trying to sow destruction everywhere."

"I don't know, Bret. I never knew him as well as you did. Definitely not close enough to see what Alice saw. Regardless, he is challenging the power of attorney, trying to remove the orders around providing your mother a ventilation machine and resuscitation if her heart stops."

My hands wouldn't stop clenching and unclenching. "I don't understand it, Howie. Saying I know him is a stretch. He was important to Alice, so I stayed a step away. Dereck ... I just don't get him or how this situation has evolved. It's not like he is paying for anything or even cared for my mother. Her dislike for him was obvious. Had Alice not forced our mother to interact with Dereck, she wouldn't have given him the time of day. So why is he even here?"

"I don't know either, Bret. But he is at the hospital, and he is being a pain in the ass. The law firm he engaged for the legal challenge is a top-notch one. Nothing is wrong with power of attorney. Your mother set it up well, but you are not listed as an agent — Alice was. She obviously cannot act in the capacity spelled out in the power of attorney, and we have used that gap to have you appointed as the guardian. Dereck has filed to reject that. It won't change anything in the short term, but he's also at the hospital all the time and may be able to act when he shouldn't."

"What do we do, Howie?" My voice was low and harsh with emotion.

"Immediately, nothing. The courts don't move fast, and I have already lodged my response to their legal move. However, Dereck is also making a move to have you declared incompetent based on your history. That's something I kept out of court previously but honestly have no way to stop it from being introduced. It's a crapshoot on what the judge's response will be once he reads that information."

"Eleven years," I whispered. "I've been out for eleven years. I got three degrees from universities. Filed for and got thirty-seven patents. I've run two businesses. Both I sold to become financially independent until the wreck. That fucking car crash. In every way, successful and a good person. Now, some judge will read I was treated for mental health — forcefully, mind you — put in the nuthouse by the same woman whose life I have control of with the medical power of attorney. We both know how that is going to go."

"Yes." Howie didn't say more. He didn't have to. It didn't sound any better to me as I knew it would look written down in front of the judge. Helplessly I couldn't help but mutter, "What does he want?"

"You don't want to hear this. You hate talking about money and your family. I get it. It's a painful thing. Your mother tried to take over your finances many times before she learned the hard way that I'm a better lawyer. But your mother isn't poor. Laying in that bed, she still has millions in her name that you can't touch — but Dereck can in the right situation. And I think he's angling to make that situation happen. Of course, it's my opinion, but I think that is the game he's playing."

"He's such scum. I don't want him to have anything."

"I know," Howie said, voice firm. "That's why I have a plan. It isn't lovely, though. You won't like it. You'll also have to travel. Go in. If you do it, though, I think we can smash him down good."

I sat back, curses flowing from my mouth.

Howard hung up.

He knew I needed time to process.

Nineteen

The call with Howie had upset me.

After committing and uncommitting code to the version control system several times in a row, I knew I was done. I was done being able to concentrate, done even trying to be effective. I walked away from the disaster I had created in the codebase and picked up my game controller. I must have finally dozed off since I came out of the fugue, realizing the boar and I were back together as a unit. The boar's senses were sharp and clear. If I could sync with the boar, especially since I felt connected to in the Flash, it would become more realistic. After Flashing a few times, I could finally sense it all, especially the volume of scents that seemed dazzling, unlike my crude nose and its appalling inability to smell anything besides sweat, tea, and a small cluster of other things.

I was belly down in the snow as the boar, but it seemed warm versus how frozen I definitely would have been. In front of the boar, the tree woman was moving slowly in a mountain clearing. From what I could tell, she followed a path in the snow. Perhaps to someone else, it would be indiscernible, but the schnozz on the boar was enormously sensitive, and I could tell she was following a pattern of pollen that was lingering in the air. She would move through it, and it would ripple, remaining in the air.

It seemed magical and probably was given my experience so far in this Flash.

I guess the boar loved to watch her since he felt very comfortable on his belly seeing her dance. My boar buddy felt different, too, like he had an engine purring somewhere in his head. It struck me — and I felt stupid that I hadn't grasped it before — that the boar was an intelligent beast. It didn't act like a normal boar at all. And a boar with some strength or power of some sort.

The reptilian hunter could melt and move stone, so it wasn't unexpected. It looked like this Flash was one with magic power or something like it. It was far from the first I had experienced, though usually I ended up dead or screwed up in most cases before I could truly sink into it.

Immerlin — the real Immerlin from a past Flash, not my virtual assistant — he had it in spades. Ostensibly, Immerlin was a wizard or something. More aligned with Celtic or Irish myth or the Earthsea novels than the roleplaying fireball type. Immerlin could speak to the world, and it responded. It was how his magic worked. It was one of the few times where I experienced the early years to death existence of someone. From the point when he was a child, I dwelled in a Flash with Immerlin. In fact, most of my twelfth year of life had been living that Flash. Maybe it was fitting since I had broken my left arm in three places and fractured both of my tibias, jumping off the roof of the house. I spent most of that twelfth year just recovering.

The last Flash with the big bird thing just kept lingering, and I was an idiot kid who thought he would fly in reality like he could in the Flash.

It didn't work.

Gravity provided a cold wake-up call.

As I watched ... her pattern looked oddly familiar, kind of like the language felt like something I had experienced before. Of course, I hadn't placed it yet, and neither had my work on the speech turned out great results, but still, I couldn't shake the sense that I had heard or seen it before.

I wanted to see more, to get closer. The boar lumbered to its feet with some snorting and did that. If I could linger in a Flash long enough and not let the fugue slide it away or just die — that seemed to happen so many times — then I could get into the Flash, and be one with whatever or whoever it was.

It didn't happen very often.

I would swear deus ex machina was hard at work killing me off if I didn't believe it would lead down a road of paranoia and self-grandeur.

Following the tree woman through the twisting paths of pollen, I found the sense of deja vu rising. Even though it was not the same — it was the same. The thought tumbled over and over in my brain, along with the steps I was taking. I'm not sure why but it consumed my thoughts. I sorted through creature after creature that I could remember, wishing I had my journals of notes, sketches, and drawings that chronicled past Flashes. I was slipping into a fugue, revolving on the thought and fading away into the gray when the tree woman stopped.

It startled me.

After bending to scratch along the boar's back, she started talking to me in the musical language. The boar snorted and squealed happily, showing the boar liked the attention. It was a strange sensation that centered me back in the Flash, pushing away the fugue. Next, the tree woman pulled a fist-sized truffle from her leafy interior and fed it to the boar, much to its delight. Then, she led it off to the side, where it consumed it happily while she returned to walking the pollen-laden path.

The boar returned to the side again to watch. I was caught between wanting to influence it to follow tree woman again and watching from the side. The boar had no such conflicts and flopped down ungracefully.

It was an odd sense of feedback that came next, almost like goosebumps or prickles that danced along the nape of the neck. I felt something stirring and moving, almost liquid-like inside its brain. The engine I felt earlier revved, sending shocks across the brain. It was stimulating and relaxing simultaneously — like sinking into a hug. So much so that the sensation floated me back into the fugue, and everything faded as I idly wondered if this is what it felt like to cultivate power here.

The thoughts lulled me into a haze. The boar's world faded and I woke up.

I was coated with sweat like I had worked out for an hour on the treadmill.

Disgusting, but I didn't wake up screaming.

It seemed like a significant improvement.

After a short bit to regroup, I shrugged off my clothes and let water from the shower roll over me. It sort of felt similar to the sensation that the boar had, though barely.

I reveled in it for a bit before doing a piss poor job of drying off and trundling over to my desk.

I grabbed paper made just for this occasion and started the process of making sense of what happened.

Or at least chronicling it.

Twenty

The work for Oniga Kai wasn't as bad as I thought. Not that it didn't take a slog through the code after I understood what they were after. It made for a long day and sleepless night, a combination I did not mind given the stress of Dereck's legal moves and mother's — love or hate, she is the person that birthed me — decline in health.

I had not Flashed for days, and it worried me. I had stayed with the boar for a bit now, several times watching the tree woman walk her pollen path or interact with others of her kind.

Flashing. It was a love and hate relationship. I'm not too fond of the bad ones but wanted to surrender completely and become one with the good ones. The boar started poorly but turned so much better after finding a companion. Plus, I had finally made some breakthroughs with Immerlin on the language and more. Linguistically we had pulled out a possible working primitive construct of the speech. It did match something from my notes, at least my early ones. I cursed my younger self for not taking better notes. Regardless, it allowed Immerlin and I to make some startling leaps forward in logic. Those same fragments I had jotted down when I was young also contained a couple of diagrams. I had thought the walking path was related to the monk, but I had the wrong Flash. No, it was even earlier than that and in the same notes as the language fragments. That, too, had been a magically inspired Flash though I could not recall what it was for the life of me.

It was blank. Of course, that Flash or series of Flashes was also when mother and the doctors drugged me with everything under the sun. So, much of that time was a chaotic drug-infused haze.

I pulled away from the Oniga Kai work and jumped over to the running work I had for IV. That was still chugging along. I cleared some alerts and tuned some of the queries before pushing away, rubbing my eyes. They were so dry I could imagine sand falling as my hands massaged them.

Not even changing, I stepped on the treadmill and had Immerlin bring up the diagrams on the screen in front of it. As I walked, I examined the pattern I had pulled from my notes and compared it to the one I had determined from watching her walk. They were very similar, different in subtle ways, but ways that my engineering attuned brain told me were critical. I wasn't going to pretend to know or understand the tree woman's physiology. I felt instead a rather insane urge — how ironic, mother would be proud —that I might influence the direction she was taking. Not top of mind and all, but I had been a passenger on this type of power growth before. So many past flashes seemed to align with this path. My notes and a plethora of material drawn from mysticism, games, and fantasy were at my fingertips to speculate how it worked. And if I was right, a combination of the two designs and some tweaks might improve the flow the tree woman was trying to achieve.

Whatever additional thoughts fell right along with me when Immerlin startled me, and I slipped. Picking up my bruised body and pride, I yelled at him. He didn't listen. I hadn't used a command word, just lots of swearwords.

"Incoming call, Kim Laysme, 90degreesright."

"Yeah, yeah," I said, rubbing my ribs where I had landed. I stumbled over to a chair, sinking into it before yelling, "Immerlin, accept the call on speakers."

"Mr. Byrne?" The voice was feminine, reedy, but not unpleasant. The combination sent my brain spinning to a past effort where I assisted with building ad placement strategies algorithms. Bingo. Quickly memory conjured up a thin woman who was always well dressed and elegant, matching the voice.

"May I help you?"

"Yes." The answer was so short that I was caught flat-footed for a moment when there was no follow-up.

"Ms. Laysme?"

She offered a short bark of a laugh. "Ah, sorry, Mr. Byrne, I was lost in thought."

"That's okay, Ms. Laysme." I slid the chair over to my table and grabbed a notepad. Wrote down the word 'upset' and underlined it.

"I appreciate that, Mr. Byrne. I'm calling about the placement algorithms you helped us with ... and a few other things."

"Go ahead ..." I wrote down 'past work' on the notepad next to it. I also sketched out a quick grid around the two words, leaving plenty of space.

"No way to be gentle here. Our CTO, Mr. Clemson, has directed me to connect with you over the placement algorithms you built last year. But, unfortunately, we — 90degreesright — were recently served legal injunction by the federal authorities to cease employing our ad services, specifically those that relied on your algorithms."

I added a few more words to my bingo table. While I felt terrible for Laysme, I couldn't help but ask, "And ...."

"And what?" Her voice sounded strange at my question.

"You just told me that the authorities served a legal injunction to your company over ad placement. How does that include me? The work I performed was on your behalf and included complete ownership of the code, work product, and any derivative use of that code. Everything was done on your hardware, with your software, and by your direction. Your legal counsel was quite clear about any sense of who owned that material once the work was complete."

A little too gleeful about it, in my opinion. In fact, between that legal beagle and a couple of 90degreesright engineers, I was ready to cancel the contract and take the penalty several times. But unfortunately, I had forgotten to take her off the safelist of accepted calls, or I would not have even taken this call, especially since it cost me a nasty bruise.

Her voice was curt but tired. "I see. Law enforcement has indicated that a cybercriminal gained access or found a way to abuse those algorithms to inject malicious ads. I think you will find this puts us in a conflicted position."

I added more words for my bingo table. I would get upset if I did not have the experience of going down this road of 'blame the contractor when something goes wrong' from before.

"Ms. Laysme, I'm certain you realize what you are implying. However, let me be clear — I have complied with all — repeat all — terms of our previous contract agreement. Everything was, as I said, turned over to you and all work performed on your equipment. If a cyber actor used your algorithms to position malware and law enforcement has asked you to stop, I encourage you to comply with them. If you need assistance with the incident response or a referral to someone who can assess how this happened, I am happy to provide you with a name for both. Any implication that I had a hand in this tragedy is treading the edge of slander."

Her voice was dry. "We were hoping that legal counsel would not be necessary."

I cut her off before she went further. "Ms. Laysme, again, I don't know what you mean or what you are trying to imply."

After a pause of silence, she said, "Fine. Our legal counsel will contact you. Good day."

She hung up.

I circled some words and fired up a browser to do quick searches. After finding enough to get a sense of events around 90degreesright's malware issues, I directed Immerlin to call Howie while I threw that info and a list of links into an email to Howie.

He picked up after a couple of rings.

"Jumping meetings right now," Howie said after he picked up.

"Gotcha," I said in return. Then, humming, I said, "Looks like I'm getting sued or something like that."

He paused, muted the phone for a minute, and then came back on. "Okay, I moved a meeting around, so we've got 15 minutes. Who's suing you and why? You trash someone's game character or something, and they finally decided to do a smackdown?"

I grinned. "Wish it was that simple. But, nope, remember when I did some work for 90degreesright a while back?"

He didn't answer, so I took it as he didn't. "I did some strategic product work for them as well as generated a couple of algorithms for them to use when building advertising placements. It was pretty cut and dry, and they couldn't see me out the door fast enough. I just got an oddball call from one of their people — take a look at the email I sent — pretty much implying I was the culprit that allowed it to happen or did it."

Howie didn't say anything for a bit, but I waited patiently as he made reading noises and randomly spouted words as he read. Finally, he said, "And ...."

I smiled. "Pretty much word for word my response to Laysme when she called. Anyway, she threatened legal counsel, so heads up, you might get a notice, or I'll forward it over if I receive one. Not quite sure I see their angle on this, but it looks like a typical act of let's blame someone else for bad security to me."

Howie's pen tapped on something, indicating he was thinking. "Any chance they are right in any fashion?"

"Nope. I did everything, and I mean everything, on their systems, with their tools, and by their direction. I kept nothing and re-used nothing, not even open source."

"Huh. So, the only angle they might have is you did the work? You didn't re-use or dig up any old code used previously — by your or anyone else?"

I shook my head. "None. It's not overly complex code, just lengthy. The logic is broken into separate evaluation components, and the output is a positioning strategy. The result is kind of a glorified map of who, when, and where to put ads for maximum effect based on the inputs provided."

Dryly, Howie said, "Not complex to you, but I'm sure others would disagree. Send me over the statement of work and any other agreements you have on it. And, to be clear, you kept nothing?"

I heard the doubt in his voice. "Nothing. Not worth it. I also didn't do another job like this because it sucked. They were not the most responsive or awesome people to work with, and frankly, it wasn't very challenging."

"I'm hoping you didn't say that to them," he said.

I chuckled. "I might be nutty, but I'm not crazy. That isn't good for business. I got it done quickly and disengaged faster. Even turned away follow on work from 90degreesright. The company paid on time, but it was a terrible experience."

"Gotcha. I'll keep a watch out. Also, before we part, I have a meeting with Dereck's lawyers in a couple of hours. I'll keep you posted on what I find out."

Howie hung up, and I stared at nothing. Any desire to work had dried up into dust. Problems and problems. Work was picking up, but so were the issues. I struggled between going to the treadmill and picking up the game controller when Immerlin chimed in.

"Incoming call, Joshua Filler, DKL Cyber."

"Accept." Joshua was with a start-up that did some innovative work in DNS. They specialize in sniping cyberattacks before they materialize, or so goes the branding. I just liked their crosshairs logo.

"Bret ... how goes my favorite consultant?" Joshua was as genial and friendly as you could get. It was even more potent since he was genuinely a good fellow. He was on my shortlist to try and visit if I could ever muster the bravery to do so.

"Consulting. What's on your mind?"

"I've got a problem and think you can help?"

"What sort of problem?"

"We have a new product that we built that sits at the DNS resolver and enhances our sniping capability. We think it's the bomb, but I want someone independent to assess it to make sure we are not drinking our own Kool-Aid and missing flaws and logic missteps that will kill us when we go to market."

"So, you want an assessment of whether it functions as expected?"

Cheerfully, he said, "You got it in one."

"Well, I can help if the timeline isn't too tight and you give me some details. I have a sense of your Sniper product already, so I would need to know how this fits in or integrates to be truly helpful."

"Awesome. All of that is excellent. Any chance for that to happen for less than forty hours?"

I pondered for a moment. "Maybe. I would need to see what you are trying to do before I could commit to that."

"That's fine. You take a look at it. Please send a confirmation that you can do it in forty hours or an estimate of what it would take. If it's forty or less, go ahead and just start."

"That indicates you have a tight timeline you need to meet."

"Sorta," he said. "The ISOI 39 conference is coming up in 2 months. So we would love to take this on the road, especially for that conference since it's a pretty pool of our target audience."

"Okay. I'll look at it."

"Excellent. I know you don't like conferences, but if you ever change your mind, just name the conference, and I'll swing a ticket."

"Appreciated, as always."

"Be talking to you." Before I could respond, he was gone. I stared at the ceiling, uncertain why I had just added even more work to my plate. Maybe so I wouldn't sleep or think about Dereck or mother?

I ordered Immerlin to let me know when his email showed up. I decided on tea but barely made it up before Immerlin told me it had arrived. I decided tea had priority and made it before turning to my desk to find ways to not think about the world and its problems that kept coming to my door.

Twenty-One

She listened while her aide continued to report, looking out the office window at the tips of buildings protruding from the clouds. Inverse Voices provided a beautiful office, but she still disliked the sense of falseness it engendered. She tidied the lines of her white suit, tugging at her the pale skin exposed on her arms. She could not wait to move up. So she could go back home. Be under the sun and exchange this pasty skin for something more to her liking.

Prompting her aide to continue, she looked out at the sun descending through the horizon and suddenly wished to not be constrained by the view its muddy yellow rays produced.

She nodded. Her icy eyes showed satisfaction at the flow of statistics about the latest attempts to identify bugs and possible candidates through VR technologies. She had initiated the idea. Anything to speed up this already slow process of taking over. She rubbed a pale arm. To get back home to Ogygia. She thought of the misty peaks before snapping the image away.

Irritated by the memories, she motioned for the aide to stop, tapping the office window to bring up a screen projection. She dismissed the views to pull up just one, with a ring gauge and paragraphs of explanation. She tapped the ring gauge and pulled up the values. Then, pulling out the nineteen that represented the majority of the ring's color, she looked at the panel view of different faces or, in some cases, square blocks with names that represented the person.

"Tell me about these," she asked.

"Yes, ma'am. We have identified the core group, of which those nineteen represent individuals where we are in the process of finalizing a contract to resolve."

She narrowed her eyes. "Change this to show the pipeline view, so I know what status they are in."

"Yes, ma'am. Do you want the view you previously had reinstated or something new?"

She didn't even bother to respond but suppressed the blank tiles to only look at the images. All the pictures were different, but if the people in them depicted one thing in common, it was the profound fatigue that lined all their faces. She dismissed it without a sound and pulled up the remaining blank tiles. Then, tapping on them, she asked, "No imagery updates on these seven individuals?"

"They are extreme loners that only socialize via the internet or are resistant to taking pictures."

She tugged at her short-cropped blond hair with one hand while using her other to select an avatar each of the profiles had used. Then, tagging them all, so images were present, she said, "In the future, identify them by an avatar or picture they have used for identity online. I don't want to see names floating in blank squares again."

"Yes, ma'am. We will return to the previous week's view."

Her hands stilled, and her ice-blue eyes narrowed. "Don't be coy with me. I know you don't like how I do things. You don't hide it, and most of the time, I appreciate that. Better the enemy you know than a hidden knife. Like you, I want to finalize this and ascend beyond this little operation. Also, like you, I have my limitations. This quirk — is one of them."

"Yes, ma'am." Sandpaper would be softer than the aide's voice. She chose to ignore it, dismissing the view and then letting her hands pause.

"I don't need to say that we need all nineteen of these to dominate, do I? The loss of even one makes an upset possible. Worse, it could lead to complete loss of control. We've handled hundreds to lock down this Realm we work in — let's not fail at the end with this tiny handful. We have all the advantages — leverage them. Right now is our time to act ahead of everyone and avoid our competitor's eyes and ears."

Not waiting for an answer, she pulled up the remainder of the gauge bar. Then, tapping on the blood-red entry, she asked, "What happened with this one in Thailand? Is it linked to our previous loss in the C-suite?"

The aide's voice regained its neutrality. "Not linked to our knowledge. But, to answer the other question, she surprised us. Negotiations went poorly, and we found out late she had a competing offer."

Long pale fingers tapped on the glass. "Do I need to get involved?"

The refusal was quick. "No, ma'am, we have it sorted out. Expect a resolution within a week, maybe two weeks maximum.""I'll be relieved if it moves as quickly as you expect."

She dismissed the view and pulled up the last one. Then, framing the face between her spread fingers, she said, "Proceed carefully with this one. We can't afford to make a mistake here."

Work until you drop.

Repeat.

That had been my stress relief before, and it functioned pretty effectively. Even though the last week had been nerve-wracking in the extreme, I'd modified it a bit. This Flash was soothing, and I missed it by the third day. Even broke out the hibiscus tea to drink by the gallon. Work kept me from thinking, but I edged in the right situation to fall asleep with the possibility to Flash. Otherwise, I would work until I planted my face on the keyboard. I woke up too many times with imprints not to know it.

In the Flash, we were moving. The tree woman and the boar and what looked like possibly a few other tree people. The snow carpeted everything, and the sky was the same haze as always. It gave me a sense of discontinuity. I never understood time and Flashes. I could sleep a couple of hours and have years or decades slide by in an instant if I had a lot of fugue events that drifted my attention. Other times barely a couple of seconds slipped by, and it was hours. I think weeks or months had gone by, but I couldn't figure out how much.

My curiosity had me poking at the boar to explore the area with its senses. The change — and the slow down it caused is probably what brought the tree woman to the boar. She was joined by what was perhaps a couple of clones of her. However, I could tell her from the rest by her scent. The boar's nose was keen enough to separate them into individuals easily.

She laid a hand on the back of the boar, scratching a place that brought obvious delight. The rest of the tree people waited patiently as she queried the boar in the musical language. My work with Immerlin had not been in vain: a few words stood out. Not enough to gist but enough to realize I was on the right track. The boar squealed and snorted, obviously in reply. I had no idea how to comprehend how it communicated — and was understood by the tree people. I noted the thought away idly for Immerlin to help me tackle and rode along with the boar as we started up again.

Our path led through the forested mountainside to a frozen stream. We followed it upwards, ascending the mountainside. The frozen water gave me a chance to catch occasional glimpses of the boar's body in the ice. Seeing the changes to its coat and general size made me estimate that at least a few months or maybe even longer had passed. I also realized the boar had a grizzled coat for the first time. Otherwise, it looked like a horse-sized Eurasian boar. I know because I spent hours looking at pictures of boars, wondering what the difference between them was. It shocked mc to realize so many types existed.

The frozen steam ended at an equally frozen waterfall. It dropped from somewhere way above, farther than the poor eyes of the boar could see. Regardless, the waterfall wasn't the focus anyway. Instead, what was locked in it took the center of attention: a tree, twisted and thick, green branches and trunk sheathed in icy armor. It gave off a powerful ponderous atmosphere that quieted the ever noisy boar into silent reverence, even locked in ice.

Once there, the tree people rooted in the soil on the banks of the frozen stream. The boar checked in with the tree woman then went away, sinking in the snow. While its vision was terrible, I wanted to see what I could. I suspected the tree people put on a ceremony of some kind. The boar did not comply but shuffled slightly. Then, a series of soft cries came from above and around us.

I realized then that perhaps it had another role — a guardian one. I was not the only non-tree person on the journey. Different birds and other ground creatures had come as well. As the ceremony started behind us, the dozens of protectors had spread out in a fan, acting as a defensive force or at least sentries.

Figuring out against what didn't take long. As the pollen spilled out from the waterfall area, the boar's nose picked up an astringent scent that sliced through it all. Then, the snow moved, revealing thick carapaces and dozens of chitinous legs.

I couldn't quite process what they were, but the boar had no such impediment, letting out a squeal as it charged at one. Unfortunately, its senses seemed to go into overdrive at that moment, and I was so swamped by the input that I didn't realize we had charged and charged again before I regained some understanding of the situation.

The boar had hooked a curved tusk into the side of one of the carapace armored things and flipped it over with a surge. The boar's entire head seemed to warm up, steaming so hard that it rippled in the cold air. A fist-sized knot pressed out of its skull, giving the heat an outlet. It formed invisibly in the air before smashing down on the underneath of the carapace creature. The wriggling legs compressed and sunk it as its weaker underbelly smashed in. The boar squealed in victory before striking it again, ensuring its death as it broke apart, parts and fluids scattering on the churned snow.

It was chaotic and unsightly, but part of me reveled in the fight along with the boar. We charged together, and the boar smashed into another one that was fighting with an elephant-sized avian. It didn't last, and the boar set off at another one.

The stone protruding from its skull never receded, and the boar used its powers several times. At first, I thought the boar was using something like telekinesis. As it used its strength over and over, I realized it was more likely gravity-related. One of the carapaces managed to hook and throw the boar. It landed awkwardly but stumbled back to its feet to charge again. When it was about to happen again, I encouraged it to lay its power down on its body right when the carapace creature went to throw it. It hurt, but the boar didn't go flying much to the creature's chagrin. The boar promptly hooked it with its tusks and returned the favor.

The boar's control wasn't fine enough to do that again, but we did manage to project its power in front of it as it smashed into carapaces. I was eager to try more things, but we ran out of enemies. Probably for the best as it was exhausted and flopped into the snow when the battle ended.

The ceremony was still ongoing, even if the pollen scents were muddled from the battle. The boar staggered over to one smashed carapace and began feeding on it. It was repulsive. So much so I couldn't help but drawback, using every trick I could think of to drop into a fugue.

I hated eating the most in Flashes. Being with the boar while it ate dead bodies ... no way!

I woke up in a pool of drool. Thoughts from the Flash made my stomach flip upside down, and I barely made it to the bathroom before everything came flying out. After cleaning up, I staggered out weak and pale, finally not vomiting.

Focusing on the language I had heard, kept nausea at bay. So I wrote down the sounds and then recorded how I thought they sounded for Immerlin to process. It helped, and before long, light streamed in through the blinds.

I didn't even bother with the idea of food. However, I did decide to try to work in some tea. Something soothing and no caffeine — criminal, I know — seemed to be about right. So I settled in and swept over the report I was preparing to give DKL Cyber. A few adjustments later, it was as done as I was going to get it, even if I didn't like all the tabled data. I sent the report by email while I queued up all the necessary supporting work files to the file upload location they provided me. Same for Justin's work. It took a trivial amount of time, and I had the rough draft sent off after a couple of additions.

Considering the two tasks done, I went back to looking at the work for Inverse Voices. I had sent a scary estimation of hours to IV on what it would take to evaluate their patent issues. Frankly, I expected it was hefty enough that she would have turned me down. Unexpectedly, outside of a few grumbles from their legal department, they had agreed and even indicated that I could extend beyond that amount if it were necessary. It left me thankful but puzzled as well. I think I'm good, but I'm not that good. I didn't turn down the work since I needed it. Still, this move, plus the stack of other oddball inquiries they had made, made me nervous of them.

All that aside, she was right to be worried. Integrating the acquired company's infrastructure into Inverse Voices' existing infrastructure wasn't too much of a hardship, but the patent implementations, well, that wouldn't be so straightforward an action.

Immerlin interrupted my thoughts with a web conference call from Howie. It didn't take long before his harried face filled the monitors.

I felt a sense of dread. "What's up, Howie?" I whispered.

"Good news or bad news?" he asked.

"Bad. Always the bad news first."

Howie sighed. "Yeah, I know, darkness so you can see the dawn."

"Yep," I said, fingers fidgeting with the already frayed edge of the desk.

"Alright then. I've made moves to counter Dereck's attempt to declare you incompetent to be the custodian for your mother. His lawyer, in turn, has made moves of his own. While I succeeded in shutting down the initial legal action, his lawyer rammed through a motion to change venues. Their approach is that your mother dwells in another county and is cared for in another county, so the case should be handled by the court of that county versus ours. You know that I try to force all cases to our county because it's favorable to our position."

My throat was like a rusty gear, but I forced it open enough to squeak out, "I do. What county..."

Howie's harried face expressed even more fatigue. "Monteage. It's Judge Ty Harris."

He smelled of burnt coffee. Judge Harris did. A flicker of an old-lined face and dull brown eyes snapped before my eyes before disappearing.

He had presided over the case that ended up with me in a mental hospital. And the one that Howie had filed to get me free.

I closed my eyes. Howie's voice pulled me out of my memories.

"Hey," he barked. "Right here, right now."

Heh. Damn those keywords that had been beaten into me. The thoughts spun on, but I opened my eyes and focused on Howie. Perhaps one of the few tricks I had taken away from the damn hospital that I used.

Howie looked ... indignant. "Don't trip down memory lane. It's a fucked up move, and I'm working to counter it, so don't take it as a lost cause. Just hold it in the background and let me give you some good news."

I jerked out what could pass as a nod. Howie didn't look any less worried, so he said, "How about I put it this way. Either you show me that you are okay, or I'll be living in your house farting on your couch for the next couple of days."

Howie knew how to make an effective threat, and I plastered on a fake smile and a limpid salute to show I was a-okay. He snorted and flipped me off. Eyes narrowed, he said, "Say it. I'm not going to let this go until I hear you say it out loud."

I glared at Howie, and he glared right back. I broke first, dropping my eyes and gusting out a sigh. Then, mimicking a robot, I said, "I'm fine. I will stay busy and not linger on this change."

"And ..." Howie prompted.

"I'll also program Immerlin to call you immediately if anything is bothering me or if I have any issues. Happy?"

"No, but it will work. Now, let me give you some good news that hopefully will balance."

Visualizing a scale tipped all the way to ground with Judge Harris' name in it, I doubted it. "Go ahead. Anything has to help."

Howie flattened out something in front of him. Probably paper, given his love for writing things out.

"Remember when you told me about the threat from 90degreesright? Well, I did some digging and networking. Thanks, by the way, for the name list you gave me of other contractors you knew worked for them too. It looks like 90degreesright have pseudo threatened a few other folks on that list. I've touched base with lawyers and talked a few more of the others to represent them on this issue. I engaged my contacts with law enforcement and made it clear 90degreesright was applying pressure in alignment with the restrictions of their ongoing lawsuit. That, in conjunction with a few favors, has blown this issue up in their face."

"That's good news," I said.

Howie nodded, eyes crinkling as he gave a slight grin. "I also am working on seeing if I can jam it to them, too. If it works, they will be paying you compensation for the mental anguish and time lost to work effectively due to their slander."

I wanted to hug him. Getting on the wrong side of Howie is what has sunk more overblown jerks than I could name. I would do anything for him.

"Howie, you are the bomb, you know that?"

He laughed, waving for me to give him more. I gave him the finger, and we both laughed. Finally, Howie said, "You owe me. I know it's not our regular time but come over for dinner."

My innards froze up, but I forced out a choppy okay. The guy is saving my bacon and is worried about me. Could I say no?

Twenty-Three

Wanting to meet up with Howie was one of my top ten things to do. Actually going through with it skewed the opposite direction. Luckily, music and the right gadgets allowed me to cope. Howie wanted to see me in person — mostly because he knew his chance of coming to the house was lower. Letting people in the house was my personal horror show. Contractors were the nightmare. Don't get me started on maintenance. Letting people near me was horrible.

I hate my brain most days.

A few days and some endless grind on work finished almost all the items I owed people. First, the Inverse Voices work was done until more scanning and log data came in. Then, everything else was done, cleaned, and in their hands to finish.

Even though I enjoyed the boar's Flash this go-around, I couldn't bring myself to go to sleep voluntarily. I'd put it off for days now, living on coffee, work, and adrenaline. I didn't want to sleep, didn't want to think about tomorrow, didn't want to work — hell, I wasn't sure what would settle the jittery sense of doom building up behind my eyes.

Flopping in the chair, I said, "Wake up, Immerlin, let's do the morning roll call."

"It's not morning," said the smooth baritone. "It's 11:37 PM, Central Standard Time. Morning is not until —"

"Immerlin, cancel. I know what time it is and that it's not morning."

I flicked my fingers and gave Immerlin a one-finger salute. "Fine. Immerlin, new email, August Derlitte."

"Email to August Derlitte, S.I.N.K. drafted."

I closed my eyes. "Email subject line is next quarter's call for research papers. Body, standard greeting, and signature line. Email body paragraph one: We are approaching the new quarter, and I'm eyeballing my schedule for upcoming conferences. I've several ideas about potential papers that I think would be good papers, especially those that would showcase the Argyle platform super well."

That got me thinking about their platform and datagrams, knowledge graphs, and their 4d exploration engine. It's not dull stuff, but it managed to take me down anyway, as I slipped out of the fugue and realized I Flashed to the boar.

It was practicing.

I think.

Given the amount of effort it was putting into smashing rocks and the snowy earth, I guess that was what it was doing.

I could feel so much this time, more than ever before. The wind lifted snow, sending it flurrying around the boar. It was surreal and made me want not to leave. To not go back. I don't know how long I could stay, but I wanted to find out. To see if I could push away the doom that Judge Harris had laid upon my heart.

The thrumming engine in the boar's brain pulled my attention back. It was revving up to smash something again, and I realized just how hard this might be. But, I had to stay in the moment, as much as I could, all the time I could. Or, I'd slip into a fugue and be right back, Judge Harris about to kick my ass and all.

The boar snorted and smashed the ground again, crunching dirt, snow, and rocks. It didn't look effective, frankly, but I wanted to understand what the boar was doing. So I threw myself in the sensation. It was weird, like a combination of a shiver going up your spine and the vibration you feel when you have an engine purring under your hand.

It stopped, ate, and went to sleep, but I didn't. While it snorted and snored in sleep, I kept messing around. After a few aborted attempts that roused it several times from sleep, I finally figured out that the 'engine' as I was calling it was the fist-sized projection that pushed out of the boar's skull in the battle from a few Flashes ago. It was some stone or hard deposit that the boar's body had produced. The stone didn't quite vibrate or even spin, though it certainly seemed that way. I had read enough fiction and lived through enough Flashes to realize this was the boar's source of power or magic. It's monster core or whatever name matched. Unfortunately, none of that knowledge or miles of fiction really helped me know what to do with it. All I could think of was miles of colorful description and little process to understand how it functioned.

Well, nothing beats the coder's path: try and try and try until you succeed or hand the project off to someone else.

From what I could sense, the boar seemed to rely on passively soaking up energy from, well, I guess, the environment. The sensation came from the movement of energy as it moved in or over the hard stone. Focusing on it seemed to build up an attraction that drew the power into the boar. I worked on that all night, not letting my attention stray until the boar woke up. It struck me as weird that it wasn't nocturnal like boars back home but whatever.

The boar returned to practice, and we repeated this cycle several times. I almost slipped into fugue but found a happy medium between backing off my attention to let my mind rest without sliding into a fugue that would send me back.

It was an old trick that worked. Self-hypnosis had been a method I had evolved to convince the doctors in the hospital. It worked here to make sure I didn't slip away.

It was the twelfth cycle of this when I realized that the boar had gotten slightly stronger doing its practice. It was also when I realized, quite accidentally, that the energy flowing through the boar's body reminded me of a network. Not a good one, mind you, but one put together by a five-year-old having a temper tantrum.

Somewhere along the line, I got the crazy thought to fix it. I wanted something to do. Desperately. Something all-consuming so I could ignore the looming sense of despair I felt for the upcoming meeting with the judge. I needed it.

Somewhere in that mixed state of thought, the tree woman had dropped by and left numerous truffles for the boar to eat. After what felt like a happy time hanging out together, the boar ate one while also absorbing energy passively like normal. However, when it consumed the truffles, they burst with energy as well. It was a seriously bizarre sensation, like fingernails scraping across your liver.

Energy welled up and exploded from its gut. Then, it swirled around and smashed into dead ends before it dissipated. Power ran around in circles until exhausted. Then, finally, it leaked out and was lost. So little made it from the boar's stomach to the stone in its brain.

Absolutely. The. Worst. Damn. Network. Ever.

That little bit entered in and seemed to strengthen and slightly modify the stone as it soaked in energy during the boar's sleep period. Then, an even smaller sliver appeared to be used to decongest or repair the network.

It gave me something that I needed to focus on desperately, and over the next couple of sleep periods, I played with the stone and energy it drew in.

Drawing out the messed pathways in the boar's body and viewing it as a network gave me what I needed to focus on to stay here.

I had already figured out that attention attracted energy. Experimenting while the boar slept made me realize I could shape that attraction by focusing on specific areas. It took a bit of visualization on my part, but it was worth it. When it used energy while practicing during the day, I traced the pathways. None of my experiences with server rooms had ever turned out great, but I knew how they worked, and I had been in them virtually more times than I could count, not to mention that I had engineered more than one network. When the boar slept, I redirected some of the energy to unclog, rewire and move pathways.

It was slow business but kept me engrossed. It got a little dangerous from time to time, as focusing so hard almost brought on the fugue more than once. When I didn't have the energy to play with, I made the time pass by visualizing ways the boar could use its power and made attempts to try and convey it to the boar. Not sure it ever stuck since it didn't change its practice much from smashing everything. However, it used its gravity to pull a rock shard down to the ground when it went flying at it after a smashing charge. That gave me hope, though it was an isolated incident.

Days continued turning into months, culminating with a change in the weather.

The evolution of pace was welcome. While I had used self-hypnosis to recoup in small bits, I was beginning to feel like I did when I was hospitalized and drugged all the time. It made pushing away the fugue incredibly hard since concentrating took more and more effort.

The snows came down thickly, and the boar began to roam more widely to find food. Somewhere along the way, the boar started to emanate heat when it got cold or wanted to melt snow. Its brain stone had changed shape several times, especially as I cleaned up its physical network. The way energy interacted with it made it shift and change, becoming more intricate and fluted.

Not only had its powers changed, but so too had its size. While it was not precisely small before, it had grown tremendously. It gained not only mass but significant density to the point where it had to use a trickle of its gravity power to keep its excess heaviness from destroying where the two of them dwelled.

The changes did not go unnoticed, and the tree woman checked on it from time to time, bringing more and more truffles, fruits, and vegetables — most of which I couldn't begin to name. Very little of it looked like earthy produce though the boar loved it desperately, based on the squeals and snorts it happily gave out consuming them.

The deep snowy time made the tracking of days disappear. The boar slept all the time now, and I worked, plugging endlessly to redirect what it soaked into fixing its physical network. After a while, I finally accepted that I had gone as far as possible with self-hypnosis.

It did nothing for me now.

Nothing.

The drugged, stretched-out feeling was worse, but I didn't want to stop.

I had almost rebuilt the boar's physical network.

I wanted to finish it.

Make it work.

The tree woman checked on the boar from time to time. When the boar went into a deep, hibernating sleep, I could sense her moving a series of double fist-sized stones around the boar. At some point during the boar's on-and-off sleep period, the boar had gained the ability to see around it for a short distance. It was worse than its already pitiful eyesight but allowed me to 'see' around it even while it was sleeping.

It was fun at first. But then, the extra input just made me more and more tired and stretched out. My mind wasn't recovering anymore, and all the information was overwhelming me. Nevertheless, by focusing all my scattered attention on the rebuilding effort, I succeeded in not drifting away into a fugue.

The stones she brought were filled with energy. I did not understand the pattern she made with them, but I did recognize they were something the boar could absorb. To use them or not use them never crossed my mind.

The energy was there to be absorbed.

After an endless time, my burned-out brain realized that we had finished.

It was chaotic and dreamlike to me, but I could feel the change. It happened right after I completed rebuilding the network. A cocoon of fiery gravity appeared around the boar, as the boar's gravity and fiery power wrapped around it protectively. It distorted everything around it, creating ripples that rapidly built into a sucking black hole that absorbed energy and sent it to the boar.

Sensing the boar's huge body wrapped in heat and gravity ripples brought to mind an image from the past when I collected cards. A dumb card game. Still, the pictures on the cards resonated with me. I had one that held a giant boar, enormous and wild, flames for boar bristles and eyes like furnaces. On-Raze was its name. A god in the card game who could create — or destroy if called to do so.

The image lingered in the sea of confusion, so I focused on it. The boar seemed tiny, like a child next to the image in my mind. I could see them side by side, the little boar before the enormous god-like picture in my mind from the card game. It was real or as real as it could be in the feverish drugged state.

When the tiny boar spoke, my mind seemed to lurch to a halt.

"Ancestor?"

The tiny boar prostrated in front of the image I had accidentally conjured.

The static image said nothing in return, no matter how many times the tiny boar asked it to speak. Instead, it repeatedly tried while my burned-out consciousness tried to comprehend what was going on. I don't know why it didn't feel far-fetched, but I could sense that the tiny boar was the boar.

The one I had been riding along with the whole time.

Somewhere in that chaotic mess of thinking, I realized the tiny boar was doing everything it could to get the picture's attention. It was using all its energy, everything, the totality of the power that it was sucking and absorbing to try and reach the image of the god boar from the card game that I had accidentally conjured.

On the one hand, I felt guilty. But, on the other hand, I felt happy.

What I didn't like was that it was wasting its energy.

It kept trying, over and over. The energy was going from it and into the picture I had accidentally made. At some point, I realized that the power wasn't lost but was infusing the image. Not in a good way, either. It was building up without an outlet. Unlike a real being, it had no way to use it. Effectively, it was rapidly becoming a ticking time bomb. Through the blurry haze in my mind, I realized that the situation might kill the boar if this continued. Instead of using the energy to advance and grow, it poured the power out. The boar was truly burning away its life force. Either the picture I had built would explode from too much energy, or the little boar would die from exhausting its life force in a vain attempt to talk to something that didn't exist.

I wanted the boar to stop.

Nothing I did seemed to make the little boar listen. My mind hammered at it, but it was too intent on the god boar picture. Finally, in desperation, I moved to the god boar picture instead and somehow sank inside. It was a crazy thought and even more insane that it seemed to work.

The disorientation was nauseating. While reality seemed to spin and flip flop in vomitous ways, I looked through the chaos and fog clouding my vision and caught its eyes.

Emotion. If I had to describe it in one word, that's what I would use — a flood of emotion.

Happiness. Fear. Awe. Hope.

So many emotions. The storm almost shredded me, but the lingering pieces of my mind managed to find the way to send the energy it had sent me back. It created a cycle, and energy pumped from it to me and back to it again. Along with it came fragments of memories, sensations, and thoughts. The pieces were muddy and dull, mixing with my recall of events. It felt heavy, like a stone pressing down, and instinctively I shared some of my thoughts. It was no more coherent, a blurry stream of memory fragments, ideas, and visions I had conjured of how it could use its powers better.

The emotions the boar sent back as we cycled back and forth with energy burned even hotter, and I was drowning, falling deeper into oblivion. The fugue was dragging me down, down, down ....

My focus was a tiny pinhole in the fugue covering everything. Thoughts were fleeting and scattered, spinning visions that would appear and disappear. Finally, I realized I was swimming in a sea of thought with no clarity and a lot of fuzziness. Fear surged, welling up and then drained away to numbness. I idly thought of the tree woman.

It resonated with the tiny boar, who restored my focus a little bit. We both seized on the thought. The connection was weak at best, but with my last bits of focus, I sent back the image of the changed diagram I had always wanted to find a way to convey to her.

That effort took everything, and I went numb, losing the connection to the tiny boar. I could feel nothing. Oblivion felt strange, without sensation.

Vague. Formless.

"ZZZZZZZzzzzzz"

A dull, off-key buzzing sliced through the oblivion. It hit it, or more accurately, I smashed it. Immerlin started barking, but I yelled back until I found the right combination of commands that shut him up.

I crushed a pillow close. A thought kept revolving in my foggy brain.

Oh, holy fuck, what had I just done.

Twenty-Four

Scott found Doc Matson exactly where he expected. Doc was either in the autopsy room, his tiny office, or smoking on the fire escape. The propped open door and smell of smoke made it easy to figure out.

"Doc, you have got to see this," Scott said, walking over waving a wad of paper in one hand.

Doc Matson sneered at him through curls of smoke. Scott didn't seem to mind and unfolded one of the sheets of paper with care. He shoved it towards Doc Matson while grinning like he had gotten lucky last night.

Flicking away some ashes, Doc Matson languidly grabbed it. Scribbles filled the paper as he expected. It was complete chaos. Scott had turned the page several times while he was writing. It probably was because he kept spilling things on it, based on the mixed colors of the stains.

Restraining from tossing the page off the side, Doc Matson asked, "What is this supposed to show me?"

"Proof, doc, more proof!"

Scott snatched the sheet of paper and pointed to a nearly incomprehensible mess of numbers and words. "I had shit luck figuring out the burn deaths or anything related to fires. Drowning was just as bad, though the guy who had saltwater in his lungs and fresh water on his clothes was quirky. Another one had a fish up his anus, but none of those looked credible."

Doc Matson puffed on his cig and flicked ashes, turning away.

"Wait! Wait, no, really, I've got more good stuff."

That got Scott a lazy wave from Doc Matson, which he took as a reason to continue. Not that he planned to stop talking anyway.

Scott flipped the paper. "Look here. See this? These are four cases I found. You know what's weird about them?"

Scott waited expectantly until Doc Matson lazily waved his hand. "Ink, sir, ink. Now, you might be thinking: 'Scott, what's weird about ink on a corpse? I've seen a million bodies with tattoos', but you would be wrong, sir, wrong. It's not ink on a corpse but ink in a corpse!"

Scott punctuated the end by raising his hands triumphantly along with his voice. Then, he dropped them listlessly to his sides when Doc Matson didn't even blink.

"Seriously?" Scott said. "I thought for sure you would love the fact I found a couple of bodies with gallons, mind you, gallons of ink in their body, from veins to organs."

Doc Matson drew on the last of his cig and threw the filter away to the pile below. He blew out smoke and looked at Scott through the haze it made. "Gallons of ink?"

"Gallons," Scott said, breaking out in a cheesy smile. "I got it all laid out on the computer. But, but that's not the whole of it. While that is oddball — believe me, one of them was found in sand up to his crotch and filled to the brim with ink, even leaking out of his eyes! But still, the quirkiest one is the group of reports I found where two people — not a lot but still — two people who were found with their organs and inner tissues liquified but the skin and bones intact."

Fishing around in his pocket, Doc Matson found his pack of cigarettes. Firing it up, he asked his question through a plume of smoke.

"Ink-filled bodies and liquefied ones. Oddball, yes, but so what?"

Scott grinned broadly again. "Ah, see, the shit gets deep here. The two guys — the blister bodies — were found in two different states and are totally not related to each other in any way that I can see. Still, according to the coroner's report, the wounds were in the same place in each case, and they died within seconds of each other. If that's not enough to be eerie, I don't know what is!"

Doc Matson held the smoke in his lungs before letting it out in a big cloud. "Those creepy tentacle videos you keep leaving open in the browser — that's eerie. Why are you so fucked up, anyway? Find a decent girl, already."

Scott waved the papers in Doc Matson's face, eyes rolling at his reference to his video tastes.

Doc Matson grabbed them in self-defense and looked at them. Scott waited, eyes glued to every movement. Finally, Doc Matson pushed them back and worked his cigarette until it finished. He threw the butt down to join the others below and looked over at Scott, exhaling his last bit of smoke.

"Got it on your laptop?"

Scott's head danced up and down like one of those dolls on the dashboard of a car. "Sure do. Including pictures and sketches of what the coroners thought was the shape of the weapon in the balloon bodies. I swear it looks like a curved beak!"

Doc Matson nodded and scratched his beard as they plodded inside. For all the grief he was giving Scott, it was strange, and he liked peculiar things. It made dealing with the dead somehow more bearable.

Twenty-Five

The nightmare was outside the door. It scratched at the edges of my eyes, but thankfully it was dark. Even past the eye mask, I could feel it, the emotion growing stronger as I got closer to the courthouse. The only concession that the judge had given was to meet at the end of his day.

Otherwise, I was going in.

Leaving my house.

Walking into the courthouse.

Howie tried his best, but nothing seemed to deter Judge Harris. Once we proposed the idea, the judge latched on it and wouldn't let the thought go. He was a monster wrapped in the scent of stale coffee.

I tried not to hyperventilate when the Tesla came to a stop. It made the chime that I had programmed in to let me know we had arrived. It magnified in my brain, echoing over and over. I couldn't keep my hands from trembling. They were frozen blocks of ice that refused to remove the eye covering.

A gentle knock on the window. A couple of more knocks. A short staccato of knocks.

It was Howie. I knew that stupid knock anywhere.

While I hated my time in the mental hospital, it had given me a few tricks. Howie and I had created a knock-tap language. A stupid, child-like thing between two kids, trying to find a sense of privacy in a cold, sterile place where laughter and fun died a long time ago.

It gave us a game that only we could play.

It kept me from actually becoming the very thing that I was accused of being.

Tap. Tapping in rapid succession. A question.

Hearing Howie outside, asking if I was okay, finally empowered my hands to move. I fumbled around until I worked the scented ointment from my pocket.

Scents helped — another trick.

A generous amount helped the mixed scent of green tea and hickory dominate. I breathed in the smells, and they soothed the shaking feeling that the wrong move would make me shatter into pieces.

I got the eye covering off and braved the color and lights. After that, I mostly ignored the blurry haze and focused on using clumsy fingers to press the door unlock button.

Howie settled into the front seat with practiced ease. I heard it behind closed eyes. His voice had a low, gravelly bur to it. I knew he was suppressing intense anger. Yet, for some reason, I found it soothing instead of upsetting.

"You made it."

Deep breath. Exhale. I nodded without opening my eyes.

"Yes," I exhaled/gasped out. I focused on the scents instead of the sights and braved opening my eyes. Howie's face was as annoyed as I expected it to be.

"I won't bother asking if you are up for this. We both know that's not the case. However, if you can do this — it will be worth it."

I think he was trying to convince himself as much as he was me. Judge Harris didn't exactly give us a choice. Either show up in person or else. The threat didn't have to be filled in. He had all the power.

My fingers spun the fidget rings I had put on. The movement was comforting. I sucked in more air, letting the ointment scents settle in my lungs. Then, letting it out, I suppressed the trembling in my voice as much as I could and said, "I can do it. I got to do it. Otherwise, what? I end up in a full courtroom before the judge? He would likely send me back to my old room at the hospital."

Howie probably slipped back in time like I did to the memory of that horrible, clinical room — on the outside seemingly ordinary but a cold, heartless bitch underneath and just out of sight — horrors lurked in the corners, especially when visitors left. And, after the visitors left, no one was around to monitor the monsters in white uniforms.

I watched his fist clench. Loosen. We breathed together for a moment, and I reached out a trembling hand to tap on his arm. I felt him flinch. It stilled my fingers for a moment before I continued. Then, finally, he tapped back.

Something about it — having a friend with me at the moment — pushed the nightmare a little farther away. We tapped for a few minutes, completely forgetting everything. Reality, however, is a harsh mistress who cut through the sense of calmness with a knife.

Howie's watch buzzed. Immerlin's mobile version spoke too. "Alert, 10-minute warning."

"Immerlin, silence the alarm," I whispered, letting my hand slide back.

"You got this," Howie reinforced.

"I know. I am just going to confront the bogeyman who dropped the hammer that put me in limbo for most of my teen years. What could go wrong?"

Howie gave a pained smile, and I didn't laugh either. It was a feeble attempt at a joke anyway.

On that failed note, we left the car. It was as dizzying as I expected, but I managed somehow. I kept focusing on the other end of the situation — Dereck gone, and this legal shit settled once and for all. Or, so I hoped.

The metal detector wasn't too bad, but when the guard's aftershave almost sent me into spasms. Luckily, Howie kept events from escalating and deflected the guard's good intentions. We made it to the front of the judge's chambers. I couldn't tell you how or the path, but we were there.

Howie grabbed my arm and tapped out encouragement. I settled my heart and nodded. Howie talked into an intercom, and finally, the door buzzed.

Howie reached to open it, but I beat him to it, using a shaking hand to push it ajar. I shakily strode forward into the dim recesses on the other side of the door.

Each step felt like I was walking to my execution. On the way, I re-applied the ointment under my nose. I almost dropped the applicator several times but managed to succeed. My heart was loud, beating like a drum in my ears. Through that jungle medley, I raised a trembling hand to push open the final door.

The scent of stale coffee and aftershave burned through the mixed scents of ointment. It made me tremble more, but I forced my legs to keep going.

Judge Harris didn't bother to look up, just flapped a hand towards the seat in front of his desk. It was kind to call it that. It looked more like an enormous wooden aircraft carrier laden with case files and papers.

After an eternity, Judge Harris pushed the papers in front of him away, threw down his glasses, leaned back, and rubbed his eyes. He got up, saying nothing, but moved over to his coffee area. After pouring cold coffee into a mug, he returned to his desk and looked at me.

I sat there paralyzed. Watching him. Doing nothing.

Old eyes probed mine, and I couldn't face them. So I dropped my gaze to the desk. It was safer.

Judge Harris didn't say anything, but I could hear him drink a sip of coffee. It was unsettling.

"I wasn't sure if you would come." His voice reminded me of rust. Metallic. Grainy. Peeling in flecks and bits.

When I didn't respond, Judge Harris said, "Do you remember me?"

I jerked my head up and down before he ended speaking.

"I see," he said. "Then you might remember that I like to see the faces of the people I talk to then."

My heart lurched. Using bravery that I didn't know I had, I lifted my eyes. I thanked every god in this world, and Flash I could remember when I saw him looking down at a case file in front of him. He looked up, eyes dark but not as cold or heartless as I expected.

He looked down again at the case file. "I'm old-fashioned, and some people would say that I'm an ass. However, I expect a certain amount of decency. Equally, I extend it back. I'm aware from your file that you have some ... issues with certain things and situations."

I nodded. I wasn't sure what else to do and was afraid to look anywhere else.

Judge Harris put his glasses on to read something and then took them off not long later. He rubbed his eyes again. While he did so, he asked, "Do you know why I insisted that you come and meet me in person?"

I shook my head. Both hands were twisting fidget rings.

"We have history, you and I. I've seen you in my courtroom almost as much as I have seen repeat criminals over the years."

My hands stilled at that comment. I wasn't sure how to take that. Maybe Judge Harris saw my confusion since he clarified.

"I'm not putting you in that bucket, don't worry. From a frequency perspective, you have been in my courtroom a lot compared to most. Several times you melted down quite spectacularly, I might add."

I repressed those images before they rose. I had no desire to relive those moments. It did make me shake, though. Judge Harris picked up on it and raised both hands defensively. "It's okay. Sorry if that brought up bad memories. My point is when I saw your case file again, I was surprised. Our last meeting with your fierce lawyer friend was pretty definitive. I never expected to see you again. But then, here comes your case file and an offer to meet, if necessary. I read some interesting things there. I went back to your other case files. I did a little investigation. You have done well for yourself in the last couple of years. In fact, very successful, in a positive, legal and good way. I found it refreshing, honestly, given the typical less-than-positive aspects of society, I normally have to wade through. So, when I read what was going on, I wondered. Would a man with such intense agoraphobia as yourself really come to meet me in person if I requested it? Maybe it didn't seem very empathetic, but I wanted to know that fact. Do you know why?"

I jerked my head left and right, mind cursing him from top to bottom. So he did this on a whim?

Judge Harris picked up the case file, looking at me over its edge. "It says here that you are the sole supporter of your mother's hospital care. That you have been the sole supporter since she went into care a year ago. The same woman who stood in my courtroom a few years back and lobbied to have you committed to an asylum. Her face that day was etched in my heart. I had never seen a woman look at her own child in such a vile, disgusting way in my life. Her words, well, I wouldn't use those on the hardened criminals that pass in front of my bench. So, I wanted to know. Not on paper or over the phone, but from your mouth."

My mouth was a desert, but after a couple of aborted swallows to make enough spit to dry it, I uttered, "She's my mother."

He cocked his head in response. "Oh? I believe she disavowed that quite loudly in the courtroom that day. Had you the fiery lawyer then that you do now, then she could have potentially lost her case that day with that statement. You are caring for this woman? In good faith?"

My mouth was too dry to speak, so I nodded. The judge, however, was not satisfied and pressed me to speak. "She ... I ... even... we didn't do well. Mother couldn't ... didn't want to deal with me. Exhausted. She just ... got tired of it. Of me. That's what led up to ... events. Afterward, when I was older ... Alice helped. She got us talking. We actually were ... trying ... trying to reconcile."

It was hard to speak of it. Alice, my angel of a sister. She had found a way for both of us, mother and I, to have a common ground. To share something for the first time in a long time. That I had found success didn't hurt. Mother always measured with money to a certain extent. It was something fundamental in her heart.

"I see. In fact, I was curious what motivations might be behind it all. From what I can determine, the care is topnotch, and nothing has been stinted to make sure your mother is being taken care of. However, see, Mr. Dereck Eisenrohr disputes that you are the right person to provide this care. He or I should say his lawyer has eloquently laid out a series of points to show you are not the right person and that this care is just a cover to gain access to a sizable fortune linked to your mother's estate."

I shook my head. Judge Harris looked at me for a minute before putting down his case file.

"It had me wondering. You get a lot of insight into human thought when you sit where I do. You learn to filter out the bull and focus on details that indicate what's actually going on. That doesn't mean you can't be fooled, but if you have the right information in your hands, you can actually puzzle out the heart of things readily enough. So, I pondered on your case for a bit. Part of me thinks that a man who feels so deeply about his mother that he beggars his fortune to pay for her medical care isn't the type Mr. Eisenrohr has painted. That this man is a person, who when that care is threatened, would even reach beyond his own frailties to stop that threat. I called you to my chambers, knowing fully well your medical condition. It's not nice, I admit it, to put you in this position. But I think it is fair. I think it is a good evaluation of your character. Are you the child who, no matter how conflicted their relationship with their parent, will aid them when they are in need? Would you even overcome your own problems to do so? I wanted to know."

I nodded. What was there to say? I didn't hate Judge Harris or my mother any less for this situation.

"Mr. Eisenrohr says you are doing this for money. What do you say?"

It was an unkind request but not an unexpected one. Words slowly tumbled out as I concentrated on not melting down.

"Mother and I were talking. Had actually gotten to the point of meeting."

Judge Harris nodded, looking at his notes. "Indeed. My understanding is they were on their way to see you when the accident happened."

I didn't want to revisit those memories, but they didn't ask. A flicker of pacing back and forth, the oddness of my house being so clean. Mother was coming over. Alice had talked me into letting her stop by. So she could comprehend how well I was doing. How successful I had become. Not the failure, the disaster, she thought. Then, calling Alice. Her not picking up. Not until the fourth time I called. It wasn't her but emergency services. The horror of realizing she had died barely blocks away. Then the guilt of not being able to walk the distance, the short few blocks that I could see from my rooftop. A smashed car, crumbled and torn, surrounded by emergency vehicles and a sea of lights.

"I couldn't let it end that way." Seeing Judge Harris didn't understand what I meant, I let the words tumble out to explain more.

It hurt.

"She was coming to see me with Alice. My sister, Alice. She was the one who always found a way to make everything better." Bitterness crept in, and the words gushed out. The guilt, the pain, the anguish of the fragility of life — and its unfairness.

"She was pregnant. Alice was. She was so happy about it. So happy that we couldn't help but join in that excitement of new life. My mother and I spoke for the first time in years on the phone call when she announced it. Her pregnancy opened the door and led to us actually realizing the other person wasn't the horrible monster in the past, and our memories made us out to be. It led to me inviting her over. To see what I had made out of the ashes of the past. Alice drove them, but they didn't make it. She somehow slid in the rain, hit a curb, and smashed into a light pole. Alice died instantly, they said. Her and the baby — gone. Mother lived, but it was close. They had to pry her free, and she was inches from death."

I couldn't help but weep, tears running along the knuckles of my hand I chewed on it furiously.

His voice pulled me back. "I would comfort you with a hug, but I suspect it would make things worse. Listen up, young man. You don't strike the religious type, so I won't bother to appeal to you that way.

Life isn't fair or balanced, and it often sucks. As long as you are in life, however, you have a chance. An opportunity. That's partially while I'm minded to believe your side of things more than Mr. Eisenrohr."

Grief can't be so easily packaged up, but I managed to stop the weeping, at least, enough to focus on what Judge Harris was saying.

"You are either genuinely upset and doing your best to take care of your mother or a consummate actor pretending to do so. I'm more inclined to the former than the latter. Additionally, just like you have been my court before, so has Mr. Dereck Eisenrohr."

His statement sent a shock wave through my emotions. I rocked forward. "What do you mean, Judge Harris?"

He took a drink of cold, stale coffee and responded. "I mean, I've seen Mr. Dereck before, on another case, cases really, if I get down in the weeds. Not with the Eisenrohr name, though. Different names, shall we say?"

Stunned, I said, "What does that mean?"

"It means he's a con artist. He is a person who preys on women. When his information came up in the system, I wasn't surprised, though I was when I saw it in connection with your name. Dereck chasing down money from women doesn't make me raise an eyebrow, though having his activity tied to a person's death and another woman in the hospital did. I'm still piecing together the connections, but his request to replace you looks like a pure money grab based on what I was told about your mother's finances."

I lowered my head. Everything was muddy. I felt hollow and on fire at the same time. All of it was stirring like a slowly boiling pot.

Judge Harris coughed. "I realize that this old man was not being very considerate of your feelings. I apologize. However, your brother-in-law is likely not who he says he is and looks to be after the estate and finances of your sister and your mother."

"Should you really be telling me this?" I bit my tongue, so it came out a whisper. Otherwise, I was afraid I would scream.

He agreed. "Probably not, but I am. It won't jeopardize the investigation, and it's damn relevant to your case. I doubt you two talk — right? I would encourage you, in fact, to bind you — not to have contact with him after this meeting until this case is done. Do you have any problem with that?"

"No," I whispered through my teeth.

Judge Harris pushed a stapled stack of paper to me. "My suggestion — and only that, mind you, given my position — you have your fiery lawyer friend take a look at this publicly available information. It will help him — and you — control the situation around Mr. Eisenrohr trying to take over the estate and finances for your family members."

I took it with shaking hands. Nothing on it really made sense to my traumatized brain at the moment, so I clutched it in one hand on my lap.

"Thank you."

Judge Harris waved it away. "No need. I have to deal with the drivel and shit of society on a regular basis. So when I see a way to do a good turn for someone who has shoveled enough shit, especially in my courtroom, I take it."

I didn't know what to do, so I muttered a second thanks and sat there, paralyzed by the emotions racing through my heart.

"Now, young man, I would love nothing more than to keep talking to you. Find out the fascinating things you have done to spin your life in a positive way. To help comfort you with the loss and possible upcoming loss. However, my life doesn't wait either, and I have a long night ahead of me."

It took me a moment to realize he was asking me to leave. Then, he finally sighed and opened the door for me, and I stepped into the foyer to meet an anxious Howie.

The door closed behind me with a click, and I started answering Howie's questions.

Twenty-Six

Howie had only begrudgingly let the Tesla swallow me back into its interior.

I was going home.

He wanted to go with me. We struggled for a bit before compromising that he would follow me home. That when we arrived, we could talk about him coming inside again then. We both knew it was a put-off, but I was over-drafted, worn out, and too hollow from the emotions that Judge Harris had dredged out of the past to care.

I set the Tesla to return home and threw myself into every comfort I could in the car, from eye mask to heavy heated blanket. Music thrummed in the vehicle and drowned away any sound that might creep in from the outside.

My mind kept reeling from what Judge Harris said and the memories he dredged up from the past. Oh, Alice, how I miss you. You would know exactly what to say, how to turn this situation into something humorous, something quirky that would make the pain all go away.

And Dereck. Or Sam. Or Klaus. Whatever your real name is. The papers that Judge Harris had provided listed several. I'm coming for you, you son of a bitch. I should never have listened to Alice when she begged me not to mess it up by digging up some dirt from your past. While I always thought you were unworthy of her, never, ever did I think you were a con artist scumbag riding on women's hearts. Once I got back home, his history and I had a date night planned. Once I had his dirty history all outlined, it would make it show up to the right people. The ones that would make sure he got a long-coming, well-deserved ending. I visualized cement galoshes, but I knew realistically it was more likely a view from behind bars in his future instead.

It's life, not some tedious Hollywood flick.

I suspect the combination of movement, sound, being overwrought caught up to me. I dropped into a fitful sleep and right into a Flash.

The boar felt different. I felt a sense of odd guilt, which didn't help my already over-drafted emotions. I had impersonated a divine ancestor for the boar — part of me expected to be struck down by fire or lightning or some such for it.

After a pause where being struck down by divine fury didn't happen, I soothed over my emotions. Getting them under control, I tried to perceive what was going on.

Sight wasn't precisely what I had. It was more a growing awareness. Something had changed since the boar's transformation. Before, I pretty much immediately became aware and participated in the boar's senses. Now, it felt distant. Disconnected. After some metaphorical fumbling, I discovered something interesting. My — well, whatever I was — seemed to be still in the picture of the godly boar I had conjured up previously. It came to light quite literally as I focused my attention on it. The picture began to glow, and the bristles on the divine boar picture I had built burst into flames.

With it came a vague, separate sense. Hard to describe, equally as mysterious to pinpoint, but with a bit of focus, I realized that other sensation belonged to the boar.

It took even more fumbling to figure out how to reconnect with its senses. But then, I thought maybe I had made a mistake.

The boar was fighting. Sounds, smells, and colorless blurs exploded. It was pure chaos, and I thought I would die from the overload. Wound up tight, my emotions stretched and thrummed like a rubber band pulled near to breaking. If I had a head to hold, I would be cradling it right now.

In the blurry mess of motion feeding into my senses, I couldn't figure out where the boar was, just that the boar was in full melee. I suspected we were in the same region from the snow, churned earth, fragments of trees, and such. But that really wasn't stealing my attention.

Everything else did.

The scents of blood and torn bodies filled the boar's nose. Its ears flooded with screaming and howls. The boar's eyes flinched as wooden spears formed from roots exploded from the ground, rocks catapulted through the air like shrapnel, and lightning ripped the ground like whips.

The urgency in the boar was palpable. Even stretched and hollowed out, my emotions synchronized with it. Blood coursed, and energy flooded the boar's body as we charged towards a creature that looked like a horse-sized pangolin. The beast rolled forward into a ball and sent a wave of scales split off towards the boar in response to its charge. Gravity powers revving at full strength, energy left from the boar, fashioning two intangible limbs, pushing the scales just far enough from it, so they missed. When the pangolin creature went to leap away from the ground to dodge the boar's charge, I could sense the boar using its gravity powers around it, making it float helplessly in the air instead of springing away from the boar's charge.

I was proud of it. That was one of the things I had conveyed to it as a way to use its powers. It looked like it listened to my ramblings.

The pangolin exploded in a rain of flesh and liquids as the boar smashed into it and compressed it with its gravity powers. Its bristles lit up in fire to burn the gore off as it pivoted to charge again.

Dodging an explosion of rocky shrapnel, the boar raced through tree people battling more pangolins to smash into something that looked like a giant rock. It rebounded, sliding back, completely dizzy and stunned. Then, through its dazed eyes, I realized it had slammed into a giant land tortoise, and the rocks were actually the bumpy, rock-like material of the tortoise's shell.

A dancing whip of lightning at the end of its flight stung the boar, shocking it aware. The boar staggered to its feet, dodging an attack from another pangolin in the process. It left the pangolin a bloody mess after a short struggle before joining the tree woman fighting the rock-backed tortoise. She jumped up, sending a spray of wooden arrows at the tortoise's weak points. Her pollen was visible in the air, trailing after each arrow, somehow helping them shift and adjust when the tree woman attacked. The tortoise moved and swerved its overlapping rock shell to avoid the arrows. The movement left the tortoise off balance, and I could tell the boar noticed it as fast as I did.

Finding the right moment where it was off balance the most, the boar and the tortoise smashed again. I could tell the boar was trying to use its gravity powers on the tortoise and failing. After several attempts, the boar finally got lucky and hit it just right, knocking the tortoise off-balance enough that the tree woman succeeded in sending a barrage of arrows into the soft flesh under its shell. It spun with lightning speed and shrieked, letting out an odd sound that seemed to mix anger and bending metal all in one. The boar got clipped and went flying, barreling through the chaos of the melee to careen into a bole of a tree, snapping it in half and sending the trunk thundering down on top of it.

The sensation was multi-layered. I knew the boar was stunned and hurt, trapped under the tree. But I also felt stunned and hurt. Pain trickled in, stabbing with needles. Blood slid across the boar's vision and juxtaposed with the blood sliding across my own eyes.

My nose smelled something burning, felt wetness on my skin.

Vision overlapped, a ghostly overlay of one world framed over the other. The eye covering was long gone, ripped away. Music sputtered disjointedly, clashing with the drizzle of rain.

My vision changed again to the boar's melee, showing me what the boar was seeing. An undercurrent to the melee that the boar's eyes were feeding me was the chaotic sideways scene of a rainy night, pavement, the smell of burning, and the sound of whimpering. Past the buckled sides of the Tesla and through the broken window was the sight of another car. The other vehicle was mainly intact, but I could see a woman dangling upside down from her seat belt and flames licking up from the backside of her car. Then, discordant, my ears heard the sound of a truck revving and driving away.

I blinked and the two scenes mixed even more. I felt paralyzed and yet mobile, looking through the eyes of the boar and my own. With horrible procession, I watched the fire creep towards the woman in the car. Simultaneously, through the boar's stunned eyes, I absorbed the scene of the tortoise crashing down on the tree woman. As the tree woman lay captured under its shell, its head snaked out, curling up, mouth open.

A storm of fire began burning in its open beak of a mouth.

Help them.

Help them, I screamed, though nothing came out of my throat.

I was paralyzed, watching as both women in two worlds were about to die; somehow, my reality and my Flash aligned to match.

The smell of rain and welling desperation evoked memories. What was before my sets of eyes mixed with the third scene of the emergency vehicles that I watched from the roof of my house a year ago. I could see all three of them stacking on top of each other, a deep-seated feeling of helplessness shackling my limbs, holding me back from acting.

No, not again. The thoughts played ping pong in my brain, gaining strength, growing into shrieks of madness.

Move, damn it, move!

The fires in both worlds moved closer to kill the two of them, and I couldn't help but think of Alice.

Who I couldn't help.

Who I couldn't even go to when she was so close.

Was I really going to let it happen again?

Watch while the world swallowed up someone again?

My heart pounded. It raced, sending heat and power to my limbs as I reached within for something primal.

It came out like a scream, and in two worlds, I moved at the same time. From somewhere deep in the twisted darkness of my soul, I found the power to move, hand unbuckling my seat belt, crawling out of the Tesla.

Then, in the boar's world, I shook off the tree pinning me down, staggering to my feet.

The boar and I both synchronized movements. I charged across the pavement to the woman in the car while the boar raged through the battlefield to the tortoise. Fire and gravity churned around the boar, and I was with him, somehow a ghostly image of the godly boar picture I had conjured wrapping around him. The tortoise let out a shocked scream as the boar wrapped in flames and twists of gravity rending the air around smashed into it.

I found myself tugging at the woman's car door, struggling to pry it open enough to pull her free. With a titanic effort, I wrenched it free, ignoring the trailing lines of fire that dropped onto my back as I crawled inside. Armed with savage ferocity, I hacked at the seat belt holding her in place. The metal piece I was using bent, but I finally cut her down and pulled her free to the wet pavement.

The rain lightly falling was soothing on my burnt back. Car lights shone on the wet street, illuminating us both. I reared my head back and roared in two worlds before collapsing.

I felt hands flip me over, and Howie's face swam into view. Sirens and more sounds came afterward, but I didn't notice any of it.

I pulled Howie down close and rasped out. "I saved her this time. This time, she didn't have to die on the street. I saved her. I saved her."

He might have responded. I couldn't quite tell though I could see his lips moving in my fading vision. I felt he was telling me good job before the darkness ate everything.

Twenty-Seven

"Can someone tell me why this operation went so wrong?"

The three ghost shapes that overlaid the fantastic cloud scene past her office window didn't respond.

The icy-eyed woman waited. One of them, the sandy-haired man, shuffled around, playing with a match, before finally answering.

"The target wasn't in Thailand anymore. So we tracked her down to a hotel in Malaysia, but she surprised us again."

"Again. Again?" Her voice sharpened enough to cut glass. "Should I add another again? Did you not realize how cunning the Homegrown can be when one of us died earlier? Shall we all agree that she has out-thought, out-smarted, and out-planned you every time?"

The sandy-haired man's features contorted. "That's not quite a true depiction of events."

"Really? How would you report the situation upstairs? What should I tell Ogygia? What's your twist on the situation?"

"Hmph."

"That's what I thought. Don't think I'll bury this for you. We all only get so many attempts before replacement happens. You might want to remember it. But don't worry, you are far from alone."

She pulled two red lights from a side menu, expanding them on her office window to put the avatars and records of the two into view.

"Which one of you idiots thought it was a smart idea to make a move on these two bugs? Well?"

The Elfin featured man snorted. "You know I authorized it. It was time to clean up. I added your 'consultant' in for good measure. I told you previously that I did not like someone poking into our business."

"Really? Somehow this boondoggle meets the requirement to keep this from the public? This mess you've created keeps us from being exposed? Really?"

"Unfortunate mistakes," he said stiffly, looking away.

"Indeed. Mistakes, indeed. At least one is outright hostile, and I suspect the second one is not far away. This mess ... you will have to own up to it. Upstairs ... the masters in Ogygia. They want to talk. Not just to me, but you too. I hope you are ready. I doubt you are going to like the outcome."

The Elfin man looked stunned and then fearful before his image blinked out.

The remaining woman and sandy-haired man looked at each other before focusing on the woman in the office.

Cooly, she looked back. "Don't worry. He won't get far. People like us, we don't get to run from our failures."

Ignoring their expressions, she pulled all the red dots to the center of the window and expanded them. Then, splitting them into groups, she sent three to the other woman, two to the sandy-haired man, and kept two for herself.

"Solve them," she said. "Do it quickly and do it smartly. All of us are coming up for review. Whether we make it to return to Ogygia or end up like him depends on our next efforts. You can use any of the available assets. In fact, muster them all. Also, I'll be going in person as well."

The other woman expressed shock. "You are going in the field?"

She smiled, staring out over the clouds and the tops of buildings. "Yes. I've been in this office too long. The situation is so poor I intend to act directly. After all, if I can't solve the situation, it won't matter much whether I'm sitting in this office or I'm somewhere, does it?"

The sandy-haired man squinted at her and then guffawed. "Fine. You are right. It's been too long since I was out and about. Maybe some fieldwork is what's going to be necessary to solve this."

The sandy-haired man left, leaving the two women. The other woman hesitated, started to say something but reconsidered and just logged out instead.

She closed her ice eyes for a moment, contemplating. Her hands followed, shutting down everything in the projection except the two dots that needed her attention. She opened her eyes again, fingers deft, expanding each bug's records out, laying it out in a tree below each person's avatar. After some contemplation, she took notes on one avatar's file before closing it down to focus on the last one.

Tapping the window, she jotted a few notes down after thinking a bit and then zoomed in on the face. It looks gaunt in the rainy backdrop of the most recent picture.

"You," she said aloud. "You, I will take care of in person."

Twenty-Eight

I couldn't move.

If I wasn't so spaced out, I might have freaked out about it. Everything was muffled and far away, like I was underwater. Strangely I wasn't alarmed by it, but I would say it was because of the drugs. I had been put under so many times when I was in the mental hospital it wasn't hard to figure out when I had been injected with medication.

That I was aware was probably more shocking than anything. Trying to move led nowhere, so I settled on trying to piece out what I could from the muted sensations I was picking up.

An angry voice that I could swear was Howie was giving someone the what for in spades. I was in motion, or at least swaying. Maybe I was in the ambulance? No, that didn't seem right. It didn't smell right. Out of all of the senses, it was working the best. The sterile, antiseptic smells were too strong. I would say a hospital.

I was moving again. A brief sense of pain and coldness. Howie's voice draining away into oblivion.

I floated in a gray haze sea before the sensation returned.

It was cold. Smells were explosive, overwhelmingly so. Gone was the hospital. In its place were snow, trees, and earthy scents.

I was back with the boar.

After a mountain of effort, I managed to get the boar to open its eyes. The boar felt as worn out, drugged, and exhausted as I did.

We were in a wooded grotto on something. Felt like wood more than stone, but I had no way to tell. Light streamed down through openings, illuminating a wide but shallow pool of water. It looked clean, so I suspect it would be a beautiful blue if the boar could see in color.

We were not alone. Tree people of all kinds were moving around the open mouth of the grotto. Many tree people were aged. In fact, most of them were ancient-looking, except for the familiar tree woman and one or two others I vaguely could recall meeting in the past.

Time passed. I noticed because the light streaming grew dim. Several of the ancient tree people touched and treated the wounds on the boar as the moon rose. I didn't realize it until then, but the boar was in terrible shape. It looks like the battle played havoc on the beautiful work I had done to sculpt the boar's physical network.

Nothing was in good condition.

The moonlight streaming through the perforated cave ceiling illuminated the pool of water. The light crawled across the water like a snake, curling and flowing like mist on the water. Several of the ancient tree people entered the pool, sending roots into the earth floor. As the light curled and moved around them in a smoky haze, I felt the platform holding the boar move. As I moved towards the pool of water, I realized several large tree roots held up the boar. They were crawling through the earth, shifting the boar into the pool. Before it met the water, the roots moved, turning the boar legs up.

The water was unexpectedly warm but still shocking. I tried to hold my breath, an absurd thought to have.

Thankfully, I couldn't blush and stopped.

The boar floated in the pool, buoyed up by the tree roots. The boar's nose was well above the waterline, and all I could see were tree branches and the perforated cave ceiling.

When the boar was in the middle of the pool, the ancient trees swayed, giving voice to an odd creaking sound. It filled the air, and light danced, joining streamers of pollen, fashioning fireflies in their branches.

Soothing, gentle power flowed into the boar. It filled the flesh, bone, and organs of the boar. The full feeling continued until I thought the boar would burst. Then, I slowly realized the boar was recovering like its body was remembering what it looked like when it was healthy.

The smell of pollen changed, surging. Then, in bursts, one ancient tree person after another sent a ghost-like version of its form in the streaming moonlight above. As I watched, even the boar manifested a ghostly version above.

I felt a tug but resisted. I wasn't sure how I would look if I followed. The boar shuffled and moved around with the ghostly ancient trees before looking down at what I swear was my soul and saying, "Ancestor?"

Caught between fear and desire, I waffled between following the tug or continuing to resist. I focused on the picture of the god boar and merged it into the image. At first, what was awkward had become more comfortable now that I had done it a few times. As I took an imaginary breath and decided to follow the tug, an immense flood of discordant sensations ripped through me.

Everything wavered dropped into a fugue, that never-ending gray haze that was the limbo between waking and flashes.

A heavy blanket lay over my senses, but I could tell I was in an emergency room. The shift jarred my mind, and it took a bit to readjust. When I could comprehend the change, I realized I was lying in a hospital bed. Lying would be a bit of a stretch since I was semi-suspended.

Eyelids wouldn't raise, so I couldn't really see. But, eventually, the murmurs I was picking up became clearer. Finally, one of the voices was for sure Howie.

"Doctor, respectfully, I want to move him."

A tired voice that must have belonged to the doctor responded. "Respectfully back, I don't give a damn what you want. You are not family and frankly have no say in the matter."

"Madam, I am the legal custodian of my client in any situation where he is medically incapacitated. Therefore, I can request he be moved to another hospital."

Annoyance crept behind her already tired voice. "I agreed you could stay while Mr. Byrne received care. That's already me cutting you some slack. You say you are his lawyer — great. You even signed the documents to pay for his medical care —also great. You say you are his custodian — cool, awesome, and phenomenal. But you don't have paperwork that supports that. I can't take your word and let you move a hurt patient out of my emergency room. Not going to happen."

Howie shot right back. "I did show you the signed document that demonstrates my custodianship and ability to make decisions on behalf of my client."

She shot him down. "You showed me a document on your phone. That's nice, but maybe I'm old-fashioned. Produce a printed copy or have one sent from your office. Otherwise, don't push my good nature any farther."

Someone else came over, and the doctor adjusted what I suspected was the drip going into my arm. It brought on a surge of sleepiness. The nurse mentioned my family had shown up to check on me. I heard Howie's sharp exclamation before the darkness sucked me down.

Twenty-Nine

I stayed in the darkness. Not true night but the limbo that went for whatever I was in when I Flashed and yet was disconnected from any sensory input. Not that I couldn't. The image of the godly boar that I had built was just past my attention, and the boar's senses were a mere thought's distance.

The problem was me. I didn't want to know. Not yet. I wished to return to the hospital. Family? That didn't leave a lot of possibilities. Frankly, only one bastard met that criteria. Dereck. Or, whatever his damn name was. Only that jerk met the requirements. I didn't want that bastard anywhere near me.

The thought brought up nausea. Not that I could figure out how I could feel it. Fuck, not like I had a stomach.

Maybe through the boar?

I don't know.

Flickers of the hospital, how it looked and smelled, the gross, antiseptic, and metallic air. The drugged, blanket-like pall that always seemed to occur when they got their hooks in me.

I panicked.

Had it been in real life, I would either be a basket case drooling from the over-stimulation or be on my way to being drugged and tied down.

It might be dangerous.

Only because they wouldn't let me free.

My mind spun, fragmented and scattered. Usually, it would be enough for the fugue to drag me back but not this time for some reason.

Some of that distress must have leaked to the boar. I could feel it searching, weakly grasping around, trying to communicate.

The thought scared me. What if the boar asked who I was? What if the boar realized I was a person and not this Ancestor he thinks woke up due to his bloodline?

It frightened me.

I was still kicking myself for building the image, accidentally or not, and pretending to be some kind of divine being. But, even if I could talk — and I was sure I could, now — I wasn't sure what to say. The connection before, where I had built the divine boar image, had allowed for a transfer of information. Even as distorted as it had been, the thoughts contained enough of the musical language that I could use that information to communicate.

It's also why I was sure it thought I was not only an Ancestor but one from its bloodline. Its intellect and powers made it obvious it wasn't just a monster or regular boar. When it transformed — or was it ascended? I guess either one could be right — and we transferred thoughts; it conveyed its heritage. It had been chased from its home by hunters. A pretty far trek from what I could gather, though what it said was pretty chaotic. The boar's capture by the lizard hunter was the end of that trek.

The boar wouldn't stop whining at me. Out of frustration and fear, I finally gave in.

"What?"

I must have conveyed some of that frustrated emotion to it because I got a sense the boar trembled. The shakiness and apprehension of the boar's mental voice when it spoke supported that.

"Ancestor? Are you there?"

Yes, but I don't want to talk to you. Too many questions exist that I have no hope of answering. I mulled on what to say while it asked again, and finally, I just gave a loud grunt. Maybe I could pull off the disgruntled grandpa persona and get it to shut up. The response must have been enough since a gushing sense of relief flowed to me from the boar.

"Are you okay?"

How do I answer that? No, I'm not fucking okay. Also, what the hell? I had never had this happen in a Flash before! Not one time had the focus on my Flash ever tried to have a conversation with me. Well, except for the monk, and that was special. So what made this time so different? Was it because I made the image in its mind? Did that create a new connection that didn't exist previously?

The thought troubled my mind, and I flipped through memories of past Flashes, studiously ignoring the boar as it chirped, asking question after question.

Finally, it got so interruptive that I barked out, "I'm tired. Shut up for a moment!"

The boar fell quiet, and I returned to going down memory lane. It wasn't easy. I have buried a lot of memories. Many of them just sucked, especially those where I was out of my fucking mind or laying strapped to a table in a room at the mental hospital after having what they called a mental break. I wished Immerlin was here, so thinking about this shit wouldn't send me down the whole path of recalling all the current fucked up events. He could find things without me having to dig so deep into the ugly shit pile of the past. I couldn't help but start shaking, panicking, and fear rose to choke my non-existent throat.

The feeling must have included the boar, too, as it started squealing and snorting in distress. Somehow that helped me calm down. I pulled my emotions into some semblance of order and managed to convey calmness. Finally, the boar quieted down and managed to eke out a voice.

"Ancestor, are you okay?"

I dreaded starting a conversation but felt compelled after sending both of us down an emotional spiral. Somehow I needed to apologize or at least provide some kind of explanation.

"Yes. Contemplating the past is particularly ... painful. I'm thinking about a way out of this situation."

The boar squealed and snorted, huffing, before finding words again.

"Ancestor, you don't need to do that for me. I will get stronger. The cultivation you shared with me I have absorbed, though I cannot do it all yet. Also, Melethe has long wanted to thank you for providing the changes to her cultivation. She has told me that the changes have quickened her growth."

So much information was in this statement that it took me a few moments to process. Thankfully, the boar patiently waited after I snorted in response.

Melethe is likely the name of the tree woman. That wasn't in the data the boar sent me previously in fragments, but it sort of made sense given I had earlier conveyed the updated diagram with my annotations. While I was happy the boar understood the visuals and thoughts I had sent about its powers, I was confused about its thinking. Why did the boar think my distress was because of it? I had to fix that. Even if I was accidentally sharing misery, I didn't want the boar to feel responsible.

"You are not to blame. If anything, I should not pull you into my pain."

The boar was quick to disagree. "Ancestor, please, do not worry about me. I would not have you waste what little energy you have gathered to wake up to worry about my feelings. It's an honor if I can share your burden even a little."

Did it seem like I was sleeping to the boar when I was not in the Flash? It made me curious, and I couldn't help but ask.

"I've been asleep for so long. Tell me what you know. How long has it been?"

"Ancestor, this child is not sure what you mean. If you are asking when an Ancestor last awoke in my lineage, it has been many generations. More than I can count."

What did that mean? I've never Flashed into a boar previously. So while I didn't clearly remember all my Flashes, I could, at least, keep a sense of them clear in my head. And me being a piggy before this wasn't one of them.

"What Ancestor and when?"

The boar barely let me finish before responding. "Trwyd, mighty Ancestor. Trwyd woke to Ascer the White Tusk, my distant relative. Under his tutelage, Ascer the White Tusk led our people to the southern mountain valleys of Coppelia. He rebuilt the cultivation path of all boars, allowing us to master the fierce spirit, the ice, and the trees."

The boar rambled on a bit, most of which was endless reams of this boar birthed that boar, who did something interesting or another; I just tuned out or put aside all of it for later. However, I did pay attention when it started chattering about the paths and cultivation methods. The boar talked about how Ancestor Trwyd's process taught them to absorb the world's powers to form a solid monster core, dissolve it into a liquid, and then dissipate it into some kind of compressed cloud formation. The process felt easy to describe but challenging to pull off.

The boar then started rambling about the Ancestors again, which prompted me to worry again yet gave me a sense of relief. By the boar's retelling, I wasn't impersonating a god after all. Not sure pretending to be Ancestor of the boar was much better, but at least I felt I might have a smaller chance of being smitten with lightning. Or whatever they used in this world to smack down heretics. But, wait, do they even follow gods here? I had to ask.

"What of the gods?"

The boar snorted. It didn't sound complimentary.

"The last of the gods decayed into nothingness or fell silent long ago. Ancestor Trwyd, when he awoke, was said to have asked the same question, wondering if it would need to battle the gods again."

That got me thinking. Didn't the tree people — what had the boar called them? Pon Cloed, that was it — have some ritual or another at the waterfall? It seemed religious to me.

"Who do the Pon Cloed worship?"

The boar let out a sad squeal. "Ancestor, they still send prayers to the moon goddess, Laioud, and the forest god, Natur. Even though the gods are long dead, they have not given up hope for their return."

I grunted in response.

Thinking of what happened after the wreck, I asked, "How much have you healed? You were pretty torn up from the previous battle."

I could sense the boar hanging its head. It squealed softly in distress. "Ancestor, I have let you down. My body is in a bad state, even after the healing Melethe and her people have provided."

I snorted. It echoed in the darkness, startling the boar and me both. The boar let out several squeals, but I ignored it to reach across the distance to link with the boar's senses. It wasn't wrong. I could tell it was a complete mess. While it was not as bad as it was previously, all the work I had done to rebuild its body was in shambles.

Ignoring the boar's calls, I followed the broken network of its body to the brain. Its stone — well, I guess in the vernacular of this world, a monster core — was cracked and outright broken in a few places. What little power it still generated looked to be exerted to keep it intact.

Instinctively, I knew that it was the key. Fixing it would allow the boar to regain past strength and even grow more. Otherwise, the boar would probably be powerless in the future, if not crippled physically.

Unsure, I poked and prodded, rapidly realizing that I couldn't reshape the core or help re-organize its broken physical state without absorbing power. The way the boar's body was currently didn't allow it to absorb anything. Tracing the tiny trails of energy it did have led me to its stomach, where it obviously ingested foods that provided power. Unfortunately, the state the boar was in would never allow it to absorb enough energy that way to have any calculated effect.

I returned to the darkness, disconnecting from the boar's senses.

"Ancestor?" The boar asked. I could hear the question in its voice.

"Quiet," I said, not wanting it to interrupt my thinking. A metallic, chemical smell burned just beyond my senses, but I pushed the input away. I wanted to focus on this, not think about the hospital. Revolving different options around in my mind, I finally focused on the image of the god boar I had crafted previously.

Thinking about the god boar image pulled me into it. The image lit up with dim light, flickers of flame dancing across the image's skin.

Sensing the energy that filled the picture, I realized that the boar had not taken back the power it shared with it earlier. I couldn't say whether it was stubborn or genius. Sensing the deep well of energy the god boar image contained, a plan formed.

If I was to play the role of an Ancestor, then I might as well go all in. After all, why not? Leaving the boar in the shape it was in was a travesty when I could do something about it.

Letting the image light up entirely and burst into flame, I used the boar image's mouth to speak. "Tell the tree people to take you outside into an open area. Make sure it is far from trees and has nothing flammable."

The boar squealed and then haltingly said, "What is flammable?"

I let out a small roar, making the dark space tremble. "Burnable. Make sure nothing can catch on fire where the tree people place you."

The boar squealed and left. I used the time to reflect on the boar's body and the diagram of its network. Based on what the boar said of cultivation, I guess the pathways I adjusted before would be meridians, but I still preferred to think of it as a network.

I mapped out what I wanted to do in my mind and then began altering the image to match, adding a bit here and there to make the boar's ability to absorb energy, convey it, and re-route when damaged more effective. After all, a good network should do all those things. It just took the right combination of hardware and tuning.

The boar returned.

"Ancestor, they are taking me outside. Melethe asks if there is anything they can do to help. After all, they feel guilty that I was harmed protecting them during their ritual."

"Tell them to stay back," was all I said.

I connected to his senses then. We were outside, surrounded by several Pon Cloed, including Melethe. The boar squealed, urging them to step back. The Pon Cloed retreated. Melethe was more reluctant, but after the boar insisted, she moved as well.

Seeing they were far enough away, I drew on the energy the boar had embedded in the image previously and bled the power out of the boar's skin, letting it swirl and cloud around its body. Fire leaked out of its pores, rising higher and higher until I crafted the godly boar's image of the Ancestor outside of its mind and into the space around the boar's body.

I looked out of the image's eyes, seeing the world from a different vantage point for the first time. The snow had already melted around the boar, showing a mix of fertile soil and rock. Luckily we were far enough away from the trees, or they would have caught fire. The tree people had moved well away, the heat I was pouring out making them uncomfortable. Only Melethe was stubbornly staying too close. I could see the leaves on her wooden form wilting.

Taking a deep breath of chill air, I raised the head of the godly boar's image and roared, forcing her to stumble back as the fire surged off the image's bristles, sending out a bloom of heat. Then, satisfied that the Pon Cloed tree woman finally moved back far enough, I looked down at the boar I had wrapped around.

A sharper scent of antiseptic brushed across my sense, but I shrugged it away. My eyes looked up to the stars that twinkled in the dark sky. The starry landscape was more majestic than Earth. I felt drawn to one pattern of stars. Felt tugged towards them. The feeling puzzled me, and I shook it away.

I had a boar to rebuild.

Six Million Dollar Boar, here we come.

Concentrating my attention, I compressed the image's shape and sunk its energy into the boar's body. To the Pon Cloed, I'm sure it looked like I stared at the sky before I shrank into the small boar. It caused the fire to compress and rage, growing as white as snow from its intensity.

Satisfied, I began. In place of working to rebuild the boar one step at a time, I cheated instead. The energy belonged to the boar anyway, so I returned the power but used the god boar's image as a template.

Literally, I was rebuilding the boar's body with its own energy, using pressure and fire to restructure everything all at once.

Definitely, definitely, was going to hurt.

Pushing aside any guilt and closing my ears to the boar's agonized squeals, I concentrated on its monster core. Before I had used the energy, it absorbed to carve and adjust the monster core. This action had led to it gaining both fire and gravity powers. However, the discussion on cultivation with the boar earlier indicated that the monster core of the various power tiers was mapped to different states. Solid, liquid, and then a kind of compressed gas. Since we were rebuilding a six-million dollar boar, we might as well spend a chunk of that on jumping it to a more powerful realm. Even if it failed, the monster core was non-functional. At worst, the attempt would destroy the monster core. Given I was rebuilding its body, it should be able to re-form a monster core at the worst if I failed.

The metallic scent returned, and I felt a jolt that shook me. I shrugged it away. Doing this would take all my concentration, and I was already starting to feel groggy. Too many actions were taxing my mind and ability to focus.

Delicately, I wrapped the broken monster core in layers of gravity, each wafer-thin layer compressing it a bit more. Going back to my elementary physics knowledge, I knew that solids have a high melting point. However, breaking up the nice repeating structures inside can speed the process. So at the same time, I pressed on the monster core to break it up, I added heat to start the melting process. Not content, I added gentle waves of movement to make it spin, using a cycle of heat, compression, and movement to speed the process.

Even I felt the agony. It made me increasingly more and more tired, combined with intense flickers of hospital smells. It almost made the panic return, though I pushed it away hard.

Concerned for the boar, I cut away a tiny amount of attention and found it flopping in agony in the dark space. It was bleeding and cracking, with pieces of its mental construction falling away.

Worried, I wrapped it in a ghostly blanket of the god boar's imagination. Using the energy to do this meant it would not have as much power to rebuild its body as I would like, but I think its mind would break and die otherwise.

We both endured the boar and I together. I could sense its monster core slowly turning to liquid and wrapped it even tighter with the blanket I made from the god boar's image in the dark place.

I felt a jolt and a strange dull sensation of pain. My attention faltered, and perception swirled, growing blurry. I heard a voice laugh and felt like I was in motion. Hospital smells assaulted my nose. Another voice chastised someone about moving too fast.

The boar's squeal of utter agony brought me back, and the hospital faded as the boar's reality overlaid it. Like the crash, it was overwhelming, and I knew I couldn't maintain it.

I increased the heat and motion to the point where I thought we would incinerate. However, it seemed to work as the monster core finally liquefied.

Everything started getting blurry and heavy as a blanket dropped over my senses. Scared and unwilling, I felt the fugue eat everything, leaving a tiny spec of perception of the boar. The boar lay, unmoving in the dark space, the ghostly image of the god boar image fading around it.

I used the last vestiges of my focus to push it into its body and left one echoing command before everything faded away completely.

"Live!"

Thirty

My first coherent thought was the voice had to be Howie's. After that, the universe grew old and faded, exploding into a new one before I figured out who owned the second voice.

Dereck.

More voices came and went, but I had a heavy, wet blanket on my senses. My sluggish brain recognized the sensation.

I was drugged.

Not just with painkillers, too.

I moved or tried to. The moment must have alerted someone since I could hear someone come over. My eyes weren't giving me anything but blurry feedback, but even though the nose plugs someone had thankfully given me, the sharp scent of Old Spice cut through.

Dereck. You son of a bitch.

May I spoke it out loud or murmured something because I could hear him laugh. That irritating, barking laugh. It sounded like a dying demented dolphin.

His voice grated on me. "Well, well, look who finally decided to show up at the hospital. Did it really take a car wreck for you to join your mother and me? How sad."

His mock sympathy made me want to vomit. Luckily, I couldn't. The drugs making me groggy were suppressing that, too.

"Don't thank me too quickly, but I ran off that do-gooder Howard. Or, should I call him Howie as you do? No? Well, that's fine. We are not best buds, anyway."

I tried to speak, but nothing came out.

"Don't strain yourself, partner. We don't have to push to make up for the lost time. After all, it's not like you are going anywhere, anytime soon."

I made more noises or at least tried to do so. I felt a hand press my eyes closed, and then something rubbed against them. I tried to protest but to no avail. Eventually, it stopped, and I blinked my eyes open.

Everything was much clearer.

"Got those disgusting eye boogers out of the way. I bet it's better now," Dereck said.

Given I could see his angular face and its poor imitation of a Van Dyke beard, I had to agree. Not that I was voicing anything. Speaking seemed to be still impaired and not just from a raw, dry throat.

"See, you are already happier. Suppose you had just come down here and done this earlier. I would have been so much happier if you had been here earlier. After all, it's been a year. A year, my brother, a year. You made me wait the whole time."

Maybe it was the drugs. I wasn't getting what Dereck was trying to say. He obviously read the confusion in my expression.

"Ah, someone is lost. Well, let me clear that up."

Dereck plotted the bed next to me, pushing me unceremoniously off to the side to make room. It pressed me against the restraints I realized were in place to hold me in the bed. Dereck tracked my eyes and saw I noticed. Dereck let a grin grow on his face.

"I see you noticed. Well, after I ran off Mr. Howard, I made clear to the hospital that you were a dangerous — previously committed and all — mental patient. That I thought it's as a crime that you were allowed to drive and — lo and behold, look what happened — you almost killed someone with your car. They were quite considerate in agreeing to make sure you were not in a position to harm anyone else."

His smiling face repulsed me. Even drugged, I found the lie he had spun abhorrent.

"Wondering how I did it? I would be if I were you. Well, let's just say that I agree that Mr. Howard is a good lawyer — probably a great one if I had to admit it. But. Yes, but — he isn't as canny as I am. You see, this isn't my first rodeo. Your dear sister — my lovely wife before her death and demise — going to see you, mind you. Well, she really cared for you in a fucked up brocon, bizarre way. It must be the mental health weirdness that runs in the family. Anyhoo, she wanted to make sure you were always cared for and had a caretaker document drafted up to cover a situation where you were incapacitated or in medical care. It's a beautiful thing, that document. Only a year old, you see. Now, Mr. Howard, he too has a document, a power of attorney. The problem is, my lawyers aren't shabby either. My document is a lot newer than the other. In legal terms, my document trumped his document. So, I'm the caretaker right now. Got you out of his nasty hands and moved to the same room with your mother. Have to keep the family together, you know. The hospital was so considerate, too, especially as I explained things."

Dereck paused as if I was expected to respond. Instead, all I could manage was a dribble of saliva. Dereck wiped it away with a cloth nearby.

"Tsk, tsk. Now, don't be contrary. You are in good hands. In fact, you get to stay with your mother for a day or two before you go to your new home. After all, we can't let people with a mental health condition run around freely, can we? Thankfully, a few people in the right places are very open to this thought. That, and the right number of Franklins in their bank account. After all, money talks."

I knew from experience that rage, while potent, wasn't going to cut through the drugs. I had lived that before. I vented a few murmurs, trying to say Howie would be serving him a serious ass whooping, but it didn't come out coherently.

Dereck patted my cheek. "No need to get all red-faced. We have a day or two to talk, anyway. After all, we have much to say. Should we talk about your sister or your mother? Hmmm, let's start with your mother. After all, she's still with us, just wasting away on the bed. Did you know she has taken a turn for the worse? She has almost rallied to wake up a couple of times, but thankfully, I've been by her side to help. All the time. When I'm not on my phone trying to fix the finances, I'm right by her side. Making sure she gets the right medicine. In the right amounts. You know how important that is, right?"

Even though the haze and profound paralysis brought on by the drugs, I managed to make a fist, not that I could wield it. Dereck tut-tutted me and patted it with one hand. Then, he showed me his phone. It was open to a bank app that displayed numbers I couldn't read.

Smiling, Dereck said, "It might be too blurry for you to read, so let me break it out for you."

He tapped on a couple of screens in the app and eventually opened up a transaction log. Pointing to it, Dereck said, "See this transaction for today? That's the last one. I've finally gotten all that money out of the little nest eggs she hid it in. And man, did she hide it everywhere. I knew she was loaded but once I started digging, whoa, did I find a lot."

Through the druggy haze, I realized he had been stealing mother's money this whole time while playing the diligent and caring son-in-law. My already low opinion of him sunk even farther. Maybe more. My slow brain hadn't unraveled what he meant earlier about medicine, but I suspect he meant poisoning her.

Dereck put away his phone. He tapped me on the forehead repeatedly with a stiff finger.

"Now, you deliver yourself on a platter. Gift wrapped and every-thing. Too beautiful. Not that you have money or anything I care about to desire. Some things I can't use, like that nutty cryptocurrency stuff and some patents. Too hard to make money from those. But, see, your delicious sister, she comes to rescue. Always looking after you, you know? She set aside money in case of her death. She sent it right into a trust fund for your benefit. Not that you used it. I would call you ungrateful, but I plan to use it on your behalf, so I'm rather glad."

I made noises that he laughed over. Fury fought the drugged feeling and lost. I tensed a little but eventually fell back in exhaustion. Dereck patted me on the chest before idly pinching and twisting the skin on my arms.

"Don't get too worked up. Don't you get goosebumps or bruises or something?"

He torqued the skin pretty hard, but I couldn't feel it except as a dull, faint pain — one decent thing about the drugs, I could say.

Dissatisfied, Dereck stopped.

"Well, that's no fun. Let's talk about your bitchy sister. My lovely wife. Did you know how much sympathy you can get when you are a widower? And a caring son that is by the bedside of his sick, ever so sick mother? I've used that sympathy to bang I don't know how many nurses in this hospital. Even got one of the nightshift doctors to provide me a little sympathy."

I tried to spit on him but just dribbled. Dereck dutifully wiped it away.

"Oh, don't be a puritan. It's not like I wasn't hitting it regularly with others when Alice was alive. And, not like your precious Alice wasn't getting something on the side, too. Hell, I've been snipped for the better part of a decade. So imagine my surprise when she came and announced that she was pregnant. I was perplexed. The vixen knew it too. I never felt happier when I heard she died."

I couldn't process that well. Maybe it was the drugs.

Dereck patted me on the cheek one more time before standing up to fiddle with my IV line. My arm felt cold, and the world started to fade. As it receded, I heard him say, "Now be a good boy and stay drugged and quiet. It will all be over soon. I'll be happy and you, well, you — who cares."

Thirty-One

The sandy-haired man walked down the street. The chill in the air made his long coat a necessity versus a fashion statement that was the norm in the city.

Not that he got cold. His hot blood had transferred over nicely, even if it didn't quite work as well in the physics here. Again, trade-offs. The body was shitty but good enough, especially coupled with his napalm blood, good eyesight, and speed, making for a solid hunting combination.

Idly, his fingers tapped on the small canister that he kept on his belt: hot blood but no delivery system. Luckily, technology to the rescue. A long metallic hose extended out of the top of the canister and through his clothes to exit at the wrist. The toggle in his hand allowed him to inject the blood or to send it out in a spray. All he had to do was find the right opportunity and mind the wind. It would be embarrassing to have your own napalm blood fly back and eat your face.

The darkened paths of the more desolate streets in the city were full of shadows. Mostly some thugs who thought they were tough or just territorial. They quickly reconsidered when he looked at them. Something about the combination of glowing eyes and his hefty firearm solved the few issues that arose. Those that didn't quite get the picture, he settled as quietly and quickly as possible.

His target was on the fourth floor. Navigating a stairway full of trash, graffiti, and human waste got him there. Darkened rooms with plastic sheets ripped from the nearby construction site served as doors. The sandy-haired man found his target quick enough, lounging listlessly in a drug-filled haze on a pallet that smelled of sweat, drugs, and human excrement.

He put a bullet in the other two in the room, the silencer muffling the retort nicely. Positioning so he could see the entire room, the sandy-haired man concentrated. One eye changed, morphing into something akin to a gem that would not look out of place on a spider. In two worlds, he eyed his prey, one laying in the disgusting pallet in a drugged stupor and the other below him, wrapped in thick strands of webbing. In one stride, he both stepped forward and dropped, striking, injecting the napalm-like fluid into the victims in both worlds simultaneously. Neither hardly registered the deaths, rapidly combusting from the inside until nothing more than a loose pile of ashes was left.

Verifying he killed both of them in two different worlds, the sandy-haired man grunted, letting his eye return. Then, calmly he walked out, leaving the dead bodies and the murder scene behind, putting it far out of mind.

In a sports car, he dialed a number. A woman's voice answered on the speakers, the soft sound of bells in the background.

"You done yet?" He asked, checking his mirrors. Nothing on the road, but it was a habit to check.

Her musical voice responded. "Hold on one second."

The sandy-haired man heard the soft retort of a firearm fire rapidly. Three times to be exact. He chuckled.

"Still using the Mozambique Drill?"

Her remarkable voice responded, layering over the soft sound of children giggling.

"It fits. You know I like to get close, just like you do. Unfortunately, not everyone can strike from miles away like the snow queen."

The sandy man's features twisted into a snarl. "Uppity bitch. I know she was chosen to be in charge, but she twists all my legs. I would love to break her slowly, feasting on her carcass after she died."

The giggling on the other end of the phone grew louder. "Now, now, calm down. You are making my children excited. They are already stimulated from removing the target just now."

That calmed the sandy-haired man down completely. He pulled the car over suddenly and jumped out, transferring the phone to an earpiece.

Eyes alert, he looked around carefully, not caring if he was drawing attention or not.

"You do know we are allies, right? Perhaps you could remind them?"

Her extraordinary voice shifted an octave higher. "What? Did I frighten you?"

"No," the sand-haired man said but couldn't help think about her horde of children, little feet adorned with bells and hands stained with blood. He didn't quite fear her, but her children could move to any-where her voice went — a fearsome combination in a world full of cell phones.

"Don't worry. I've fed them recently. The children are just a bit worked up. I'll see you soon after I care for the next target."

The sandy-haired man shuddered long after the phone call ended.

Thirty-Two

The darkness was welcome. The first thought on my mind was the boar lived. Then I snarled right after, thinking about when I woke how I was going to punt Dereck to the damn moon when I returned. He was seriously underestimating Howie if he felt some kind of legal dance would get him what he wanted. It annoyed me and was easier to focus on than the thoughts that he was potentially slowly killing mother in some fashion or that he might have had a hand in Alice's death. His hints weren't clear enough for me to clearly grasp those thoughts. I didn't want to go down that trail yet.

Not yet, at least.

Dark bitterness welled up inside. Hah, send me back to that hell? No way. Howard and I had long thought through those scenarios after I had gotten free. We cooked up dozens of counters for that shit — Howie knew I would rather die than return to that endless abyss.

I used that comforting thought to close the door on my other, more fearful thoughts and looked around. The image of the godly boar was a ghost, barely visible in the darkness. I could sense the boar was healing. Its monster core was a pulsating pool of liquid, waves from the energy that the boar was absorbing, causing a constant wave action that stirred the pool's surface. It was fascinating, and I watched it mindlessly for a bit. Touching it seemed unwise given the transformation healing the boar was undergoing. I tried connecting to the boar's senses but gave up. It seemed like the boar was almost completely shut down.

The darkness was neither comforting nor unsettling. It just existed. Restless, I merged with the divine boar image. It had next to no energy but made me feel better. Drifting aimlessly made me feel useless. I knew that the situation in the hospital was in good hands; Howie had never let me down. Still, it made me anxious and uncertain. I wanted something to chase the fears that kept nibbling at my mind away.

Idly, I remembered that the boar had mentioned his Ancestors. Once it was born, the thought took hold, and I pondered on the concept. Could there possibly be a person existing in the bloodline of another? Of a race? I mean, sure, I had listened to plenty of documentaries about finding traces of ancient man in DNA for sure. Ancestral memories weren't exactly a unique concept. Most cultures had some form of it. But, a representation of a living, breathing entity with its own sentience and powers? At home, not a likely scenario. Here? Who knows. The boars and I suspect the rest of the world had some kind of alchemy they could perform on their bodies. Completely changing them out, in fact, at times, like what the boar was going through right now. While I had definitely accelerated the process due to my interference and the boar's wounds, it wasn't something that it did not expect to happen in the future.

I contemplated the idea, toying with various ideas, tossing them out when they didn't make sense, keeping the elements that did. Eventually, it struck me. With the cultivation alchemy, the boar might renew his body over and over again. This system looked to refine blood, muscle, bone, and more again and again. It was constantly changing and upgraded. So, it had to be a constant for something to survive that process. It might seem like a jump — something my coding partners had yelled about many times when I first started coding — but I inferred the link to everything was with the monster core. While I didn't have the opportunity back then when I was talking to the boar to dig into this topic as much as I would like right now, it did make sense that boars that didn't cultivate didn't have an Ancestor wake up. While I definitely couldn't support it with logic, it felt right, like that was a crucial part of the puzzle.

Which got me thinking. The elements that constructed the monster core had to be present through all the body alchemy, even though the transformation of monster core states from solid to the eventual gas. That formation of the monster core wasn't static, either. The process continued to either grow or transform the arrangement of matter in the monster core. It was pretty fantastic when I thought of it.

The arrow of my thoughts was pointing towards an idea. Vague, but taking shape. I just was a little uncertain if I should test it.

When the boar had talked about its cultivation path, it had noted that most monsters fashioned a core in their brain. The Pon Cloed tree people did something similar, but many other races created a space in their body and used it to contain energy instead. The boar indicated they did both, creating a monster core and spaces, though they didn't use the spaces for cultivation. The darkness that I seemed to exist in was precisely one of those spaces, proportionally balanced and symmetrical to the boar's monster core.

I found that tremendously interesting, for obvious reasons. When I was first rebuilding the boar's physical network, I originally rerouted numerous pathways away from these locations since they seemed to create latency and loss in the boar's physical network. Then I put many of them back. What I found when I shifted away from them was the formation of the monster core slowed dramatically. I didn't suss it out then, but I noted that those spaces played some part in creating the matter and eventually helped form and enhance the monster core. The jump my brain had made was that these locations might be where any past Ancestor was dwelling.

After a bit of internal struggle, I decided to go poke around. I also realized how bad I had gotten at doing nothing. Being idle was driving me batty, and sitting around and staring at the darkness did nothing but bring up memories I was trying to suppress until I could do something about the situation.

Decision made, I shifted my attention to the space I was in. While I put the possibility as close to nil, it made for a good benchmark. Measuring the darkness was ... wow, difficult. After failing a bunch of times miserably, I finally decided to fill the darkness of the space. When I had rebuilt the boar the last time, I had increased the number of pathways to this space. It pumped in a decent amount of energy, though the majority of it was just as quickly being pulled out to assist the boar's transformative healing. Not letting that stop me, I gently massaged the energy into a gaseous state, staying connected to it while filling the darkness.

It gave me a very full feeling. Sensing through the energy let me feel the dimensions of the space. The space was pretty smooth, though that was a poor approximation. I didn't exactly have a good sense to explain what I was sensing, so touch would have to do. I found a few rough locations, if you will, to touch. Several of these were right underfoot.

A bit of experimentation made me realize they were formations of memories. The formations seemed to represent fragmentary snippets of thoughts, actions, and events. A very broken visual of the boar's transformation replayed before my mind. Mentally I rocked back, stunned. Some of those fragments didn't deal with this world. That bothered me, and without realizing how, those deposits scattered. I pulled back my attention and tried again. After breaking another deposit, I understood. Intrigued, I tried the opposite and tried to create a deposit. It took some time and energy to figure out, but I succeeded.

That woke up the beast that could code all night without blinking or bathroom breaks. I reorganized and sanitized a few bits of information related to home that didn't belong. I got in a rhythm that didn't break until I stumbled across a memory that wasn't mine or the boars.

It was pretty apocalyptic — a harsh burning sky. Reality cracked like glass, opening jagged fissures — scenes of amorphous figures struggling through the cracks.

I wanted more, but it wasn't complete. The other deposits held information, but it was incoherent. Reaching the end of what I could find in the darkness space, I gently reached through the boar's body, sending my mind along the pathways until I arrived at the next space. Much of the boar's body was in flux, so it was a bumpy ride. What I remembered and visualized didn't match what was present, so I got sidelined and redirected dozens of times before I finally arrived.

The space was different than the darkness. Less connected, for sure. I filled it with energy and sensed the dimensions. Significantly smaller, but it contained many more deposits. Intrigued, I selected one. Then another. Then more, astonishment growing each time. I expected to find memories of the past. Instead, I found pretty articulate visuals that lined up with the information I had conveyed to the boar earlier, including data on the transformations it was currently undergoing.

It was a library, of sorts, constructed and fashioned in some unknowing fashion. Underneath the current data on the fire and gravity powers the boar had, I uncovered more disarticulated fragments of the cold powers the boar mentioned. Nothing about the other two the boar said that its people were taught and not organized by any means.

Maybe it was madness or the insane desire to tinker, but I couldn't help but organize it. I tidied up the deposits with gentle precision to make them more consistent before hungrily looking for another space.

In rapid succession, I moved through all but one of the places. Each was significantly smaller than the first two and contained very little beyond snippets, none of which was very understandable. The last place had a hint of danger, or so my mind insisted. That made me cautious, but curiosity was entirely in charge, hitting the crazy button nonstop.

I gently entered, treading cautiously. I didn't immediately expand out energy but floated, passively taking in what I could first.

Previous deposits had a sense of color. Most felt eggshell white, with varying tints of yellow and a tiny few hints of earthly green and browns. The deposits here were angry red and deep purple, with thick ropy black veins and scattered familiar white and green deposits.

I think I found one.

After a short debate, I left and came back, clad in the image of the godly boar. Slowly I increased the energy flow, letting it flicker and burn, warming up the space.

Something stirred in the deposits. Energy pooled and whirled in eddies until they fashioned a set of eyes. The sensation of age, of time, lay across everything like a heavy blanket, choking and confining. A voice from across time asked, "Am I needed?"

Stunned, I found it hard to answer. The presence, in relation to my own pitiful image, was overpowering.

Again, the voice from across time asked, "Am I needed? Do I need to fight again?"

Realizing that not saying something might be worse, I finally spoke. "No."

Shorter is better when you don't know anything. The presence of the Ancestor receded, replaced with immense tiredness.

"Do I need to awaken?"

That wouldn't do. I can't have the actual Ancestor wake up while I'm out here pretending.

"No, Ancestor. I've already awoken in this child to guide it."

Through the profound fatigue clouding the Ancestor, I could pick up a bit of curiosity and relief. "Then I shall sleep longer. Does my blood still exist? Does it beat in the hearts of the people to this day?"

My heart jumped into my throat a moment before I responded. "Yes. This child is of your blood."

I figured the boar must be, given it was carrying the Ancestor in its bloodline.

"I am content," came the hoary voice.

I agonized over saying something proactively, but the Ancestor filled the silence before I could do so.

"I do not recognize you. My heart does not resonate with your image. Of who's line are you descended?"

If I had a heart, it would be beating in the red zone. Time to spin the lie and hope I don't get caught. With fake pride, I belted out the backstory for On-Raze.

"I am On-Raze. I drank the blood of giants to steal their flames. Swallowed the cores of dead worlds to have their weight. I burn enemies with my gaze, trample them beneath my hooves, and cut them fore and aft with my tusks. I am On-Raze, and in life and death, my family shall never suffer, for I will rise and rise again, to lead them to victory."

A dry crackling laugh came from the Ancestor. "You brag well. Nevertheless, I have always hated the giants, so I salute you. Your line must have crossed with mine in the past."

"It is so, Ancestor."

Tiredness returned to its voice. "If you have already awoken, I shall return to sleep. One is enough, and you are younger. I feel the fresh scent of your youth. I will let you guide this child. Do so well. Do not let me wake up later and find you have failed."

I nodded, and the heavy presence slipped away. While I sat stunned, the energy and then red and deep purple deposits disintegrated. The power it created was titanic and flowed into On-Raze's image.

The flood was more than I could handle. After that, everything dissolved into nothingness no matter how I flailed about and tried to hang on.

Thirty-Three

The ceiling looked familiar. Someone helped me raise my head to suck liquid through a straw. When I laid back, the scent of vanilla and coffee caressed my nose. My blurry eyes focused on a plump body with toffee skin, cheerful features, and a lavender-hued nurse's outfit.

"Malika?" I croaked out.

"Hello, sugar. You just rest a moment so I can get Howie."

I sunk back, blinking. The drugged feeling was mainly gone, though it was still lying on everything like a light haze. Malika and I go back a bit. When I exited the hospital years back and still needed in-house care, she was the one that had worked with me. I had come back to take care of anything I needed medical-wise, so I wouldn't have to go to the hospital. Like Howie, she was one of the people who didn't set off my agoraphobia. Like him, she's also one of the few that I felt comfortable allowing in the house for short periods. Of course, it didn't hurt that Alice was the one that introduced us both years back.

Thinking about Alice got my brain tumbling, slowly, only interrupted when Howie vigorously moved into the room.

My room, I noticed.

So we were at my house versus the hospital.

"Glad to see you awake," Howie said.

I nodded weakly. Malika helped situate the bed to sit up and then slipped out. Howie looked me over, and I returned the favor. He looked tired. Like he hadn't slept for days.

"You look like shit," he said.

I let out a cough. "Back at you."

Howie found a chair, flipped it around, and leaned over the back so he could be close to the bed. "You awake enough to talk?"

I nodded. I needed to know too much not to fight for information even if I was still feeling the haze from the drugs that someone had pumped into my system.

"Okay. It's been a bit chaotic, so it's a lot to cover. First off, it's been a couple of days since the emergency room visit."

I protested. "That long?"

Howie nodded. "Yes. Before you ask Immerlin or me, I rerouted a couple of calls for you and made sure your clients understood you were temporarily out of pocket."

I nodded my thanks. I wet my mouth with saliva before scratching out, "Thanks. I knew you had things in hand."

Howie gave a tired chuckle. "Handling your clients was the easy part. That snake Dereck and his lawyer — they did a number on us that I didn't see coming. Luckily, we had made preparations in the past. I couldn't stop him from having you moved to your mother's room or kicking me out. At least, not on the first day. Once I got Judge Harris involved and the information he provided in front of the correct law enforcement officials, that changed rapidly. I was able to have him arrested before he had you moved from general care to mental health and behavioral care. We already had a good amount of dirt on him. Finding him in possession of sedation drugs upped the ante. Once the police had his phone and its information, Dereck was pretty much sunk. The phone contained enough data to show he was not only stealing money from your mother but also texts messages that supported a confession that he was attempting to kill your mother and indirectly you."

I laughed harshly, which led to a bout of coughing. Howie helped me get some water before we continued.

"Serves him right," I rasped. "Please tell me they are going to put him away for life."

I could already see the tired, distrustful look on Howie's face. "The case is solid, but you know how the court system works. They are working on a plea agreement to nail him."

I didn't want to brood on that. But unfortunately, the court system fails more often than it delivers justice. So I wanted to hope the dice would land on justice this time.

"How's my mother?" I asked.

Howie nodded. His tired features had that set that told me the news was not good. "She's not in immediate danger. I can't prove it, but I think that bastard was injecting something into her IV line or having the nurse he was smashing do it for him. I've moved her from the hospital to another facility with equivalent care. At this point, I don't trust any of them. The hospital was very accommodating, as well. They wanted nothing to do with the mess and helped."

"The lady from the wreck — did she come out okay?"

Howie smiled. "Good work, you moron. But don't give me a heart attack young, you know! She's fine, to answer your question. I understand she has asked to meet you in a different setting. If you feel up to that at some point, it should be trivial to arrange."

I hesitated. Then shook my head. "Maybe later. Over video or something."

"Up to you, partner. Now, that's the majority of necessary items to cover. Next, you and Malika have a date with a sponge so that we can save the rest of the list for later.

That made me blush. I also realized I stank of stale sweat and medicine. "Bastard," I said, making a weak attempt to bat at him.

Howie laughed. "I can't believe you blushed. It's not like it's the first time. You know Malika has seen it all before. Appreciated it, too, from what I understand."

"Shut up!" I said in a harsh whisper, glancing at the doorway.

"Too easy," Howie said, chuckling. "Don't worry. She's not listening. You know she isn't — never has when we talk. Now, rest up, and I will be back tomorrow. In a couple of days, this will be behind you, you will have the house to yourself again, and we can stake that asshole Dereck out in the desert sun for the ants to feast on."

That vision chased away the embarrassment to come with the sponge bath but also made me remember what Dereck had said.

"Howie," I said. He must have picked up something in my voice since he leaned in.

"I wasn't totally out of it when Dereck had me sent up to mother's room. He taunted me — pretty much shit talking like you would expect. He did, however, say a couple ... of things."

"Like what? Not sure anything he confessed to you while you were in a drugged state would be admissible."

I bit my lip. "Not like that. Dereck ... he said he was snipped, you know?"

Howie looked puzzled and gestured. I could see he didn't make the connection I wanted him to make.

Looking down at the sheet covering me, I said, "He had a vasectomy. But ... Alice was pregnant."

Howie got it then. He tipped the chair back like he does when he's thinking about something. "Bret, I think between the two of us, you know your sister better than anyone. I like to think I'm a close second. I can't, for the life of me, see your sister cheating. Even on an asshole like Dereck, I don't see it."

"Me either," I fumbled out weakly. "It doesn't make sense to me."

Carefully, he said, "Alice asked both of us not to dig into Dereck. Ever since her boyfriend Tom, when we dug up all those pictures of him and showed her, she has been adamant for us to back off. Still, you looked at him a little bit, didn't you? I know I did."

I nodded. "Not deeply, just a skim across the surface for the obvious. I regret not digging deeper."

Howie snorted. "She would have torn the hide off of you if you had. She had a nose for smelling when you lied, and we both know it. So you would not have been able to keep it from her."

I gave a small laugh. Howie wasn't wrong.

Damn, I miss her.

After a moment of quiet, Howie said, "I can find out. It shouldn't be difficult now his identity is clearer. Unless he went to some back alley joint, there are bound to be records. Or, I could encourage the authorities to give him a complete checkup. Should be plausible to get done."

"Okay." I wasn't sure what else to say.

Howie looked at me, cringed a little, and asked, "Then what? If it's true and he is snipped? It might lead to something you don't want to know."

I stared into the sheet. All I could see was Alice's cheerful smile.

"No, Howie, it will lead to where it needs to go.

For Alice, I can accept any outcome."

Thirty-Four

It took a week before I could get everyone out of my house. Even then, Malika scheduled a visit every other day to check on the bandages. I didn't have many, but the burn on the back and shoulder required maintenance, or it might go wrong. I protested but failed to convince her or Howie that I could do it alone.

Sleep had been fitful, ugly, and drugged. I had not Flashed the entire time, which was making me anxious to the point where I had voluntarily even tried to sleep and make the Flash happen.

The case with Dereck was moving at glacial speed. Howie was working on determining if Dereck was capable of fatherhood.

Armed with the jitters and just vague easiness, I finally returned to work. A trivial amount of effort finished up any lingering work. The last reporting to Inverse Voices had already gone out. It was extremely quiet on their end. I didn't even get the standard auto-reply. Given my access was cut off, I suspected they were either very unhappy with what I had done or that I disappeared for a bit without contact. The money still showed up, so I wasn't too torn up. Working for them had put me on edge anyway.

That left me with a decently long list of calls to return — most of which I planned entirely on ignoring. A few, though, needed a touch. So, I settled gingerly into my chair, arming myself with some warm tea.

"Immerlin, call, Marlin DeSoto."

"Calling Marlin DeSoto, Senior Director, Face D/NT."

As the phone rang, I recollected the triplet of calls Marlin had left. I had done some work for them a few months back, primarily second stage analysis and product predictions. But, in his typical clipped manner, Marlin had pretty much demanded a return call. If I didn't know him so well, I would have thought he was pissed. But, it was just his everyday speaking style.

It went to voicemail and dictated a message. I made it about halfway through when Immerlin announced he was already returning my call. Sighing, I killed the voicemail and connected.

"Bret, I need you to do some work."

Blunt as usual.

"Hi, Marlin. Been a few months. I'm doing well, by the way. Recovering just fine. How about you?"

Marlin snorted. "Glad we got that done. Now, I need you to reprise the earlier report you did for me. I need something more tactical, more focused, with a bit more tactical emphasis."

As he talked, I pulled up the previous work I had done for him. The summary brought it all back after I read over it. I wasn't sure how I could have targeted more accurately than I already had. Aside from scratching an "X" somewhere, I couldn't have made a more precise map.

"I need this report to show that the FF/6 offering made the difference in the first and second-quarter numbers. That the boost in revenue we saw in those quarters is directly related to the sales efforts we made for FF/6. So the number has to show that the bump in revenue was directly linked to the FF/6, and we couldn't have hit those numbers any other way."

"Marlin, you never gave me sales numbers," I pointed out. "You insisted they were not ready when I wrote the analysis report. You provided calculated percentages, but the math underneath them was not clear."

"Can't you use them to say something along those lines? Right now, the analysis you did doesn't provide the support I need. Lacking that clear cut line to FF/6 puts my whole department and FF/7 that's in the pipeline in jeopardy."

"I can't say that when I don't know. That's why I didn't. Using the data you provided me would have made FF/6 look worse than it did, which is why I didn't. I recalculated the numbers and built the impacts. The math and calculations are in the supporting documents to the report."

"Hmph. Just write me a second report that says without FF/6 inputs into gross sales, the company wouldn't have seen a 50% rise in revenue for those quarters."

"How can I do that without the actual numbers?"

"Because that's the actual result I need," Marlin said bluntly. "Without something to that effect, Face D/NT is going to defund a chunk of my department. They have decided to ax my core products supporting the service lines because some other consultant decided we were too fat as a company. Too much all over the place with our offerings. The current thought is that if they cut four of our products — most of my department — from the service offerings, that sales will only go down by ten percent."

"Wait. Your core products are the FF and DR series. So unless you changed something, that means you have six, no seven, products active right now feeding into sales. So you are saying ... they think if they cut out four of your products, any of the four, that it will only impact sales trivially?"

"You got it."

I wish I didn't. What fresh insanity was this? Marlin's department is easily the source of three-quarters of the company's profit-bearing revenue. Cutting any one of them would hurt a lot more than a ten percent sales drop. I almost couldn't believe people in decision-making positions were this stupid. Or dumb enough to listen to a consultant without vetting or verification.

"So you need a short report that addresses sales elasticity, directly linking the impacts of each of your products to sales and revenue benefits?"

"Yes."

"I need sales numbers and actual costing values."

"I can't —"

"Give me last year. Hell, give me two years back. Given the track record from the percentages and my past reporting for you, it should be enough to paint the picture. I can label it as not final and still illustrate the impact enough. But I can't do that without data, and I don't know if I can show a clear fifty percent. But I'll do what I can."

"I can send you the last two years, but you will have to say they are not final. Preferably you can reference an outside source as well. Two or three if you can."

"I can do that."

"Fine," I said. "I hope this will help. However, Marlin, let me remind you that I'm not a product placement analyst or business analyst. My specialty is analysis but with a security bent. So this report might not tip the scales as you think against another consultant with a better pedigree."

"You let me worry about that."

Marlin hung up, and the numbers showed up a few minutes later. Between Immerlin and I, we sliced, diced, and cut them up. I knew I wasn't going to get him a perfect fifty percent, but I should be able to eke out a picture of close to forty percent. That was stretching every condition right to the edge of plausibility.

That took me half a day and worked nicely to keep my mind engaged. Then, Immerlin interrupted me with a reminder. My hands paused on the keyboard. They trembled a little. I pulled them back, leaning into the chair, wincing when it pressed on the bandage over the burn.

I did a couple of breathing exercises and fumbled a comb through my hair. Then, deciding it was as good as it would get, I tapped the web meeting button.

She was already in the meeting and had her video on. She looked pretty. My mother would have said she had lovely bones. Her voice was lower than I expected, slightly hoarse, either from smoking or perhaps the car wreck.

"Hello? Is this Bret?"

I said, "Yes," and mustered the bravery to press the video button.

She giggled when I came into view.

"Oh, I like the long hair. More handsome than I expected. Are you into computers? It looks like you work with computers a lot."

I was a bit flustered but muttered, "I do. All the time. How are you?"

"I'm fine," she said with a giggle. "Sorry about my voice. I have serious asthma, and the pollen count is high. It's playing merry havoc on my voice right now."

I nodded, showing that I understood while not having the slightest idea. Then, like an idiot, I said, "How are you?"

She tittered and said, "I'm fine. It's Sharon, by the way. I have the advantage since I talked to that hunk of a lawyer, Howard, earlier. He told me your name was Bret already."

Mentioning Howie helped me relax. Her mentioning Howie was a hunk made me chuckle, though I kept it off my face. Story of my life to be the sidekick to his handsome self.

"Howie and I go way back. He's pretty much a superhero."

"That seems so fitting for him. Howie. Yes, he completely seems like a Howie. I can see him being a superhero. Not that you are a slouch, yourself."

I waved a hand, face red. Then, changing the subject, I said, "I just did what any person would do in the situation."

She laughed. "I wished that were true. I've heard too many stories where people leave or keep driving when they see an accident, even if they are the ones that caused it. Let me tell you. I have got a girlfriend who ...".

She kept talking, on and on. I had a hard time keeping up, much less comprehending it all. Eventually, I found a pause to get a word in. Mainly to get her to stop gushing so hard.

I said, "Sorry we could not meet in person as you wanted."

She stopped talking, and her face brightened, her finger fidgeting with her hair. It was pretty long, at least mid-back. I hadn't noticed when I was pulling her out of the car.

"Don't worry about it. Howard mentioned you were struggling medically and that face-to-face meetings were not something you could do easily. I think that is why I'm even more appreciative that you crawled out of your car to pull me out of mine. It would be amazing and heroic in any situation, but to have to overcome even more — I think you did an amazing thing. But, of course, I'm pretty biased, too!"

Our conversation continued, but it was apparent to both of us after all while that I was uncomfortable, and we didn't have more to say other than the wreck. So, after revolving around that topic a few times, we parted ways.

I put my head on the keyboard, thinking that I was going to be alone forever. A perfect situation. What seemed like an equally perfect woman to connect with to have something meaningful. I just couldn't finish that last mile to make it happen. Hell, I couldn't make it past the first one hundred feet. Who was I fooling?

One thing did stick out that made me lift my head. To ponder on, for a moment. Sharon mentioned that she had been swiped by a large truck. The vehicle clipping her is what sent the two of us careening into one another. The problem was, that wasn't how the incident report read. She laughed it off when I pointed that out, saying that the insurance adjuster had cautioned her not to mention it. Saying it would just confuse the situation. Nothing at the incident report from the police on crash supported a third vehicle being present or that our two cars had done anything else but collided with one another.

I remembered the sound of a car, too. I wasn't going to claim some shadowy hand was present, but it was odd. That was too many coincidences for my taste.

Thirty-Five

The sandy-haired man kicked the pile of ashes, letting the wind scatter the little that remained. Usually, he would leave an intact corpse, but it wasn't necessary this time. The icy bitch had been right, even if he hated to admit it to himself. The hound he just cleaned up had betrayed them. Many of them had. Most of the damn company had somehow turned by the Homegrown, and they had missed it.

He put the large tank down. The stockpile of molten blood he had stored up wasn't going to be needed anyway, so he splurged. He brought out the big guns. Contemplating it, he wiped the sweat trickling down his cheek with the back of a glove.

Disgusting.

Sweat that is. I still haven't gotten used to it.

The wind was cool, a gentle caress on sandy-haired man's skin. He looked up at the moon shrouded in the clouds. The air between him and the moon seemed so stifling. He yearned to be free of it and back in the cold, crispness of home. The wind was whistling through spider silk — the stir of the trees. Ethereal fog moving and breaking on the web strands, like water on the shore.

Ogygia. Why, oh why did I have to be the one to earn a strand of Fortune back then? Why had it landed on my webs? Why had I picked it up? Where has it led me besides so far from home? Stronger? Sure, but to what end? They are the ones who reaped the benefits while I had to do the dirty work.

The wind picked up, stirred the leaves, and shook the trees. Behind the rustling of leaves and scratching of the branches of the trees was the soft sound of bells. The sandy man's back clenched, muscles writhing and contorting before he forced them to relax. He didn't bother to look behind him but just stared at the cold air stirring in the trees in the wooded draw below him.

"I wondered if it would be you." His voice had a catch to it, even as he made a wry smile. The only answer he got was the wind and the tiny tinkling sound of bells.

"I must admit, it was a toss-up between you and the ice bitch. I wasn't sure who would show up for the clean-up. Once I realized that so much had been compromised, I figured no one would let me stay neutral. Any chance you can let me go? I'll bow out. Go home. I can give up and just disappear."

His answer was a low child's giggle. The sandy man shook his head, letting one eye change. Reality shifted and a vast expanse of trees shrouded in mist with strands of thick webbing draped everywhere appeared. He looked in the trees around him in both worlds. The sound of giggling children rang out, and he could sense small hands tearing through the silk of the webbing. The vibration was unmistakable.

"The price you asked for better have been worth it. You must know this is going against Ogygia. So who was it that got to you?"

Silence. The slowly increasing volume of bells ringing in the wind in one world, the tearing of silk strands in the other. The sandy-haired man's mind spun furiously. "Think of it as my last wish. So, who was it? Carcosa? Edolin See? Tsalmatt? Or, was it — wait. No ... it couldn't be any of them. The reward wouldn't be big enough. It would have to be something so ... valuable that it would be worth the risk for the reward. It's him. It's that consultant, isn't it? I should have known immediately, given that cold bitch's response to him almost dying. Can't collect if he is dead, can you?"

Bells rang more clearly, interspersed with giggling. Through it, his ears picked up one footfall after another, breaking twigs and rustling leaves. The pace didn't change, but the sound grew louder. In the other world, he moved shuffled to the tops of the trees. It didn't stop their trek. It just changed the focus on their movement.

He paused, letting his features grow slack. "I'm right, aren't I. Only one reason I can think of that would cause either of you to turn. It's not just that he's a Homegrown, is it? Paradigm, right? I can't think of anything else. It's no wonder."

He had nowhere to turn. The forest was his home. Against someone else, it would be his strength. But, against her, every tree, every leaf, and even the wind was marshaled against him.

The sandy-haired man rolled his neck. He slipped to the ground in the other world. In this one, he ran both hands through his sandy hair to put it back into place. He listened to the soft sound of bells grow louder in both worlds, joined by tiny gigglings, like invisible children playing. He realized the footsteps had stopped behind him. Across the two worlds, he could feel the warm caress of something breathing, something so close it was almost touching.

The sandy-haired man closed his eyes and then smirked. "Be a darling and at least leave my progeny with a chance. And, I hope you don't expect me to beg."

The sounds elevated, wrapping around him like the wind. Tiny hands tugged at his body, holding him down. His features loosened, one eye gone, erupted in a plume of gore. Three enormous tree roots penetrated his thorax in the trees decorated with fog and spider silk. The sandy-haired man and giant spider fell forward in two worlds, not feeling the pain or having any more care in either world.

Thirty-Six

Staying productive, as always, kept my brain gainfully employed. The list of calls to catch up on never dwindled but seemed to multiply instead. I chopped at the work stacking until I made a sizable dent, but it never seemed to stop growing. It didn't stop me from trying to shrink it, though.

My two shadows named Malika and Howie finally faded away, satisfied I wasn't going to work myself into a stupor or not care for the burns and end up back in the hospital. That took a combination of smooth-talking and frustration to make happen. Having either of them in the house was starting to drive me up the wall. Watching me dissemble when they were around was pretty deciding. Howie almost wholly moved to web meetings. Malika still had to come in person, but that was also winding down.

Car insurance paid out, though not nearly enough to replace the Tesla. So I made sure and bought back the wreck. I didn't want anyone to know that I had tinkered with its software a tiny bit. After all, the car company had not built the Tesla to interface with virtual assistants. Immerlin, however, I took with me pretty much everywhere, so it had only taken some time and elbow grease, aka, coding and physical access to the vehicle, to fix that finally. No company wanted an amateur tinkering around in their closed software environment, and I had no desire to have someone accidentally or otherwise figure out the changes I had made. They had been both physical and digital. Luckily, insurance adjusters are not trained to find the modifications I made, even if they come with a specialist from the company in question.

Let's just say the changes weren't evident to the everyday guy.

Work filled the spaces, so I didn't have to think. I did actually work until I couldn't work anymore and staggered over to the pallet I had thrown down on the floor near the desk. Even the pain from pulling on the healing skin around the burn didn't keep me from falling into it face first and finding my way to the abyss of sleep.

The darkness within the boar was a welcome discovery. It had been too long since I Flashed, and I was apprehensive. The sensation was a bit different than before. The image of On-Raze I had built always felt two-dimensional. To my credit, I initially visualized an image from a card game. Only when I had left the darkness to manifest in the boar's world did it take on any kind of complete shape. Whatever the Ancestor had done, fixed that. I was now entirely in a full 3D form, which was surprising when I opened my eyes in the darkness. The furnaces of On-Raze's eyes illuminated the space. The fiery bristles were not far behind.

Shocking was a word that hardly described the feeling. However, some flailing around helped me realize it was a functional version of the On-Raze as I had envisioned.

At least, physically.

After some hijinks and goofing around with the new body, I concentrated on linking up with the actual boar.

It took a few tries. Eventually, I succeeded. Cold wind and snow were my rewards. The boar was in a rugged, wooded area, light snow still on the ground. The boar's new body and mine could have been twins, minus that he was much smaller, and his boar bristles looked like shards of flint protruding from this skin versus fiery sparks. The boar's nose told me that we were no longer at the tree woman's valley. It was a confusing muddle of scents that hinted end of Winter, and the beginning of Spring was not too far away.

I suspect my fumbling around alerted the boar to my presence. It found a place to drop, nestling in the snow, and met me in the space where On-Raze dwelled.

"Ancestor!" The boar squealed with obvious delight.

I animated the On-Raze image, illuminating the space. The joy on its porcine features was unmistakable.

"I have visited you many times, Ancestor. But, you slept, and I worried that in healing me, you had used up all your life."

I snorted in response and settled down. Then I bold-faced lied. "I'm here and will always be here. I won't take actions that I cannot do."

The boar ate it up. The boar also started talking, squeaking, and jumping around, telling me about the healing process, waking up, and understanding all the changes. I listened until I couldn't deal with it anymore and said, "Why are you not in the valley of the Pon Cloed tree people?"

The boar snorted. "Ancestor, I may have strayed far from home, but even I felt the Call. I knew if I stayed longer, I would not make it in time."

Not wanting to let the boar know I had no idea what it meant, I just grunted. I debated how best to have the boar tell me about the Call. It went and solved the issue before I could even ask.

"Ancestor, look," the boar said. In the darkness, the boar fashioned a vague haze, roughly a topological scene, though one so difficult to read that it was apparent the boar had never seen an actual map. I could sort of make out mountains, hills, and a river, but the rest was a goopy mess. One mountain peak was bowl-shaped. Maybe an old volcano? Hard to say. As the boar chattered and I focused on it, I could feel a kind of pull towards the bowl-shaped mountain.

"I cannot tell distances from this," I said, a bit smartly. Traveling had never been a delight for me in any world or time. Knowing how far I had to go was one of the few things that made the journey more tolerable.

The boar looked downcast. "Ancestor, I can only sense the Call and get a vague sense of how to get home. I have failed you."

I grunted and shifted to my feet. Then, looking down on the boar, I said, "Sense it again. I shall join you."

Excited, it struggled to its feet with a happy trumpet of squeals and snorts. I could feel it focus, listening, not with its ears, but with its liquid monster core and the spaces in its body. They resonated together, connecting to something I could not sense but yet, could at the same time. It seemed that the stronger one was, the better the antenna they could create to pick up the sound that was the Call.

Tossing aside my evaluation of the situation, I traced the feeling, following the sound.

I looked upon mountains, hills, trees, and rivers out of thousands of eyes. The world unfolded, dizzying in conception, as I experienced reality through thousands of boars, seeing out of their eyes. I could make out different places, different viewpoints, all along the path from where the boar currently was to where I suspect its home lay.

If I had been in my own body, I would already be covered in vomit. It was a chaotic, disturbing mess. No wonder the boar's map home was fuzzy. The enormous influx of input from the different boars was nearly impossible to understand. I tried to fly up, hoping I could see from the sky. Maybe get another vantage point. The only thing that rose was my stomach, which flip-flopped a few times. Seeing that didn't work, I took a different approach.

The impression of what was being conveyed looked to have happened across a sizable expanse of time. The boars who were sharing this path home had not necessarily walked the way together. Different times, different boars, some on target, some straying from the track. I used that understanding to my advantage.

I focused on a group of boars that strayed and ascended one of the higher hills nearby. I looked over the land below through their eyes, using what they saw to fill in the more fuzzy sections of the boar's map. Seeing that it worked, I moved from group to group, looking over one place to another, doing my best to clean up the map.

A group of giant bees chased one cluster of boars and ended up hiding in an outcropping on a mountainside that gave an excellent overview of the path. A different boar — foolhardy but damn strong — got lost frequently, swimming in rivers, getting lost in snowy ravines, and off a cliff or two. I suspect he survived, if for no other reason than sheer stubbornness.

I updated the map each time it made sense, and I continued until exhaustion overwhelmed me. Then, finally, the fugue began biting at the edges, and I slipped back into the On-Raze image. My fiery bristles were dim and flickering. Eyes almost wholly shuttered.

The boar was still caught up in the Call, but the map was significantly more precise now. I regarded it, committing the terrain to memory as much as possible before the fugue rose and consumed me.

Home.

The word turned in my mind when I woke up. It was dark outside. Immerlin told me it was two in the morning when I asked.

Home was a complex concept for me. I had no place that really resonated with me as home. If it were a person, it would be Alice more than my mother. She unconditionally cared for me. Alice was the person who stood up for me — no matter what. She made the courtroom battle to commit me to the hospital happen. Not that I blamed her for it. If she hadn't, mother would have packaged me up and made me disappear. Only Alice's fierce resistance and the fact she was an adult that could contest what was happening gave me a chance to stop it. We both failed, but it paved the way for Howie to get me out later.

I heated water in the kettle and made tea. Between cups, I jotted down notes and sketched out everything I could remember. Then, breathing in steam from the cup, I got on the treadmill. I walked slowly until my thoughts took on some semblance of organization.

Home.

Alice.

It was the middle of the night, but I still called. He would pick up. He always did.

I wasn't wrong, either. Howie's voice sounded sleepy when he asked if I was okay. No surprise, given the time it was.

"Howie, let's talk about Alice when you get time in your day."

I could hear him stop moving around on the other end. Then, finally, he asked, "Do you want to talk now instead?"

"No. Give me an hour or two in your day tomorrow, if you can. I probably should have waited to tell you properly, but I want to settle some things that I have been putting off. If nothing else, everything has made me realize you can't push off some things without a cost."

"Okay. Or, perhaps most importantly, are you okay?"

I sucked in a sharp breath. "Yes. Go back to sleep, and let's talk tomorrow."

Partly joking, partly annoyed, Howie said, "Did you seriously just call me in the middle of the night to tell me to call you tomorrow?"

I felt a bit sheepish but copped up to it. "Um, yeah, I guess I did."

Howie regaled me with a list of profanity that would make a sailor proud and hanged up.

I made more tea and kept walking. Finally, both the boar and I had a path to take to find the way home.

He had a map given by his Ancestors.

I needed to find one of my own. Unlike the boar, my mother wasn't going to show me the way with a handy map. I would have to find that path myself.

Thirty-Seven

Howie came to my place versus calling. Seeing him outside, I had a moment of petulance and almost didn't let him inside. I had just gotten my own zone back. Letting someone in made me shiver. So I pushed the complex emotions down and buzzed him in any way.

"Immerlin, soothing music mix 67, all speakers, volume 5."

"Playing music mix 67.

I busied myself making kukicha. Howie wasn't a tea fan, but he tolerated kukicha. I kept some chilled, so it didn't take much to warm it up. You just couldn't boil it. It made it taste horrible if you did.

"Bret."

"Howie," I said, setting out two cups. He walked to the other side of the kitchen counter, putting down a slim laptop. Like Howie, it was clean, proper, and neat. Everything I wasn't.

We didn't say anything else, keeping the ritual, until the kukicha finished warming up. I poured a cup for both of us, put the kettle between us, and pushed Howie's cup over. He took a few sips, short pauses in-between, while I inhaled the steam rising from mine. We stayed silent a bit longer until I broke the silence.

"Immerlin, block all incoming calls."

"Incoming calls blocked."

Taking that as a sign to begin, Howie put down his cup, laying his hand on his laptop. He didn't open it like I expected but paused.

"Bret, you positive you are up for this? It really hasn't been that long since the wreck, hospital, and Dereck's hijinks. You and stress are not exactly great bed partners."

I put down my cup. I reflected a moment in the silence to show Howie I was thinking about it, then nodded. "Yeah, Howie, we need to chat about Alice. And probably a couple of other things. I've been burying my head in the sand a bit too long on this topic, though. Look what that got me."

Howie grunted and tapped his laptop cover with his fingers. "Dereck is a grifter, so you can't take the blame on that one. We both know Alice pushed us not to dig into him overly much. Can't say I blame her given the royal treatment we gave previous boyfriends."

I waved him off to show I wasn't accepting that excuse. Howie poured some more kukicha from the kettle and saluted me with a raised cup to make peace.

I smirked and saluted back with my cup. It needed a warmer, so I poured some of the hot kukicha from the kettle too.

"I wasn't sure what you were going to ask, so I brought along the information I thought you would want."

"Thanks," I said, motioning with the cup for him to open the laptop and show me.

Howie looked at me closely, looking for something in my face. An expression or guidance, perhaps. The twitch of his cheek told me he didn't see what he was looking for, but Howie opened up the laptop, nonetheless.

"Let me run down things from the top," he started. "Alice had done pretty well in the real estate business and had some good investments. She had a tidy sum coming in, most of which she didn't use from what I can gather. Instead, much of it went into her investments, which are a pretty generous spread of stocks that pay good dividends, some tactical real estate buys, and the cryptocurrency you had pointed out. To both of us, mind you. Like me, she capitalized on that and made a solid killing when it rose. In fact, she and I merged our cryptocurrency accounts a bit beforehand, so that's stayed in my hands. Plenty more I could say about her financial affairs, but I suspect this is not what you are looking for, is it?"

I shook my head, though I was curious about a couple of things. "First, how much did Dereck manage to put his hands on?"

Howie grimaced. "Enough. He liquidated most of her real estate — mostly for crap deals, too. The majority of her liquid assets are in his hands. It will take months, maybe longer, to unswizzle that mess. Traceability is hard, and if I weren't already very familiar with how Alice organized her assets, I wouldn't have even been able to tell you what we just covered. I've worked with law enforcement to provide records, accounts, and historical information, but I wouldn't hold your breath. The only real data I have on finances for Alice is the trust fund she set up."

My voice sounded a bit rusty to my ears. "How does that sit? Did Dereck get access to it as well?"

He shook his head before I even finished asking. "No. That I can speak to authoritatively, it's been in my hands since her law firm transferred it a month or so after ... she passed."

Howie coughed, and we both went silent. We both consumed a cup of kukicha in silence before we started again. Each sip felt like drinking memories of Alice, her smile, her tiger approach to life, and unceasing energy.

Howard broke the quiet atmosphere. "Alice set up her life insurance to pay into a trust. Originally, Alms & Metaroon would have handled it, but Gregory Alms came down with pancreatic cancer and stopped practicing. Albert Metaroon referred it to me to take over since he couldn't handle Greg's work with him gone. He also knew Alice, you, me, and how tight everyone was. He was sure I would handle it well."

I said, "He wasn't wrong. You are in the one percent, if not at the top."

"I wouldn't go that far, but I do think I do okay. Enough to keep your dumb ass out of trouble most of the time."

"Most of the time," I echoed.

"Exactly. Outside of whenever you dig legal pitfalls on your own, I keep the wolves away, your money in your hands, and your ass at home and not in some out of the way corner of nowhere."

We clinked cups to that.

"So, Dereck never got close to the trust. Alice had a sizable policy, which paid out millions into the trust. Aside from paying the maintenance fees, it hasn't been touched and has increased an okay amount due to the investment strategy tied to it."

I waved my hand dismissively that I didn't care. As long as Dereck didn't get to it, I was content.

"Don't be too quick to cast it aside. It could solve a few problems, and you should consider it a real option, since we are on the topic, to handle some situations. For example, the care provided to your mother."

I grimaced at that thought and looked down at the counter. Howie waited me out. Finally, I gestured for Howie to continue, though I kept looking at the counter. Not sure what I hoped to find there. Maybe the answer or something.

"The trust is enough to cover her care for a while. Years potentially, even with the move to a different facility. It will be cheaper for better care in some ways since the hospital was stacking on the charges for long-term care."

"Just take care of it, Howie," I said, not ready to bring up my eyes. I missed his nod but heard his response saying he would take care of it. What he said next, though, got me to lift my head.

"Really, though, I suspect you will be interested to know I chased down some interesting things when I went back over her records to give to the police. One of those was she was paying for a storage facility. Prepaying, too. Had allocated money to pay for years, in fact, almost close to a decade."

I grunted. Alice did quirky things. Not sure why it was interesting.

Howie smirked. I could tell from his voice. "I know that doesn't sound impressive, but Alice liked to be organized. Like all of us, she had a good amount of transactions going on in her accounts. And, unlike you or I, Alice liked to account for and annotate everything. So she had dozens of transactions, some small, some pretty good-sized, basically every month that she marked with 'BB'. Sound familiar?"

He got my attention and for me to raise my eyes. Then, looking at his somber grin, I asked, "What do you think that means? I don't recall having anything that required a monthly amount from Alice. Could it be a reference to something she noted as linked to me but didn't tell me about it? Seems a pure Alice-like thing to do."

"I don't know," he said back. "I know Dereck didn't seem to pay attention or care about it, from what I can tell. I've tracked down the location and plan to stop by to take a look. I'm curious too."

I tapped the edge of my cup with a fingernail. It didn't make the sound I wanted, so I set it aside, choosing to fidget with a spinner instead.

"Doesn't that ... seem like a pattern of buying things, like stuff? So why put my name by it? Did the transactions have any data around them or say who from?"

Howie grunted, losing the smirk for a concentrating look. "Yes and no. Most were not very understandable. At least not to me. Some were from online sources. I suspect artists or something."

Happy to have something to do, I said, "Leave me the list."

Howie handed me a ream of paper with circled transactions. I stared at the stack of paper. Finally, he said, "You are the analyst, right? Have at it."

I groaned and took the stack of paper. "Thanks. It looks like I have some scanning to do."

Howie snorted. "You mean Immerlin has some scanning to do."

"If only it were that easy. Someone still has to load the paper, deal with the issues of getting a good scan, and then make sense of the OCR'd copies, so they turn into some kind of useful picture."

Miming mock shock, Howie said, "You mean Immerlin can't do all that already? You are really letting me down with this A.I. stuff!"

"Hah! Like I've said over and over, Immerlin is a lot of things, but an A.I. isn't one of them. I wish he were because I could use another friend."

We both laughed. It lightened the atmosphere.

Howie said, "Seriously, it will be faster just to stop by. I'm planning on going tomorrow. I've got some time in the afternoon. Want to come?"

Hands flexed subconsciously. Outside wasn't friendly at the moment. I'd been pulled out of my house to the courtroom, had a wreck afterward, and almost committed to a hospital again by Dereck. Leaving my home seemed like a very, very bad idea.

"I'll pass," was all I could cough out.

That response ended the talk, and after some mindless discussion, Howie left. Before he did, Howie reminded me that he would be offline tonight and to stay safe. Howie had a date with his girl, and she made it clear that no interruptions were allowed. He gave me an apologetic smile, but I just gave him two thumbs up and wished him luck.

Some mindless scanning later, I had a couple of hundred images that I queued up to turn into text. Luckily, I was pretty adept at that particular subject. After some manipulation and a bit of code, the pages rapidly became something I could work with more readily. It didn't take long to lay out the corresponding 'BB' transactions. Approximately thirty percent came from one source from what I could gather. The rest were all over the place, the majority equating to online transactions from dozens of shops, I would suspect.

It's not like I had a handy goto list that told me what transaction line item mapped to what storefront, but I queued up Immerlin with the data to see what could be drummed up with some rudimentary searching. It's incredible what's possible to find on the Internet if you know how to look for it.

While that was spinning, I looked at the one source that made up almost a full third of the transactions. Some of the notes Alice made also contained the capital letters 'QVD'. It wasn't familiar to me, and digging around didn't bring much to light that made sense. Not knowing what it represented made it hard to shrink the search space into something smaller. The amounts were consistently in the hundreds, a few bumping up to around one thousand. The transaction pattern didn't make sense to me. The times she made them didn't either. A pattern of behavior, yes. Something coherent? Not yet.

I did find it interesting that Alice had paid a private investigator a couple of times. I almost missed the transaction until I realized the scratch next to it looked like something I had told Alice about when we were young. I had flashed into a creature that looked like a snake with eight eyes up and down its length. The eyes had double eyelids that would close laterally and horizontally. I had trouble drawing it, so I always made a wiggly line with four 'plus' signs on each side of its length. We used to joke about how awesome it would be if it were in our world. The snake creature could find all kinds of stuff and look through the world's layers to see things otherwise unseen.

When Alice worked with Howie to get me out of the hospital, she used a private investigator to help with some work. I remember she drew the snake thing when she sent me letters. Later, she used it again when a private investigator looked up troublesome clients that cropped up from time to time.

I tore through the house and poured over her documents but couldn't find or identify the private investigator. I couldn't remember either, which was driving me nuts. I started to have Immerlin dial Howie several times, remembering only at the last moment that he was out of pocket.

I fretted for a while, pacing and thinking until drowsiness ambushed me, and I gave in, letting sleep win.

Thirty-Eight

The darkness was comforting. Flashing to the boar had turned to something I looked forward to, like a warm blanket on a cold day. Still, the puzzle wrapped around Alice had me yearning to wake as much as I wanted to stay. So I let my thoughts drift, but the fugue did not rise to take me home. Even after failing over and over to bend Flashes and the fugue to my will, I still tried. Sometimes I so desperately wished it was within my control.

The boar had gotten stronger. I could sense differences in the energy flowing through its body and read it in the deposits that had built up. The Call was more robust, too, creating some kind of synergistic effect with the boar, the chief reason why the deposits had grown so much. So perhaps the Call to return home was not only a journey but also a means to strengthen boars as well.

It intrigued me, and a quick thought brought the map we had worked to clean up into sight. It hung in the darkness of the space, and could I see we had traveled some distance since the last Flash. Either the boar was moving at incredible speed, or more time had elapsed.

Time was freaky in Flashes. For me, a night of sleep could be seconds in a flash, or years could go by. Hell, one time, each night and its Flash was probably the passing of centuries. Even then, I couldn't quite tell how much time was going by in the Flash. What is time to a rock, any-way? It had been an oddball flash, existing as some strange thing that felt like a rock. That flash episode happened while Howie and I were at camp, making for a hellish summer filled with near drownings when the camp councilors made me canoe or swim.

I suspected weeks, and maybe months had come and gone. On one level, I felt okay with it. On another, somewhat upset. In the past, when a Flash lasted long enough, time would accelerate inside the Flash.

More often than not, I — we, the creature I flashed into and I — would get killed. It happened so often that I sometimes suspected some Deux Ex Machina in the background, manipulating my life. Every counselor, doctor, and therapist told me it was just my imagination, just like all the Flashes. Quirks of thought, fodder of an active imagination. That I was broken and sick since it took over my life and made me non-functional. From my viewpoint, they were right and wrong, more on the error side. While I wondered what was real and what wasn't, I liked to think it was real, even if just for me. It was my personal movie, even if the films were more of the horror and nightmare varieties than romcoms and adventures.

The best Flashes were those where I didn't die, at least abruptly. I would flash until the creature passed of natural causes or until I just flashed into another creature. It felt like I had met some unseen milestone that acted as a trigger when that happened. Even though I have flashed my entire life, I still haven't figured out the rules, if any, existed anyway.

Not liking my maudlin thoughts, I connected to the boar's senses. I sensed nothing but rugged terrain, rocks, and trees. Spring was in full swing, with all the right colors and scents laid out like a tapestry. The boar was moving and not alone. He had companions, at least a dozen of other boars. All of them were significantly smaller and less, well prominent specimens, their bodies more like when I first met the boar. A mixture of pride and guilt grew at that thought, and I stayed a fly on the wall, listening but keeping my presence to a minimum so the boar and his companions wouldn't notice.

It soothed the chaos in my brain, and I soaked it up. The group rested, ate, fought, and met others who joined them. I stayed in the background, saying nothing. The boar seemed to have a growing circle of companions — friends I dare say — something I never had. The group of boars all felt the Call.

Something made very apparent in the mornings, when they would awake nearly as one and look towards the direction they needed to travel, giant noses taking in equally sized breaths.

The trek and their little adventures along the way slowly let me settle into a fugue. I felt it coming on but didn't fight it. Before I knew it, the light caught my eyes, waking me up. I blinked and realized I had not closed the blinds over the window in front of the treadmill. No harsh alarms, no heart exploding mania — I even felt somewhat rested. I wondered, on one level, if this is what ordinary people feel when they genuinely sleep at night.

Kukicha yesterday meant tea today. I set the kettle on a timer and worked the treadmill. I won't say I felt refreshed after I finished my morning walk, but it gave me an odd resonance that made me feel satisfied. Work buzzed by in a blur mainly focused on Marlin's request. The numbers were fighting me, but I was slowly winning. Late afternoon cast its waning light through the window when Immerlin alerted me to Howie calling.

"Howie."

"Bret." Howie's voice sounded strange, a mix of puzzled and something I couldn't place.

"Did you get the question I texted earlier? About the name of the private investigator that Alice used?" I asked.

"I did but haven't looked into it yet. Bret — "Howie's voice stopped. I could tell he put his hand over the phone instead of muting it. Then, after a moment, he came back.

"Buddy, I know you don't feel like getting out of the house, but is there any chance you could do it? This — I'm not sure how to describe what I'm looking at and think you need to see it."

The thought of leaving the house made me tremble, and I put down the cup I had lifted before I wore the tea inside it. A vehement 'No' came out before I could even fashion a coherent response.

"Okay," Howie breathed back. "Let me send you a video call, then. I'm not going to describe this, and I want you to see it. So take some breaths and hold on. I'll call you back."

I got up and made tea instead — Ashwagandha tea. A taste I didn't love to death but helped soothe jangled nerves.

Moving and doing something familiar helped reground me to the present. I had taken to having sudden trembling and near panic attacks when I thought about it too much. Sometimes it was okay. Other times, I just fell apart at the thought.

Howie's phone call came faster than I wanted, but I took it anyway. Immerlin put him on the big monitor at my workstation so I could sit down. His face was huge, filling up the screen.

"Bret, can you see me?"

"Yeah, Howie, your head is enormous. It makes you look like one of those giants from Attack on Titan." My attempt at a joke was just that — a bad effort. Howie made a face and pulled the phone back. In the background, I could make out some kind of glass window and the blurry scene of trees and cars going by on the road through it.

"Alice rented one of those temperature-controlled storage facilities. I'm outside the door. I had to use a bit of legal strong-arming on the facility to get them to open it up. She had a digital entrance code and a physical lock on it. I found the code in the legal notes with the previous lawyer but not the key to the lock. Had to have them cut it off."

I drank some too hot tea and coughed. Then, when I finished trying to breathe tea, I said, "I'm fine with whatever you needed to do, Howie." The anxiety was already falling away now that we were connected.

"Figured you would be," Howie said. It looked like he would say more, but he stopped and started walking. On the way, he started narrating.

"I'm at the door." Howie moved the phone to show me a door. I'm not an expert or anything on physical security, but it looked solid enough. He unhinged the lock but moved the phone to face him when he opened it. Light came on. I could tell from how it changed the video.

"One sec," Howie said, moving something. He moved in and out of the view of his phone's camera, so Howie must have set it down.

"Okay," he said, coming back into view. "Let me flip to the other camera on the phone, so you can see why I felt you should see this."

The picture flipped, and I could see the scene of an organized — not surprised, given it was Alice's place — storage space, filled with boxes, crates, and similar shaped things, all draped in a variety of drop cloths and coverings. The draped cloths were pretty uniform in color and appearance, so Alice must have bought them in bulk or from the same place over and over again. The mundaneness of the room made me sigh, letting anxiety fly out with it.

"Damn, Howie," I cursed. "I thought you were going to show me a freezer full of dead bodies or something from the build-up you made. What the hell?"

Howie gave a low laugh. "Not quite. However, look at this."

Simultaneously, he tugged one of the drop cloths from the closest item. It was a crate, or the skeleton of one, wrapped around a framed painting. That didn't intrigue me as much as what the painting inside depicted. Even though the thin paper cover made it a bit blurry, I would recognize that nightmarish shape anywhere. It was exactly what I had described to Alice a few years before she died. A horrible flash that I didn't care to remember but had felt desperate to tell someone about so it would quit eating at my brain.

"Howie ...?" I whispered. "What. The. Hell."

"My reaction, too." He covered it up and pulled off a few more, revealing other paintings. More images. I didn't recognize all of them, but many were depictions of something I had described to Alice or close enough.

The storage room was divided into sections, and Howie moved opened a box. It contained a stack of pencil and ink sketches, each one separated by thick waxy paper or tinfoil. Howie pulled them out, laying several of them side by side.

I didn't recognize the scene at first but then realized the temple featured in the background of several of the sketches looked like something I had told Alice about when we were smaller. One of the sketches showed the temple with a star on top. One with multiple spikes, like a compass rose.

I restrained the urge to run to my journals and asked, "Howie, what is all this? How did Alice ... ?"

"I don't know, buddy. I don't know." Howie's face came back into view. He looked calm but unbalanced too. "I opened a number of the containers in here before I called you. Alice has paintings, sketches, wood carvings, porcelain work, ironwork, comics, and dozens of other things. All of them showed images or scenes that ... well, look like something you have shared with me."

Howie kept the camera on him but moved through the storage room, fumbling with a container before flipping the camera back around. He revealed another painting, an ethereal landscape, mist lingering over water, hints of shapes in the mist. The layering of the oil, the shapes it made, and the presentation gave it a sense of music, of a beckoning that was luring you into the watery depths.

"I remember the day you described this picture to me. That you had a flash about being seduced by mermaids and that the mermaids had drawn you into the mist and the sea. It stuck with me. I dismissed it at first, but then I saw the moons reflected in the mist. As you described, one of the moons was odd-shaped, with a circling of asteroid fragments from an old wound that formed an octahedron shape. What are the odds that someone would paint the same scene, with the same exact highlights you told me years ago when we were kids?"

"I don't know, Howie," I said, touching my face. That Flash had ended horribly. I pushed on my cheeks to make sure they were still there. Those mermaids had eaten the soft bits of my face first before turning to other delicate parts, keeping me from drowning with their magic. After that, I couldn't break away from the Flash until the sailor died. I had come up screaming and didn't stop for days.

"Have you ever told anyone else about that flash?"

"Alice. Mother. Though not in any detail."

Howie covered it back up and walked back to the entrance. He flipped the camera to his face. "Bret, I first thought she was having people paint the things you described to her. I could see the artwork was from different people with different styles, just by flipping through things. I don't have to be an art critic to see that. But I'm stumped on the other material. It doesn't compute to me that she would have wood carvings or metal work done. Comic books and at least one crate of what looks like hand-written or printed manuscripts. Those don't make sense to me."

I closed my eyes and leaned back, doing my best to control my trembling.

"Howie," I whispered, "it makes sense if she was collecting it. That she was finding it versus asking for it to be crafted."

Howie's fingers rapped on the door, and he sat down suddenly, not minding the mess it was making of his suit. "Finding it? Like, realized other people had made material that lined up with the Flashes you told her about? Maybe she saw a painting or picture and didn't think anything of it, but when she kept finding more and more of it, she started collecting it?"

"Exactly that," I whispered.

"Buddy, I can't help but tell you I'm a bit creeped out. You and I have always talked about what your Flashes might really be. I've never sided with the doctors that they are just your overactive and fucked up imagination. Seeing this, and know there is even more that I haven't even looked at, is blowing me away."

"Me too, Howie, me too." I pinched my cheeks and chin. The slight pain was welcome. Suddenly, I knew what to do. Leaning forward, I said, "Howie, bring it here."

Howie looked shocked. "All of it?"

I nodded. "Everything. Hire a moving company, have them take a picture, and map out where every box was. Then, bring it all to my house. Hell, I don't have a car at the moment, so I have a whole garage that you can be used to put the boxes."

"Are you sure?"

"Yes," I said firmly. "I want to see it, touch it, and pour over what Alice found or made. Then, maybe I can figure out what she was doing ... and maybe what some of this might mean."

Howie looked hesitant but said, "Okay. Just do me a favor, okay? Don't think about this too much yet. At least, not without me, okay? I know my brain is going all over the place, and I want to approach this logically, at least as much as we can."

I laughed. It sounded like a crow. "Oh Howie, I've already contemplated that someone had her killed over this and felt the guilt from that. I wondered if I drove Alice to her own special kind of madness in trying to help me. I'm already there and back again, plus a hundred other thoughts. None or all of them could be true, no matter how outrageous my thoughts bounce back and forth. I can only promise not to do something stupid. How about that?"

Thirty-Nine

Concentrating on work was next to impossible. I made some half-hearted attempts and finally stopped. I closed the disaster I had made of the analyses — it didn't matter the client. It ended in the same endless spin. I suspect it was the sound of people moving downstairs. They were putting the boxes from the storage facility into the garage, and it just grated on me incessantly. I finally escaped to the roof to put more physical distance between me and what was going on, with noise-canceling headphones and a tablet, of course.

I paced and looked through the information. I was decent — if not good — at finding things. Mining Alice's old social media posts and having access to her email account did wonders in figuring out her old itinerary. I suspect, just like most other people, they had no idea how much data corporations were collecting on them. Not without their consent, of course. Corporations asked. People just didn't understand or didn't care what they agreed to give away.

Alice was no exception.

Howie had dropped off her phone. It had stayed in his possession since the crash that took her life. It still hurt to think about that happening, but it somehow seemed easier to say aloud, with current events being what they were.

I leaned against a solar panel and finally wrestled the data into something like a map I could understand. Earlier attempts had been frustrating. I wished so much that Immerlin was something closer to his namesake or one of the Hollywood yarns on A.I. I could use the help.

Immerlin wasn't and didn't exist, at least not in the way that fantasy movies like to menace. Still, I needed to see where she had been going. Maybe it would help me make sense of her movements. To build out a better picture of what she had to be involved in with these art purchases. I wanted not only to figure out what was going on with the artwork in the boxes being deposited in my garage but also ... the pregnancy. While Howie and I had set that aside for the moment, I was still looking for leads, just like he was.

Shrugging that thought aside for the moment, I focused on the map. I had Alice's days and her appointments in layers, hoping it would help. But, given that she did a ton of meetings, I wasn't sure it was the right approach. Too many plots on the graph were just as bad as too few.

Any semblance of what logic I had put together went up in smoke when a phone call rang on the tablet.

It was Howie.

"What's up?" I answered. I didn't respond with fake cheer. Howie knew I had asked for this but was wise to the fact that it was upsetting the hell out of me.

"They should be done in an hour."

"That's good news, "I said.

"Also. That private detective you asked me to look up. Her name is Schuster. Siobhan Schuster. The outfit is called SSD, which I guess is a play on her name."

That's right. Hearing the name gave me a voice and a face. Her voice was a bit rough. I remember that from being with Alice when they were on the phone. I kind of visualized her as a hard-bitten, tough woman, physically. Bad on me. When I did meet her, the contrast between that mental vision and how she really looked surprised the hell out of me. Ms. Schuster could have put more than a few models to shame if she wanted: athletic, trim, and armed. Not only with a pistol but equal amounts of prim and gruffness as she needed it.

"You have a number?"

"Already sent," Howie said, doing it as he said it. "Also, I've chatted with her briefly and explained current events. Especially how it involves Alice and Dereck. Come to find out. She had a hand in the information that ended up in Judge Harris's and law enforcement's hands. I'll let her explain it. She's expecting your call."

I left the roof and went to my more secure office: no reason, just better soundproofing and comfort on my part. I dialed the number manually and fidgeted while it dialed. Finally, after a couple of rings, a pleasant young lady picked up the phone.

"Hello, this is SSD private investigations, Mischa speaking. May I help you or direct your call?"

Clearing my throat to get the lump out of the way, I said, "Hello Mischa. May I speak to Siobhan Schuster, please?"

"Okay, sir. Is she expecting your call?"

"Yes. Please let Ms. Schuster know it's Bret Byrne."

"Oh! Siobhan said to send you right through if you called. One second please."

I waited, and Siobhan answered.

"Schuster."

"Hello, Ms. Schuster. My name is Bret Byrne. I'm Alice's Byrne's brother."

"Bret. Hello, it's been a bit. I never got to say how sorry I was to hear about Alice's passing. I know you two were close. Very close."

I took a breath in to steady my emotions. "Yes, yes we were. I think Howie — pardon me, Howard Kearns, my attorney — explained why I was calling?"

"Yes. Not to mention Mr. Kearns provided all the documentation needed, including an order from a judge to ensure that I knew there was sufficient authority and legal backing to have this conversation."

"Good." Damn Howie, way to go the extra mile!

"However, usually, I do this kind of thing in person, not over a phone. Mr. Kearns indicated that you still have medical problems that make that an issue. Something about ... a vehicle accident?"

I suspect it was an occupational hazard to pry for information out of reflex. So I laughed, uncomfortable, and not trying to hide it.

"Ms. Schuster — "

She cut me off. "Siobhan. You are making me feel old calling me Ms. Schuster."

"Okay. Siobhan, I suspect you and Alice have talked about many things over the years so I won't beat around the bush here. Howie is going out of his way to protect me, but I remember you were a guest many times at Alice's house and a close associate, if not a friend. Or, at least she told me so. I want to shoot straight with you. No, it's not the car wreck keeping me from having a more intimate meeting than over the phone. I'm not a sob story kind of guy, so I won't bore you. I do have Agoraphobia, which means I'm prone to intense anxiety and panic attacks when in the presence of people I don't know, especially if the situation is equally unfamiliar. That prevents me from meeting most people, as you can imagine. I have recently had an accident, and my brush with Dereck Eisenrohr — who tried to have me committed to an asylum and potentially murder my bed-ridden mother — has me more than a little on edge."

"I appreciate that you are clarifying things, Bret," she said. "That's a bit more information than I had before, and it makes me slightly more comfortable talking about your sister's affairs. I'm sure you are aware at this point that Mr. Eisenrohr is, if you don't mind me using a professional term, a scoundrel. Alice suspected this, which is why she engaged my services to investigate him shortly before her death. Sadly, she did not authorize me to share this information before her passing, so my hands were relatively tied until I found a way to pass it to a law enforcement friend who could leverage it into another case that involved Eisenrohr."

That had me confounded. "Wait, Alice knew Dereck was bad news?"

"Yes," Siobhan answered.

"Alice engaged you to investigate Dereck?"

"Yes, again," Siobhan said.

My brain spun on that for a few moments before I said, "Why didn't she do something about it? Divorce him or something?"

"I suspect that was an action rapidly in the making before her death," Siobhan said dryly.

"Why did she even get entangled with this guy," I wondered out loud, stunned by the revelation. I had always thought Alice didn't know he was a snake.

"That might be a question that only your sister could answer. However, please don't think ill of me saying this — Mr. Eisenrohr was an associate of your mother. Dereck Eisenrohr and your mother had previous engagements that I don't have details about, but I do know that she was the pathway to introduce the two together. I happened to be at that meeting as well and was party to seeing the initial meeting."

Another crippling blow that made me want to hate mother more. I pushed the angry thoughts aside.

"So mother was the person that introduced the two of them?"

"To my knowledge, that was the first meeting, yes."

"Why would my mother even know Dereck, anyway? I can't visualize her knowing him at all."

Siobhan cleared her throat. "Your sister bought a lot of art, as well as real estate. Mr. Eisenrohr, for all his scummy faults, was talented in picking more esoteric art and making money from it. Probably one of the few legitimate things he did."

After a short moment of stewing, I put two and two together, realizing that if Siobhan was present, maybe she knew about the art deals Alice had made.

"Siobhan, would it be fair to say then that you helped Alice procure art, and that's why you were there?"

"Sort of, yes. I was there for another reason, but yes, I helped Alice acquire art, sculpts, and other decorative items many times. Your sister had particular taste in artwork, and I helped her chase down more than one piece of art for years."

"Years," I echoed.

"Years," she affirmed. "At least, for the last four to five years, I've helped her track down quite a few pieces. She frequently kept a running list of descriptions of pieces for me to match regularly."

That threw me, and I couldn't help but ask, "Did she ever tell you why this art or another or talk about it with you?"

Siobhan paused, then spoke. "I'm not comfortable talking about that over the phone. If you like to meet in person, I can go into more detail. What I will say," she said, overriding me interrupting her, "is some of that artwork was tricky. Not in a legal purchasing perspective, but in that they were linked to law enforcement cases or just suspicious circumstances."

"You can't leave me hanging like that. What does that mean?"

I could hear the firmness in her voice. "Actually, I can, and I am not going to fill in more blanks. You meet me face to face with or without your lawyer, and I'll tell you more. But not over the phone."

"This is turning very cloak and dagger," I protested. "Its artwork, for goodness sake! Do I need some legal document or authorization from someone to have you tell me?"

"No. I am just not going to say it unless we are face to face. I don't care that doing so might make you more uncomfortable. That's your business, not mine. If you want to know, meet me, and I'll tell you. Now, I have an appointment in a few minutes. Do you have other questions I can answer in the meantime?"

I rocked back, squeezing my hands, torn between wanting to know and not knowing. "Can I encourage you to meet with How — Mr. Kearns — to convey this information?"

Her answer was firm. "No. It's you or no one."

"I find this grossly unfair."

"I don't care," she said in response. "You are not my client. I don't have to tell you anything. Legally, nothing compels me to share even this much information. I could have just told you she and I worked together and kept it to the basics. I'm choosing not to do so because I liked Alice. She and I go way back, and I think she got a raw deal. But that's it.

She didn't save my firstborn and isn't a bestie. We worked well together, which is why I'm willing to bend a bit here. I'll say it again. If you want to know what I know, meet me in person. You can set the place. Maybe that will make it less uncomfortable."

"Fine," I gritted out. "I'll figure it out and get in touch."

"Good enough," Siobhan said and hanged up.

I called Howie right afterward. He picked up on the first ring.

"She will only tell me the real details in person," I said between gritted teeth.

Howie grumbled, cursing softly under his breath. "What do you want to do, buddy?"

Even though the thought was driving a spike of anxiety into my liver, I said, "We need to know. She said I could pick where, but it can't be at her office. Or, my house. That's a no-go."

Howie breathed out. "Okay. Then my place. You know it, and I can be there to manage this. It gives a measure of control over the situation."

"Okay." I grimaced and asked, "Can you set it up?"

"No problem. I've got it. Let's find out what's going on together."

"Thanks. I truly want to know. I'm tired of being in the backseat and feeling passive in all these situations that turn bad. I want to be ahead for once. It's just too fucking oddball. If I didn't know better .... "

Howie finished the statement for me. "... you would feel like this was someone out to get you? Yeah, buddy, I understand. But, hell, I'm on the outside looking in, wondering the same thing. A bit too fantastic to be fiction, if you get what I mean."

"Yeah," I said, looking at the wall. It didn't reveal anything to me, but I wished it would.

Forty

Doc Matson motioned for Scott to stop talking as soon as he busted through his office door. Then, when Scott looked like he was going to speak anyway, Doc Matson threw the pen in his hand at him, striking him in the chest. Scott looked hurt but sat down.

Seeing that Doc Matson was still on the phone, Scott flipped open his laptop and started scrolling.

That got him an eye roll. Doc Matson made a mental bet whether it was porn or not. He finished the call and slammed the phone down, rubbing his ear. Scott didn't start chirping about whatever latest strange thing he had found or thought he saw, which raised the odds he was right.

Agilely moving around the desk and finding out he was right didn't make him feel any better. Doc Matson slapped Scott on the back of the head and flipped the laptop shut.

"Really? You little shit! You couldn't wait to do that outside my office?"

Scott rubbed the back of his head sheepishly. "You know I get bored easily!"

"Every time I start to get even the slightest bit of respect for you, you do something to send it swirling down the drain, you know."

Scott gave him a 'what did I do' look that got him another slap on the back of the head. Then, fishing for cigarettes, Doc Matson headed into the Autopsy room and pulled open the fire escape door, kicking a brick he kept around to keep the door open into place. Scott trailed after him like a lost puppy, rubbing his head regretfully.

After firing up a cigarette, Doc Matson asked Scott, "You watch John Wick?"

Scott seemed to come to life with the question and started gushing about the movie, much to Doc Matson's disgust.

"I'll take that as a yes, then. Do you remember how Mr. Wick shot people?"

Scott looked at him oddly but nodded. "Up close and personal. It made for a gritty, cool style of fighting."

Doc Matson sighed and took a drag. "More specifically, do you remember how he fired? What his way of shooting was called? I know it's not mentioned in the movie, but you are damn movie buff on top of everything else, and I figure you have probably looked it up."

Scott looked puzzled, and his hand twitched towards the laptop he had brought along. "Uh, he shot them everywhere. Head, foot, shoulder, whatever he could get a bead on."

Letting out the smoke from his lungs, Doc Matson said, "Mozambique Drill is the answer. Two to the body, one to the head."

"That's so cool, doc. I didn't realize you watched the movie too."

That got him a look that called him an idiot. "I haven't watched the movie, just had the movie explained to me ad naseum over the phone all last night and today. Unlike you, I don't get days off. Just called in."

Scott had the heart to look guilty for a few seconds. Then, he brightened up and asked, "Do you want to watch John Wick together?"

Doc Matson threw the lit cigarette at him, making Scott yelp. When Scott knocked it away and started protesting, Doc Matson had a new one fired up.

"No, you idiot. I have a morgue with a couple of bodies to get through. So does a few of my compatriots, which is why I've been on the phone. Guess how many bodies that we have in common with that triple shot pattern, huh?"

"What?" Scott's look was a mixture of shock, amazement, and giddiness. Then, when he realized that Doc Matson was waiting on him to guess, he ticked off fingers and finally said hesitantly, "Ten?"

"No."

"Twelve?"

"Nope."

"Really? More?" Seeing Doc Matson nodding, Scott said, "Twenty! No, thirty!"

That got him a look of disgust. "No, seventeen, you dork. What's wrong with you? Isn't that enough bodies that you have to beg for twenty or thirty?"

Doc Matson grumbled, but Scott didn't mind him. He flipped open the laptop and pulled up the information in the files after carefully saving his place in his video to take care of later.

"Holy Shit, doc, twelve of them died in the same building in Seattle. From what I see in the files, that group worked for the same company. The rest are scattered across the U.S. and all over the place. But that only makes fifteen."

"Yep. At least one more in Germany and another in Belgium. That phone call you almost interrupted was a guy I know in Singapore. Same pattern, similar situation. Also doesn't count another possible eighteenth. That one had been out in the woods for a few days, maybe a week. Animals got to it, so the upstate coroner isn't sure if it fits the pattern."

Scott look awed. "Doc, doesn't this mean it's a serial killer?"

"Well, dork, that's the question. I'm going to do my part and help figure that out. The timeline roughs out to a potential match for a person to have flown from Singapore, through Europe and then to the U.S. Could be the opposite, too."

Somewhat awed, Scott asked, "Does that mean the authorities will establish a task force?"

Doc Matson grunted and stubbed out his cigarette. 'Don't know. Maybe? Not like we are going to be a part of it."

He moved towards the Autopsy room, and Scott suddenly realized that Doc Matson had said a couple of bodies were in the morgue. That was code for fresh ones that he needed to work on and do an autopsy.

Scott caught up. "Doc, does that mean we have some of those bodies here?"

He whooped when Doc Matson nodded, which got him another slap to the back of the head.

"What's wrong with you, Scott?"

"Nothing, Doc! I was just excited, that's all."

"That's not normal, you know. I'm almost sad that I told you in the first place."

"Doc!"

Scott got ignored, but he followed along, looking around like he was on a treasure hunt. He looked confused when Doc Matson left the Autopsy room and went back to his office. Scott got here right in time to have a folder shoved into his arms. He trailed after Doc Matson as he went back to the Autopsy room. That got him a look of ire, so he shied back. Then, realizing the doc wanted him to look at the file, Scott popped it open. Then, Scott started exclaiming.

"Wow, o wow. Really?"

Seeing Doc Matson nodding while scrubbing to do the autopsy, Scott said, "Seriously? Another chillcicle? What's the odds?"

Doc Matson didn't bother to answer him. He had too much work to do even to bother trying to answer Scott. He also knew Scott would go crazy, even set aside his porn, to figure out everything he could.

He ate up this kind of thing.

Forty-One

I don't travel well. Anyone that knows me knows that too. Not having my car made it even harder. I wanted to know, however, and shoved it down as hard as possible. I was bundled up like an Eskimo to cut down on outside inputs.

I slipped into Howie's car when he showed up and didn't think about anything.

It wasn't any easier today than any other day. I just had more reasons to give my brain the finger. The shape of this looked ugly. I would love to say I was hot under the collar about family being taken advantage of, and blah blah blah. But, really, I was pissed about Alice. Not only had she been taken away, but this kept looking like it might not be the accident I thought it was. Dereck and his bullshit aside, something else seemed to be going on.

Even Howie agreed with me.

If you step on something in the grass and it stinks, there is a good chance that it is crap.

I wasn't sure what the hell Siobhan was up to in this scenario. Her cloak and dagger shenanigans weren't winning her any awards for friendship. I had beat my brain up all day trying to remember what I could recall about her.

It wasn't much. Searches showed me that Siobhan's agency kept busy and was comfortably in the black as far as revenue went. Nothing I knew how to find hinted she was dirty or whatever the correct term was.

We got to Howie's house an hour before Siobhan's appointment. Being early let me get over the shakes and focus. It didn't take near as long as I feared, thankfully. I circumspectly hid Immerlin's mobile hardware in the house with Howie's permission. I wanted him to record things, but not be obvious. So I used the laptop until it was time.

Howie met her at the door so she wouldn't ring the doorbell. There was a reason I didn't have one at my own house. It was one of those triggers that made the anxiety shriek with joy. Howie had removed his doorbell a long time ago for me.

Siobhan looked like I remembered her, a little bit older from the lines on her face and a lot more muscular than I recalled. It was more input than appreciation. Taking it in but not letting my brain get overwhelmed. I closed the laptop, and she joined Howie and me at the table. Hickory coffee was not her favorite, I suspect. Even I could tell she accepted the cup out of politeness but didn't touch it.

Howie broke the ice by pushing over some legal documents. Siobhan glanced at the pages but didn't touch them.

"Thank you, Mr. Kearns, but I don't need more copies of what you have already provided."

"Okay, then. We are here, present, face to face, taking a great step forward to do so, in light of my client's medical issues."

"So I see," she said coolly, looking at me. It made my hands shake, so I put them under the table.

Siobhan was kind enough to pretend not to notice. "I suspect you feel I'm being unfair in forcing you to meet me in person. Allow me to say that I am only going to that extent at the bequest of my client, your sister, Alice. She instructed me to do so and use my own judgment on whether I should provide you with something she left in my care. I'll tell you frankly that I hate — completely despise — these types of requests. I only accepted the request because she was a very long-term client and friend to my agency."

We both nodded. Howie asked, "What rubric did Alice ask you to use? That Bret be able to meet face to face?"

Siobhan gave a small quirk of her lips. "Something like that. I'll skip going into detail about that since it's not something I need to convey. To be fair, Bret's condition, however, was a part of that evaluation. Personally, as I said, I don't like this or the work she detailed to my agency in the last year of her life. So I'm here to resolve details about both of these things and wash my hands of the entire affair."

Her attitude was annoying. Part condescending and part — I don't know, arrogant? I could feel displeasure emanating from Howie too.

"Fine," Howie said. "Let's begin with what Alice left in your care."

"Sure," Siobhan said coolly. She took a key on a ring with a metal tag attached from her pocket and pushed it across the table. "This key was left in my care to pass to you if I felt you met the right criteria. It opens a storage facility. The address is listed on the metal tag. Inside, I suspect is information or whatever Alice wanted you to know. I don't know the contents of this storage room or why she arranged to have the key provided in this manner. However, I can tell you that she put the key in my care roughly a month before she died in the car crash."

Howie and I looked at each other, and he took the key. I suspect we were both thinking the same thing.

"Can you tell us anything else concerning this key?" Howie asked Siobhan.

"No. That's what I know."

"Alice didn't mention anything else when she left the key in your possession?" Howie wasn't going to let her off with that.

"As I mentioned, she provided me with the details on when, if ever, I was to deliver it. She did not say or indicate that she thought her life was in danger. If anything, she was cheerful and in good spirits. Alice acted like depositing the key in my care was just another item on her to-do list to get done that day."

"I see," Howie said. We stared at each other. I was uncomfortable. Howie and Siobhan crossed swords with their eyes until Howie finally spoke.

"Fine. You mentioned other information, as well?"

I wanted to push her but didn't have the ability. Maybe Howie could and had a strategy that I wasn't picking up.

Siobhan said and looked at me. "Yes. Your sister Alice used my agency many times to track down pieces of artwork, investigate real estate buyers and sellers, and other people. Pretty much normal stuff, but not all of it. Alice liked a certain kind of artwork, something that I believe had to do with you, Mr. Byrne. On more than one occasion, she indicated that the artwork and like items she procured had something to do with you. At first, I thought it was for you, but I quickly realized that was not the case."

"Can you tell me more about that?" I finally choked out some words.

"Perhaps." She looked at me sideways while pulling out a stack of folded notes from her inside pocket and pushing it across the table. "Your sister would never send what she was looking for by email or text. She always wrote what she wanted longhand or gave me a sketch, with cautions not to scan, copy or otherwise disseminate it. Every time we met, she had me destroy any past notes. These are the last ones that she sent me. Previously, you accused me of being cloak and dagger on the phone. On this topic, your sister was quite the adherent of sneakiness when acquiring this artwork. For reasons that I did not understand or frankly care. She paid well, your sister, and that was my primary concern."

I pulled the folded notes to my chest with shaky hands before Howie could snag them. I looked them over while Siobhan kept talking. Alice's clean and organized handwriting unfolded before me, all characters beautifully spaced and perfectly aligned with one another.

One page went into great detail about a scene. Nothing I remembered off the top of my head, but seeing the triple moons described reminded me of a Flash that happened about two years before, maybe later. I had only mentioned it in passing to Alice, thinking I had seen the triple moons before when I was younger. The second page was a sketch showing the triple moons over a tall plateau, and some monolithic stone arrangement lit with power or perhaps gates. Something Siobhan said pulled me from staring at the paper.

"Wait," I said, interrupting her. "You said you found this painting?"

"Yes," she said plainly. "Like many other scenes described in sketches or handwriting, QVD was a source that painted them, or at least it looked like it. At first, I thought your sister was playing some kind of tax game or something since she would ask me to find art that seemed to show up not long later from QVD magically. Which, she would, in turn, buy, sometimes at prices that did not make sense to me."

"Who is QVD?" I had to ask. It made my mouth dry, but I got the question out.

"From what I can gather, a Vietnamese-born lady who lives in Thailand. She creates a good amount of artwork, at least in styles your sister was looking for in her art. She accounted for a sizable volume of assets that Alice purchased. Quan Van Dich is the name, QVD is her signature on art or online posts. As I said, I thought perhaps your sister was running some kind of shell game for a bit, but after investigating had determined that she was absolutely beyond my skills to penetrate or was truly just using some kind of inside information. Luck just didn't cut it in my books to be that accurate to the images that were being painted."

Howie asked, "Was it just artwork?"

Siobhan shook her head. "No, all kinds of work. Nothing illegal, mind you. Sometimes it was out there. I spent months tracing some guy in Japan who was drawing obscure manga that she wanted to collect. Another time it was buying unpublished manuscripts from some dead guy's estate that never had gotten published. It was both interesting and creepy. In fact, it got more unsettling as time went on, and I started pushing back a little."

"What do you mean?" I had to ask because I was building a fearful hypothesis as she kept talking.

Siobhan leaned forward slightly and lowered her voice. We followed along subconsciously. It's instinctive in us when we share something secret or sensitive.

"Every good investigator learns to pay attention to their gut. Mine was telling me something, and it wasn't until I went over all the work I had done that year that I came to a realization. Your sister buying some dead guy's manuscript or work was business as usual. But. She would make purchases a bit too often when the person recently died or passed away pretty quickly afterward. I'm not saying anything to impugn my client because I checked and didn't find any link between Alice and this activity. It just made me suspicious. And very much not willing to do the work anymore. It was obvious to me that someone was feeding information to your sister Alice. I had no idea who. I thought it was you, to be honest. But, after speaking to you on the phone and now meeting you, I doubt it. I'm betting it's someone else."

"It wasn't me," I croaked out. Howie affirmed that in a legalese voice. Siobhan gave us both a flat smile. "I'm inclined to believe both of you. I also want out of this mess. You have the key, which ends that engagement. That job is paid for, so you don't have to do anything. I'll just close that on my end. After this meeting, I want to wash my hands of the whole affair. In fact, if you don't mind me being blunt, I don't want to see either of you again when we are done."

"No offense taken," Howie said. I nodded mechanically. My brain was caught up in thinking.

Howie began quizzing her about Dereck. I tuned out, not caring. Put him in a deep hole and fill it in, and I would be happy. He knew my concerns and asked Siobhan. I stared at the handwriting and the sketch, looking them over repeatedly. I knew this scene but didn't at the same time. I suppressed the urge to call Immerlin and waited until Siobhan asked me if I had any questions. I shook my head and blanked out until Howie saw her out. When he returned, I pulled Immerlin out from where I had hidden him and broke open the laptop.

Howie sat down and just watched as I flipped through pictures. Once the movers had finished and I shook off the malaise that having them in the house caused, I got to work unwrapping and taking pics. It had been a weird trip down memory lane in many ways and an exotic uncovering of things in other ways. Finally, after a while, I went numb and just opened up a box, took a picture of what was inside, and rattled off the name Alice had put on the package, along with whatever came to mind when I saw it. I ended up making a small dent in what was there but nowhere near capturing it all.

I had that stack of images open, flipping through them manually while Immerlin was looking as well. But unfortunately, I didn't remember seeing the artwork in the sketch. Siobhan said she found it, but I wasn't seeing it in the imagery of the boxes I had gone through.

The Immerlin chimed, the best he could do in his mobile form, and I pointed the mouse at the results. A couple of images tiled across the screen. Not the one that Siobhan mentioned she found, but plenty of linked ones.

I leaned back. Howie leaned forward before he realized that my teeth started chattering. Once Howie saw I was having a reaction, he closed the laptop and pulled me to this couch. After getting me warm and forcing me through the ritual that ground me to the present, and not never never land, as the one doctor had called it.

"Howie?" I quietly said when I had gotten control back.

"Yeah, Bret?"

"I know you didn't get a great look at the images before I fell apart, but I did. You know what I saw?"

"No, Bret, what did you see?"

"A scene that I knew. One from my Flashes, but at different vantage points. Like different people might be looking across the same place."

"You think so?" Howie's voice sounded strangled.

"Each of those painted scenes was done by someone else, on different dates, and in different styles. So, Howie, why was Alice collecting this stuff? What did she know or who was she talking to?"

Howie was silent before saying, "I don't know, buddy. I don't know. It wasn't me. It wasn't you. Your mother wouldn't spare a brain cell to keep track of your Flashes. Anything on record from court transcripts would be old and not detailed enough. Could someone have gotten into your journals?"

"No." Impossible. I had more safeguards around it than Fort Knox. Even the information I gave Immerlin was encrypted. I doubt NSA would bother decrypting my journals and send them to Alice to use to buy other peoples' artwork.

We sat quietly, contemplating. Then, finally, I said the thing that had been spinning in my brain for a bit now. "Howie. What if that is really from other peoples' perspectives? That they saw what I see in my Flashes. Not once, not twice, but often, as if they also lived it as I do. That this Flashing situation is not insanity but some strange thing where we — this group of people and I — are visiting other worlds. Sounds crazy, doesn't it?"

Howie gave a strangled laugh. "Crazy. Not the word I would use. What is the Sherlock Holmes quote? When you have eliminated all which is impossible, then whatever remains, however improbable, must be the truth?"

"Yeah," I said.

"Want to hear my equally crazy thought too?"

I nodded. Howie laughed. The laugh had a bit of crazy that I recognized.

"Remember how we used to joke that it was some giant conspiracy and that someone was trying to kill you? I mean, you have had more accidents than anyone I know. I looked it up once, you know? Not Guinness world records level of accidents but really, really up there. When I think of this, what Alice was doing leading up to her death, Dereck's actions, your recent car wreck — hell, dozens of other things, it seems like someone or something is out to get you. Not just you, but everyone linked to this — call it an ability — to cross worlds. Didn't Siobhan say that the artwork that Alice collected was linked to the deaths of the authors, painters, or creators? So much so that even she was bothered by the correlations she was making. I can't even believe I can say that out loud and feel like it might really — I mean really — be true."

"You should try living it," I retorted feebly. We laughed, but I felt even more scared. I couldn't help but feel we had the edge of something beyond dangerous, and we were close to seeing something that might destroy us.

Howie got up and brought back beer. He offered, but I shook my head. He opened both of the bottles, alternately drinking from both.

I stared at my hands. "Howie, I would so rather it be a zombie apocalypse or something. At least I would know what to do."

"I know, buddy, I know. Not like we can hunker down and nail boards over the windows. You either got to decide they are watching you or they are not. If they are, then they — whoever they are — will react based on what move we make next."

"Yeah. Not like I'm going to order a bunch of weapons. They don't hand out gun licenses to anyone with a history of mental illness."

"Too true. How stupid those doctors are going to look when we prove to them that you are not crazy after all."

"Huh," I said, picturing one particular doctor. "Yeah, it would be sharp."

Howie took a general swig, draining one bottle. "I'm thinking this is more L.A. Noire than Call of Duty or some Jason Bourne flick."

"Or Borderlands. Or Taken. While role-playing as Liam Neeson seems like it might be fun, I don't want the situation that goes along with it."

"Me either."

"So, now what?"

Howie looked at the other bottle then put it down. "We chill for another hour or so, and then I take you home."

"That's it?" I felt mixed up inside and strangely compelled to do something with all this new information.

"Yeah. What can we do? Dart off half-cocked? We don't know enough to act yet. We need more information, like what Alice was really involved in here. No kind NPC grandpa is going to show up and make that happen. No magic rings, almighty systems, no gold finger. It's not a video game or an online novel. We have to figure it out ourselves and try not to die or get disappeared in the process."

"Sounds tricky," I said, voice lowered.

"What are you worried about?" Howie cajoled. "You have been playing this game and winning for years now. Why would you think it suddenly became different? Because we got ahold of some nebulous information that points to something more dramatic? Put your analyst hat on, buddy. Until we shape what this means, we keep close to home and proceed like normal."

I nodded. I didn't feel better, but it was a plan, at least. I needed to know, and the only clear line of information we had was the artwork and things that Alice had collected.

Howie said, "Not to add to the spin but have you thought yet about whether Alice ever contacted any of the people who made the artwork?"

That pulled the shrinking thought that had been lurking in my back brain into the open. "Dammit, Howie, I was trying not to think about that. What if she did ... and that had something to do with her death?"

Howie shook his head. "No, I don't think that's it. I don't know for certain, but I don't think so. I'm wondering if she contacted anyone, yeah, and we both are sitting here wondering slash outright saying we believe there is some big shadowy organization out there playing games. I'm just not seeing the math that points to knocking off Alice. You? Now, that I can kind of see. Too many accidents in your life to be completely random bad luck. Plus, you are a jerk, you know."

That injected levity — forced or not — had us exchanging verbal jabs. We went on for a few minutes before it finally died off.

"Listen, buddy," Howie started. "As I said earlier, I don't think this a poorly scripted Hollywood action flick hand-built to spoon-feed the American masses. It's our life. There is some crabapple shit going on, yeah, and I — it shakes me to think about this one, but I am falling in love with the idea that when you Flash, it's the real deal. Some true blue world-hopping craziness. Not just that you do it, but others do the same thing as well. That's some madness to accept, you know?"

Part of me wanted to tell him he should try living it, but I didn't. It's not like my life wasn't splashing all over him and his life. I suspect he had lost or turned down more opportunities than I could ever know to be my friend. It choked me up a bit, and I struggled to change the subject. Then, finally, it hit me.

"Howie, this is going to sound like shit or an afterthought, but Alice's pregnancy ... anything?"

Howie smiled, looking up at the ceiling. "I was afraid of saying anything too, not wanting you to think I had short-shifted things on that end. But, yes, I have a lead. You sure you want to talk about it right now?"

"Is there a better time?" I retorted.

"True, too true. Well, dear Alice frequented a fertility clinic before-hand. I don't have the timeline figured out yet, but a clear enough line exists between her going there and announcing she was pregnant. I just still can't put Dereck in the equation to figure out the why."

"Well, balls." My brain was spinning. This pile of shit kept getting deeper and deeper.

Forty-Two

The boar was waiting for me in the darkness when I grew aware. The stress from earlier had not faded, but something about seeing the boar and thinking that everything was real — really real, not imaginary just hit home. I pondered on that until I realized the boar was upset.

It was obviously not a master of emotions since I could read the anxiety and worry the boar exuding without much effort. I lit the image of On-Raze, coming alive to its eyes, and asked, "What worry weighs on you so?"

"Ancestor!" The boar squealed, snorting as it lumbered to its feet, boar features lighting up in happiness.

"For you to wait upon me here, it must be something."

Happiness slipped away to fretting. Snorting and shuffling, the boar said, "Ancestor, it has been months since we last spoke. I had worried over your long sleep."

"I've slept for long periods before. Why should I be worried this time?" Based on my estimation, we should be close, if not within the bowl of the mountain that the Call set as the boar's destination.

The boar grunted several times. "We are getting closer to home. I've met many other boars that are returning, heeding the Call for the gathering. Among them are three that also have had an Ancestor awaken."

Competition? Or, rather, someone that could call me out? Damn. I couldn't help but ask, "And ...? Does that trouble you?"

Shaking his head and squealing, the boar said, "No, Ancestor. The more Ancestors that wake up, the better for all of us Olgavelli. Having four Ancestors awake means our people can be powerful and strong." The boar then went on and on, describing what the Ancestors looked like in the other boars. It tickled me that they were color-coded. One, by his description, was rust red, the other speckled with white, and the last near pitch black.

The boar saying Olgavelli over and over again ... now that I think about it, that was the name of the boar's ... race, I guess. It still looks like a big pig to me. Hard to think of the boar in any other way.

"What are their names?" I asked.

"Ancestor Teleuichi, the Crimson Sun. Ancestor Invarog, Star Caller, and Teacher. Ancestor Beryellas, Eater of Undead, He Who Gnawed the Winds."

Wow. I thought I was a bit extravagant in names. I'm not sure what all that is supposed to mean. How do you get a title like that? Eater of Undead? The visual it conjured looked disgusting. I grunted in response to the boar's naming of the Ancestors.

The boar hesitated and then said, "A few moons past, all the other Ancestors appeared, speaking through the boar's blessed with their presence. It seems they had been talking to one another and were curious about you, Ancestor. I told them you slept a lot, only coming out sometimes instead of constantly being aware like they are."

Oops. That seems dangerous. I have no desire to be forced to swap tales with three old bastards who were the real deal. I had sweated the previous brush with the Ancestor that I ran into on the inside of the boar's bloodline.

"Good. I tire easily. What attention I have, I would rather spend on you."

The boar looked proud, letting out a series of snorts and squeals. "Ancestor, you spoil me, and I appreciate it."

"Hmph. You had best."

The boar conveyed what I guess was a smile or whatever goes for that if you are a boar. The boar then became a bit more subdued and said,

"The other Ancestors asked that when you awoke that you would seek them out."

I let smoke trail from the nose of On-Raze and bluffed, "I'll consider it."

The boar nodded and acted like my response to the request was expected. "The other Ancestors asked about my past, what had happened, and about you. I gave them your name and told them of your glorious past. They were confused and could not place you, saying that you must be old, ancient even to them."

That's one explanation I should have thought of already. It seemed like as good of an excuse as any, so I nodded. Considering this might be real, who honestly knew?

The boar squealed loudly, slipping from mildly downcast all the way back to happy again. Of course, if the boar were human, I'd have already labeled him as bipolar.

"They asked of my past, and I told them how you had helped me, taught me, and even saved my life more than once, manifesting in the battle that time with me, and even rebuilding my entire form to look more like your own. But the other Ancestors did not respond to the story as I expected. Ancestor Invarog cursed you, saying you had burned the kindling of your life force to do that. He swore and said you were shortsighted, not seeing or remembering the whole reason the Ancestors chose to give their lives to the Olgavelli. That your life force was much more important than any single one of the Olgavelli, no matter how beloved."

I couldn't help but bristle at the comment. That meant On-Raze's image lit up too, exploding into flames. I conveniently pushed aside the point that Invarog was actually the boar's Ancestor. In my mind, it didn't matter. Who the hell was he to tell me that I could not save the boar. I was not too fond of the thought that the majority was more important than the minority or the one. Ages-old fucking discussion that was easy to justify when you were not that one or the minority getting the short end of the stick. I had lost Alice and was feeling picked on already in my world. Who the hell said they could kick me around here?

I could not help but ask angrily, "What did you say in response?"

The boar snorted, both scared and angry. "I cursed the Ancestor back. As an even older Ancestor, I said that what you did was not for him to judge. That only you could determine the worth of your actions."

I stared at the boar, caught between prickling irritation and astonishment. "How did the bastards take it?"

"Badly. I cursed an Ancestor. The rest of the Olgavelli was not sure what to do. Ancestor Teleuichi attacked me, catching me by surprise. Ancestor Invarog did something to seal away my power. Right now, I'm buried in the ground. They have not decided what to do with me."

I snorted. I might be a fucked up mess in the real world, but here it's not the same. The original Ancestor in the boar's body had given me all of its power, which wasn't slight. Furthermore, I had rebuilt the boar to feed in even more energy, so I was overflowing with enough juice to kick up a storm.

Ignoring the boar for a moment, I sensed his situation. The situation was like he said, he was neck-deep in earth physically, and his monster core shackled, bound in what looked like tiny stars revolving through different constellations. I didn't bother trying to puzzle them out but ate them. On-Raze was the creator and destroyer. It was time the other Ancestors got to meet him so they would back off.

I manifested around the boar in the earth, letting the fire of On-Raze's bristles grow so hot the ground disintegrated around him. I ignored the other boars that started running around, focusing on the three larger ones that rose and moved defensively. Part of me wondered if there was a link between size and power in these guys. It seemed like the bigger the boar, the significant their strengths were.

Well, in that case, let me show them how big On-Raze can get.

I manifested On-Raze separately, pulling him from around the boar. I expanded On-Raze until he crested the top of the nearby trees, dwarfing everything around. I let out a challenging snort at the three Ancestors, daring them to come forth.

The three boar's eyes changed, and they grew as well. They didn't leave their host but made them expand in size. Nowhere near the size I took on but easily doubled in bulk.

I could read the anger and confusion on their features.

I imagined attacking the Ancestors, smashing them down, and crushing them. To use them as a target to take out my anger and spite at the world. But, I also knew it was a bad idea, so I restrained myself instead.

I just stared them down.

We played the staring game for a while until one of them, the darkest one, blinked its eyes and spoke.

"Who are you?"

I looked at him with On-Raze's furnace eyes. I let my name and story rumble forth along with all my power.

"I am On-Raze. I drank the blood of giants to steal their flames. Swallowed the cores of dead worlds to have their weight. I sear enemies with my flames, ending them in ashes. Those that do not fall before flames, I trample beneath my hooves and cut them fore and aft with my tusks. I am On-Raze, the Eternal. My family shall never suffer in life and death, for I will rise and rise again to lead them to victory. Darkness cannot confine me. Death cannot hold me. Sleep can force me to bow down, but I always awake, again and again."

The Ancestors visibly shook. Two of them couldn't hold up under the strain of the power I was releasing. All the other boars had long fallen prostrate. Only Beryellas, the pitch-black one who initially spoke, still stood. Primarily because I could sense he was using the wind to keep his boar body from falling flat.

I couldn't help but spin more of On-Raze's tale, adapting it on the fly.

"I was ancient before the Olgavelli was more than a thought. My brothers and I felled the giants so the world would have a space for our children. When the stars rained from the skies, we ate them to keep the poison within from breaking the land. I chose to bow to sleep so it would not consume the destiny of our people. Do not measure me with your youthful understanding. I was hoary and aged before you were a spark. I am On-Raze. Of my brothers, only I still remain since I cannot be vanquished. I can only be made to rest. I am On-Raze. Who are you to me?"

The dark boar finally fell. I stared at the Ancestors again, until stubbornly, the three lowered their heads ultimately. Satisfied, I rolled back the pressure and returned to the darkness in the boar. I'm sure they wanted to speak, but I didn't care. Or dare to do so. One-sided, I could spin the story how I needed. If they started asking questions or lining that up with their knowledge of history, it could all fall apart.

I could tell the boar was talking, communicating with the Ancestors and the other boars. I ignored it to think. If this was real, then I needed to take it more seriously. I had been going through the motions for too long. While even I wasn't one hundred percent sure, I wasn't going to think it wasn't true. If I was going to take this role, I needed to think about how to do it.

Do you want an ancient Ancestor? I'll give you one.

An Ancestor filled to the brim with knowledge. I might not have much to my name, but I had a headful of past Flashes. That got me dwelling on past Flashes and what I knew about fighting, tactics, and the ilk.

The fugue nibbled at me, but I pushed it away. All my knowledge was scattered and incoherent. I accidentally brushed up against one of the crystal deposits and had a flash of chaotic memory. That sparked a thought, and I returned to the smaller space containing the Ancestor's original bloodline. While that Ancestor had dissolved many of the deposits when it transferred power, just as many remained. Enough to give me a conception and a framework to build on for my idea. Thinking of it as code, I got to work rebuilding, laying out, and organizing the information, infusing my scattered understanding and thoughts. Building something like but different from the deposits as a construct.

I kept at it until the boar returned.

"Ancestor, the others are quite apologetic," said the boar when we met. He suppressed his glee but somehow managed to convey it with his mix of snorts and squeals.

I grunted and said, "Forget it. Bullying children is no fun. Now, focus all your energy here."

The boar was quick to accommodate. I used the influx of energy flowing and built crystal matrices in the darkness space. It was exhausting, and the boar tapped out rapidly after trying to help me.

Continued at it, even after the boar left, and I could tell vaguely we were journeying again. I liked that since the Call brought in even more energy to take advantage of in my construction. It was going to be bold, but I liked it.

The work made me tired, and I pushed off the fugue many times before I finished. My attention was tattered and fragmented when I finally stopped the coding effort.

A coder lives and breathes code.

Give a coder a problem, and he writes code to fix it.

And writing code to fix the problem is precisely what I did.

The boar was resting, but I woke him up to come to the darkness space. Or, perhaps it was best to call something else in the future. The boar looked around at the crystal matrices in wonder. It was pretty magical. I had to admit tiredly. Like a glass structure in constant motion, it created endless geometric shapes as it processed and condensed the information the original Ancestor left, that I added, and anything inherent in the bloodline. I even figured out how to decode some of the mechanics of the Call. Then, I incorporated the information I discovered into the code of my new creation.

I walked the boar through how to interact with the crystal matrices, so it could access the information whether I was awake or not. It included visualization methods internally and, if the boar used energy, how to manifest ghostly images externally to teach. My coup de grace was the option to condense a pellet that the boar could expel and give to another boar to have it learn as well. That took a lot of effort to build but wasn't the most complicated thing. Ego and vanity took over at some point, and I created a visual history of On-Raze's story. I just couldn't help it. It took more than a bit of poetic license concerning the original story, but I think it was a pretty good yarn.

Flummoxed was not a big enough word to describe the boar's response.

Boars don't weep, or I suspect it would be in tears.

Fugue washed me away, but I felt a rare sense of accomplishment.

Forty-Three

If I had gotten unsettled after meeting Siobhan, connecting with the boar soothed me back to being functional.

Howie had been right.

We didn't know enough to start jumping at shadows and making moves. Even if I was convinced now that someone or something was out to get me, it made me nervous, which showed in my work, but I was on the tail end of reporting anyway. I had fired off the reports to Marlin that he had requested before I met with Siobhan. Marlin had come back with some changes that I managed to kludge through and get finished. I just needed him to do the final review, so it was off my plate.

I had more work in the wings, but I didn't want to do anything new at the moment. Nolan Randy, a name I had a hard time taking seriously, but it was the guy's actual name; he had called and emailed a few times. Nolan worked for the Auto-ISAC guys. In the past couple of years, we had many talks about cars, and he knew my interests well. Nolan trying to get ahold of me on the heels of the Tesla's wreck made me a bit suspicious of making contact back. I wasn't worried that he knew I had modified the car. Hell, it wouldn't be him calling if someone dug into that thorny issue. I'd have either the cops or Tesla's legal department putting a foot up my behind. Not Nolan. I was just uncomfortable, but Nolan was a bulldog. If I didn't respond to him at some point, he wasn't the type to let it go. We knew too many of the same people, and he would find a way.

"Immerlin, New email, to Nolan Randy, subject, long time, buddy, body greeting Nolan, first paragraph, Nolan, I've out of pocket at the moment. Maybe we can connect in a few weeks? The accident took a lot out of me, and I'm in heavy recovery and just doing the minimums until I feel better, standard signature. Send email."

"Email sent to Nolan Randy," Immerlin responded.

Hoping that curtailed his inquiries a bit, I went back to work on my own issues. I got up from my desk and walked over to the nest of monitors I had created. The problem with the artwork that Alice had collected was that it was too visual. It didn't lend to an easy transition to text for me to parse and analyze like I typically approached problems. The digital real estate I had between a couple of monitors on my work-station wasn't enough to see the breadth I needed. I had pillaged from every room in the house to move monitors into the front area. I had even pulled some out of storage. Hell, I even bought a few more. While it looked like shit, to quote Howie, it did let me finally see the way I wanted. It just took two dozen monitors to do it. Of course, doing the wiring for all of that made a nasty nest of cables, computers, laptops, and mini-computers — tied into Immerlin.

I had software processing the pictures I took to look for artwork that had text, symbols, or characters of any kind. That was building a list of artwork I needed to re-process. Unfortunately, the pictures I took before weren't sufficient in most cases to read the information I wanted.

Some of the inventory had already been data-mined. Between my own journals and what had been processed, I had already discovered some commonalities. Of course, matching up scenes like this isn't a simple process. Easy for the human brain, challenging for a computer one. Still, identifying language snippets and symbols wasn't as hard, and I had already discovered a couple where it matched in my journals and on the picture.

I was also compiling a list of people. It was a list of names, initials, or online personas that had created the artwork. Correlated with their works, I hoped to learn something. Like, if the people who painted, sketched, or made art that matched my own Flashes — whether they also Flashed. But, equally, I was a bit scared. I was fearful that I would make a list just to find they were all dead. That, alone, was a discovery I wasn't sure I wanted to know.

Still, I wanted to risk finding out that scary answer. I wanted to ask those people about what they wrote, sketched, and painted. See if they struggled with this happy slash horror situation as well. And yes, it is really both horror and happiness. No matter how much Flashing has ripped up my life, it has also opened up vistas and realms that I could not begin to imagine.

Which was the point.

I no longer wondered if it was my madness. If anything, settling that question relaxed something deep inside me that I didn't realize I was clenched. Maybe it changed something. I don't know. I didn't Flash last night, which made me wake up with mixed feelings this morning.

I missed the boar a bit. It was at a crucial point in its life. Thinking about how I might actually be making a change in its life made me want to be more involved than ever. It wasn't just an escape.

The thought took shape and wouldn't leave. I moved over to the one machine I hadn't sucked into my vortex of computing the artwork. My search from last night was still there. If I was going to build a legacy for the boar, I wanted it to be the best I could make. The wall of text was a bit daunting, but whatever. It held a litany of military texts, economics, laws, and too many books to count. I wanted to absorb everything I could and pass it on.

I had learned long ago that memorizing by rote didn't cut it for me. That's why I had a couple of self-hypnosis induction techniques to help. I really evolved them to remember all the details from my Flashes, but I found them beneficial when coding. I memorized millions of lines of code, sometimes doing this. Unless I constantly reinforced the memorization, it faded, but not completely. I fought and induced sleep the same way.

Slipping into the state I wanted didn't take long, and I stayed there until Immerlin pulled me out with an alert that Howie was calling. I accepted long enough to tell Howie I would call him right back. My bladder was killing me and wasn't going to wait. So after I got the bio break I needed taken care of, I returned Howie's call.

Howie picked up on the first ring.

"I'm at the fertility clinic. It took some work, but I got them to give me the records. Alice had an IVF procedure with an anonymous donor. No idea who. Not likely to find out, either."

I was baffled. Not hurt. Just confused. Hell, Alice having a child was beautiful. That's why her pregnancy pulled us together, even starting down a road to have my mother and I mend fences. I wasn't so crass to think Alice got pregnant just for that. She wasn't that shallow.

"I don't get it," I said.

"Me either," Howie responded. "Something in this equation is missing for us to understand what Alice had in mind. Not sure what was going on, other than having a child not with Dereck, it looks like."

"Yeah, I think so."

"I hope you are ready for this, too. Alice froze eggs, too."

I felt confused. "Wait, Alice had some of her eggs frozen?"

"Yes. Not sure about the details since the clinic was less forthcoming on this subject. I did gather that the procedure and storage were paid for and that Alice funded the full ten-year storage of her eggs. She also did the same thing to the sperm she used to become pregnant. It was frozen and paid for at the same time."

"I can't say that makes this less confusing."

"Same. But, get this. I am sending it by text. Look at this bank account number. I've been staring at Alice's financials, and this is not one of her known accounts. This bank account needs to be looked into, buddy. Maybe it can help tell us what's going on."

I looked at the account Howie sent. I didn't recognize it either, but I could chase it down. At least to the bank and go from there.

"I'm on it. Anything else?"

"That's not enough?" Howie asked.
"No, it's plenty," I responded. "Stay safe."
"You too."

Forty-Four

The boar wasn't waiting in the darkness this time. I slipped into the On-Raze image and moved around. It felt good to be back. I had worried for a slight moment that I wouldn't return. A quick check showed me that the boar was sleeping. I felt a bit awkward at first: the boar was in a pile of other sleeping boars, something that created an odd sense of feedback as they moved around. I cut off from the boar's sense and contemplated the matrices I had made for the boar.

I saw a couple of places where I could do better, so I tackled those. I multitasked simultaneously, incorporating the knowledge I had memorized in my world into visuals for the boar. You can't have human concepts dominating, you know. That meant changing things, casting them into situations that featured the Olgavelli boar people, not humanity. It was tiring work but satisfying. I continued until the boar appeared.

"Ancestor, you have woken up."

"Yes," I said, finishing off a visual from Sun Tsu's Art of War. I made it into something from a boar's perspective, of course. But, hopefully, it would be of use to the boar or future generations.

The boar looked around, a troubled air growing around it. "Ancestor ... I appreciate all the things you are doing for me. But, I'm ... worried."

That got my attention, and I stopped, lighting up On-Raze more brightly. "Why do you worry? What troubles you now? Have the other Ancestors caused trouble again?"

"None of those things, Ancestor."

"Then what?"

The boar settled down on its belly. "We are close to home, the origin of the Call. Everyone expects that I will be the one chosen during the ritual and that you will be the selected Ancestor. No one doubts you are the eldest and most powerful of the Ancestors awake. It only makes sense."

Maybe to you. What ritual? What does being chosen mean? How to ask for that information without tipping my hand. The boar must have got unsettled due to my silence.

"Ancestor?" He asked plaintively.

"I'm here," I said. Then it struck me how to do this. "Yes, I'm old, so old that I cannot remember the last boar before you. I sleep long periods. I've forgotten more knowledge in my sleep than the Ancestors know combined."

Snorting, the boar said, "I'm sorry, Ancestor. You have done so much for our people over the years between sleep. It was Ancestor Trwyd, who woke to Ascer the White Tusk that created the ritual. At the end of his rule, he created a way to define the next leader of the Olgavelli. I feel ashamed to say this, but not all the Ancestors are ... unified. The ritual ensures the strongest candidate for ruling the Olgavelli is chosen, but it also selects the greatest Ancestor."

I was feeling a sense of oddness from the boar. The boar was letting off an air that said it might be a negative thing while saying it was positive with his words.

"I see. Also, I feel you are not saying everything, too."

The boar was quick to apologize, snorting and squealing up a storm. Then, finally, the boar settled down and told me more.

"The Ancestor chosen during the ritual has their power amplified, as all Olgavelli, including each woken Ancestor, gives up a portion of their energy to them. The chosen Ancestor uses the power to revitalize their life-force so that they can live longer."

While I'm sure the mechanics were a bit more complicated, I got the gist of things.

"Why does this make you sad?"

"Ancestor, I can hide nothing from you. Yes, it makes me sad. But, to extend your life force is a good thing. I just ... will miss you."

"Is that so," I said, curious. "Why would you miss me? While I sleep, I always return."

"Yes, Ancestor," the boar said, dipping his head. "I fear the ritual will make that sleep very long. After all, it returns you to the bloodline to extend your life. I have asked many others, and they say the older the Ancestor, the longer the process takes. In some cases, the chosen and the Ancestor did not meet again."

My feelings were mixed. I had lived through many Flashes. Or, really died in a lot of Flashes would be more truthful. But, on the other hand, knowing this was another world made me want to leave a legacy even more than ever. Something of me left behind. This ritual sounded just right, though I was sad that I might not meet the boar again. It was a strange, wistful feeling I was not used to feeling.

I laughed, or more accurately, gave out a long, harsh snort.

"Look around," I said, lighting on fire and gesturing with my snout. "Do you think this is for show? That this matrix I have given you serves no purpose? I won't speak to the ritual, but I know my own heart. Ancestor Trwyd may have given the Olgavelli the ritual, the Call, and many things, but I give you more. This matrix is to give you all that I am, my memories and soul, so that it will always be around. Be at the edge of your snout to revisit, learn from, and treasure. Do you forget who I am? I am On-Raze, and I cannot be stopped. Even if I am scattered, I cannot be conquered. In death, I will live. In sleep, I will be here, with you and all the Olgavelli."

The boar snorted in response, squealing and dancing.

I added a final word to hammer it home.

"Forever."

Forty-Five

Any satisfaction I had from the night before in the Flash with the boar slipped away when I read the article that Immerlin had flagged for me to read when I woke up. It was long a habit to keep tabs on companies I had worked for and liked. Not only was it a source of new business, but I often had friends there. I was still groggy when Immerlin read off the headline but snapped awake fast enough when I heard the words' Inverse Voices'. I halted Immerlin and pulled up the news directly on a monitor on my workstation. I kept reading and re-reading the article.

An unknown assailant killed twelve Inverse Voices employees on Sunday, the latest and most egregious in a spate of deadly U.S. mass shootings, prompting the state's governor to ask: "What the hell is wrong with us?"

Authorities did not immediately offer many details or a possible motive for the shooting, which looks to have unfolded at 6:30 PM Pacific Time at the company offices on the fourth floor of the Angelico Building, in the heart of Seattle.

There was more to the article, but Howie returned my phone call and pulled me away from reading it over again.

After I read it off to him, Howie said, "Bret, isn't that the company you were working with?"

"Yeah, Howie, it was." I was stunned and a bit afraid. My gut was churning in acid, and my thoughts couldn't help but wonder if there was a link.

I heard Howie's fingers tapping like jackhammers. Mechanical keyboards. Howie loved them, though I don't have the same level of fandom for them. Finally, after listening to him type for a few minutes, I couldn't help but ask, "What do you think this means?"

"I don't know. Suspicious? Hell, yeah. Definitive, no."

I mulled over that, and we brainstormed together for a few minutes on the phone. I heard Howie's secretary in the background.

"Go back to work. Let me spin on this. I'll do some digging to see if anything extends to other people I have worked with recently or if something connects me to them that makes them something we should worry about. I'll keep you posted as usual."

"Fine. Be extra cautious."

"I will."

Not sure what to be cautious of, but now I was spun up. So that ... too many coincidences were starting to look like correlations to me. I'm not going to say that my working with Inverse Voices led them to murder kill employees there. That seemed too implausible.

Checking up on the status of other companies and people are I worked with on contracts in the last couple of months helped put that worry to rest. Still, it worried me, so I checked again, looking at mass murders and single versions, branching out for the last couple of months. I cross-checked with everyone I worked with or knew. Found out an associate that I hadn't talked with in years had died, but it was a natural cause. Only Inverse Voices and I had a nexus.

I plugged in some other thoughts and keywords, running searches locally and on the Internet for possible correlations. While looking through the data, a local search result caught my eye.

A couple of the creators attributed to the artwork that Alice collected showed up related to some of the stories that Inverse Voices collected. One or two I might have chocked up to just similar thinking, but the list continued to grow as my search churned through the notes from the artwork boxes.

I let that search continue and took the current list to look up those people. I crossed that with their status, finding several of them were dead. Not just passed, but a few had died in the last couple of years. It gave me a sinking feeling, but I learned not to act on partial information long ago. It wasn't enough to say it might be connected, but my intuition was screaming it mattered.

It seemed prudent to set up a separate search to populate a list of all known Inverse Voices contributors. It took a moment to do so, and I automated that to go to Immerlin to incorporate in the identification process of the artwork creators or notes attached to them.

A picture was firming up that some of these people had died in oddball or spectacular ways. One person had been frozen into a block of ice. Hit a refrigeration truck while driving a water delivery vehicle, somehow managing to rupture the nitrogen tanks and the water supply simultaneously. That combination, the lousy weather, and too many factors for me to calculate seemed to have created a situation where he got turned into a solid chunk of ice. It made my many close calls seem tame in comparison. Not to mention inspiring a total lack of desire to get in a car anytime soon.

I texted Howie on impulse. He responded, saying he was fine, though he sent questions marks when I included an ice cube emoji. So I sent him the article about the guy being turned into a chunk of ice and a note to talk about it later.

Picking up the search, I wondered how many more I would find.

Forty-Six

Night and sleep had arrived faster than I expected. I had a few successes and many more failures in my searches. Working helped keep my concerns at bay, so I went until I dropped out. I just didn't fight the onset of sleep as I did previously. Having something to look forward to, I mean really look forward to, made a difference.

The boar was shuffling, snorting, and squealing like crazy. I melded into On-Raze and said, "Be calm."

"Ancestor!" The way the boar snorted and squealed made me feel if he were human, he would be teary-eyed and have snot running down his face. "I wasn't sure you would wake up in time."

Had the boar already arrived at his home? Crap, I wasn't ready. There was a lot I wanted to bring back and put in the matrices. To experience. This ritual that the boar described sounded a little final to my ears, so I wanted more time.

"Has the ritual started?"

The boar looked somewhat embarrassed. "Yes. Long ago. I'm in the moment of solitude, where I'm to speak with the Ancestor and learn the ways of ruling and any other advice. But ... Ancestor has been asleep, so I have stayed here for several days now."

"I take it that is unusual? How long does it normally take?"

"Usually a day at most," the boar whispered.

"Hmph. It just means we have a lot to say."

"But Ancestor, we haven't said anything until now," the boar whispered.

I laughed. "True, but the Olgavelli don't know that. Now, tell me about things outside. What happens next?"

"Yes, Ancestor. After this moment of ... togetherness, we approach the stone. After a small moment of thanks to all the Ancestors, I ask for its recognition. It will light to show it acknowledges me. You merge with the stone and receive the blessing of life force so you can live longer to guide our people."

"I see." Well, not really. The ceremony seemed rather bland, frankly. But, if this was the last hurrah, then let's spice it up a bit.

"Listen to me. If we have kept the boars waiting, then we shall fix that. However, I do not want Olgavelli to think less of you, so I have a surprise for everyone as we move to the monument. Do not be surprised and just keep slowly walking. I want everyone to know and feel the majesty of On-Raze. For them to sense how privileged they are that I chose you."

The boar snorted, looking sideways uneasily at the compliment. I gave it a few more details to mind before connecting to its senses.

We were in a hollow, a combination of loamy earth, falling waterfalls, and crystal and reddish stone columns. I found the decoration intriguing, especially one gigantic stone that contained many whorls and arcs on its surface. The boar explained that each new leader would add a new scar to the rock's surface. Most were at the base, with a few halfway up the stone.

I found the idea exciting and touched it with my nose as On-Raze. I was surprised to realize the stone was actually the tip of a larger column of rock that extended deep into the ground. So deep that it connected what felt like was a thick artery of power in the earth. It made me realize that Ley Lines were probably a real thing in this world. A bit of additional focus and messing around made me realize I could affect it slightly. Not much, but I didn't need much. Especially given I could tell this stone linked into the Call of the Olgavelli.

I might as well begin here. I manifested On-Raze, wrapping the image around the boar. I instructed him to scar the stone. When he did, I seared the stone with fire. I adjusted some of the power flowing in the rock, directing it into the cut, creating a small circuit to fuel the fire to burn for as long as the rock existed. Unlike the other scars, no one would cut through the one we made without adjusting the power flowing into the rock as I did.

"Ancestor, is this okay?" The boar was stunned that his scar kept burning. In fact, he looked a bit upset by it.

I pulled away from his body and looked at it with him. "Oh, yes. It's more than okay. Are you ready to be a star?"

The boar looked at me quizzically, and I realized he didn't know what that meant. I was going to point but realized I didn't know the way out. So, in order not to feel stupid, I said, "Go. Walk out. Let's begin."

We moved past a serpentine wind of stone and crystal pillars to a giant grotto. The centerpiece was an enormous angular crystal stabbing towards the clouds on a small island surrounded by shallow water. Around that tiny island with the crystal were thousands of other boars, some like I expected, others in more exotic combinations, even a few that looked to be partially made up of one element or another, from fire to swirling rainstorm.

It was impressive enough that I almost forgot the plan. The boar made it a few steps before I jumped into action. Then, as the boar slowly walked forward, moving in what I guess was a regal step for a giant boar, I manifested On-Raze.

A low roar of snorts and squeals accompanied my appearance. It grew louder and louder as I stepped on air and started walking, growing as I did until I was nearly as tall as the grotto was high.

My goal was not to bully like before, so I did not unleash my presence. Instead, with each step, I left behind a moving visual, a movie, in total dimensions, color, and sound, telling the story of On-Raze. Each step showed a scene: On-Raze struggling to grow in a hostile world, his brothers and sisters dying so he could live. On-Raze battling the giants, falling and rising over and over, until he grew strong enough to drink their blood and tame their fire. The rain of stars from the void, the poisonous stars that fell on the land. His harrowing journey, full of pain and endless sorrow as he swallowed the stars so they would not poison the land. The mass of boars quailed in fear when On-Raze inhaled the void between the stars after that deadly silence fell from the sky to try and eradicate the world. The crowd of boars rooted for him when he battled Death to ensure the life of the Olgavelli. I wasn't sure how Death looked in the boar's world, so I kept it shadowy and hard to discern. It was defeated when On-Raze chose to breath it in, so it could not escape and slay the Olgavelli. From a moment of awe to outright explosions of squeals and snorts, the Olgavelli was completely caught in the tale.

In all the battles, On-Raze would not stay down. It was not that he did not fall. On-Raze did so, over and over again. What he wouldn't do, was stay down. Every time he was knocked down, On-Raze stood back up. He fought again. This cycle was the key that led to his victory time and time over.

The Olgavelli loved it, and the sounds of the Olgavelli boars rang out strong and loud, only quieting when On-Raze finally stopped. But, even then, he refused to fall.

He just stopped.

From gods to giants, On-Raze fought all foes of the Olgavelli. But, in the end, what he could not battle was the consumption of Providence. It required a sacrifice to refill the Providence that the boars had exhausted, and On-Raze chose to sleep so the Olgavelli could have a destiny.

In doing this, I realized that directing a movie is hard. It took a ton of concentration to orchestrate the scenes of On-Raze going to sleep, standing lonely but defiant with the boar's last steps in the shallow water around the giant crystal. When the boar stepped on the small island, I followed, shrinking to fit. Then, while he stepped forward to the angular stone, I stopped, and we turned to face the rest of the Olgavelli.

I didn't have to say anything. I just stood, silent and defiant, before the crowd. Let a heavy, ponderous moment weigh on the Olgavelli before I let On-Raze dissolve into ashes carried away by the wind.

The impromptu movie touched even me. I rejoined the boar, realizing the boar was weeping. I felt a need to comfort the boar and let the boar know I was still there. Finally, the boar took control of its emotions and rubbed against the angular crystal, cutting its skin and letting blood splash out. It continued around the crystal, anointing it with boar's blood.

That gave me contact with the crystal, which I used to probe it. But, perhaps I shouldn't have, since I found an incredible force present. One that completely pulled me out of the boar.

Like when I first touched the Call, I found that I could sense the multitude of Olgavelli. An image of On-Raze projected above the crystal. Tiny fractions of their life forces were flowing towards the On-Raze picture, and I could sense the crystal was burning like a sun.

The image I had created of On-Raze was slowly changing, becoming even more solid under the absorption of the life force. I also felt that it was separating from me, becoming something individual instead of something I was. It didn't feel painful or odd, just different. Senses faded along with the separation until nothing remained.

A thought from a million miles away wondered if I was dying. I didn't see any tunnels, wings, or lights, at least not until I opened my eyes.

The low light of the display on the monitor read 3:33 am. It was dark and quiet, like I felt inside. I didn't feel upset or even tired. Just ... strangely settled. Like something had changed, but I couldn't say what.

Deciding laying here wouldn't solve anything, I got up. Food, exercise, and coding would do the trick.

They always did.

Sadly, I didn't get there. The display blinked out, along with anything else I didn't have connected to emergency power.

That cut into the calm feeling I had, though it didn't entirely dispel it. I hid under my desk and tried to remember where I had put my actual phone. Immerlin must have been cut off when the power went out since it didn't answer me yelling for it.

Realizing I couldn't remember and had long cannibalized the damn cellphone to integrate with Immerlin anyway, I gave up trying to find it. The room felt oppressive, and I grabbed the granite paperweight that Alice had given me as a weapon. It felt solid in my hands, and I managed my way to the stairs. It was halfway up the stairs that I thought about using a tablet. That got me cursing, and I worked my way back down the stairs, rooting around until I found it.

Still not liking the stuffy and oppressive room, I used the camera for a flashlight and made my way up the stairs. I opened the door to the roof to the sound of gunfire. That freaked me out, and I hunkered down for a few minutes, shivering, dropping the tablet, sending it tumbling down the stairs.

I cursed the shooter and my luck. Not wanting to move, I crouched, waiting. The shooting sounded distant and moving, not direct at the house or me. I found bravery somewhere inside and crawled out on the roof under the solar panels. For some reason, the idea of going back down the stairs felt wrong.

I peeked around carefully, hiding behind and under solar panels, realizing that a couple of blocks around me was black. The power outage took out more than my house, which made me feel better for some reason. But then, gunfire rang out that sounded close. Each time it did, I froze, waiting for it to end.

Piecing out the pattern to the gunfire seemed impossible I couldn't help but look for it. I had a savage thought growing that maybe someone had come for me.

I hoped I was wrong.

Forty-Seven

"It's time," the ice-eyed woman thought, touching the electrical pole. Frost spread from her hand, snaking up the electrical pole to the lines. It circled around the power lines like a cuff, turning alternate directions with jagged, icy teeth until it severed them. The power flickered out around her and for several blocks.

That was unfortunate. I had only wanted to affect one house, she thought, looking toward the multi-story house nestled in the several block radius that had lost power. Ice eyes flashing, the woman stepped forward but dodged before she finished, just turning her body enough to let the bullet hit her in the shoulder instead of the chest. It spun the woman around, and she kept enough clarity to turn the wet ground into ice that she could use to slide into cover behind a car. More shots peppered the vehicle as she did.

In another world, she knelt behind a chunk of ice she had conjured from the water moisture in the air. The clouds that lingered were heavy with moisture, making the action trivial to perform. A long-fingered, angular steel blue hand pulled the hardened wood splinter from her equally hued body, letting a spray of bright purple ichor leak from the wound before freezing it solid.

More wood needles flew at her, and she dodged and conjured more ice blocks to avoid them. It was a strange dance, her leaping and moving on the clouds, occasionally springing off the tops of buildings that protruded. Even with her oddly geometric body, it looked exotic and beautiful. The angular woman could not see her foe, just hear the giggling of small children and tiny footsteps. That made retaliating difficult, not that she didn't keep freezing portions of clouds, send sleet-filled showers raining down, or send icy spikes flying in different directions.

It was a strange entanglement, spread between two worlds. Then, finally, one of them broke the silence.

The first to speak was the angular woman wielding ice. Her features were an extended version of a person, making her head very narrow and diamond-shaped. The lips were gash that uttered, "This is pointless."

"Not really," came the subdued response, full of bell tones and punctuated by the queer giggles of invisible children.

"How about we share?"

"What, we split him down the middle and all. So you get a leg and arm, and so do I?"

"You know what I mean. Why be obtuse?"

That seemed to set off a crowd of giggling, invisible children. The gentle bells responded, forming words. "Lack of choice. My lack. Ogygia cannot succeed in this world."

That statement sent a moue of disgust across the elongated pointed features. It also prompted a star-shaped projection of ice around her. One that trapped and froze several small doll shapes. They fell into the clouds after she snapped the ice into shards. It also got her a wooden dart in the leg, which she pulled out and cast to the side, freezing the wound shut.

"You are not strong enough to stop Ogygia. In this world or the other one. We both know that. Just like we know, you cannot win against me. You know this."

"I do. Sure do. I'm not trying to win."

"Then why bother? Are you trying to delay? Good luck. Who is going to help you? Who hasn't died between the two of us?"

"Allies come in all shapes."

"Is that so," came the angular woman's reply. Her ice eyes flashed, and she said, "So, you have allied with the Edolin See? Not the ally I would have expected."

Another star-shaped projection of ice killed off more dolls. It earned the woman a wooden dart in return. Plucking it free, she said, "Are you truly expecting the Edolin See to enter this fight? I've killed them. I exterminated all their allies. Well, except for you, it seems. As we speak, the battle in Ogygia rages to show them that we own this world, not them. Return to the fold. I can forgive your intransigence this one time. After all, you have helped me clean up some rats as well. In the ashes, why not take over? I will be returning to Ogygia when this is over, after all. Then, you can direct things in my place."

The giggling started up again, the dolls tramping through the clouds toward her. The bells rang sadly. "You make it sound so simple."

"It could be."

"But it isn't," the bells said, among the giggling. Instead, more ice exploded, freezing dozens of dolls, more wooden darts to pluck out of steel blue flesh.

"Then you can die."

The bells rang.

"I will. So, too, will you. Did you think either of us was free? Did you think that claiming the Paradigm for yourself wouldn't be noticed?"

Back in the world, behind the low stone wall, the pale woman sent a snaky trail of ice across the ground and up the walls of nearby buildings. It gave her a blurry but decent enough view of the area, as she used it to look around. A bullet ricocheted off the stone wall, sending powdered fragments flying. She dusted them off her clothes then frowned when the powder clung thickly to her fingers. She stared at her hand in dawning horror and looked across worlds.

In the clouds, she stopped being defensive, sending an immense explosion of ice in all directions, entombing everything. Nothing was spared, extending beyond her sight in all directions, even freezing the buildings far below the clouds.

She swam through the ice before she came to the wisp of green locked in ice. She stared at it, and it stared back. Then, in two worlds, she said, "I'll kill you. Don't think you can escape debt."

In both worlds, the wisp spoke back. "And I, you. You won't harvest the Paradigm."

"You fool," the ice-eyed woman said, shaking her head. "If you die here, how long can you survive there? Unless you harvest the Paradigm, you won't survive in that world. But you can't, can you? I can see the binding on you on here, which means it exists there, as well."

"Does it matter?"

"Not really. I'm just thinking you are talking too much."

"Yep." The ice around the wisp puckered, turning inky and black. The ice woman surged away, swimming the ice to escape the spreading inky ooze, her attempts to sever the inky ice from her ice failing. It moved faster, surrounding her in inky ooze. The ice woman shielded herself with layer upon layer of ice, cursing as she did. Eventually, the black-coated ice fell through the clouds, just like her equally bloating form fell to the iced mud in the other world.

A bullet followed shortly afterward, striking her fallen body in the head. Then a couple more rang out, hitting the body. Like the shooter had to make sure she would stay down.

An ashen-skinned woman slowly limped over to look over the body. She leaned against the wall and slid down, eyeing the body the entire time. The movement broke open wounds that were otherwise frozen, causing her to start bleeding heavily. She touched the blood with her fingers and giggled. The sound slowly trailed away, and she motioned tiredly with one hand. A small doll trotted over, letting out the tiny sound of bells, looking like a miniature version of the woman. It had a cell phone strapped to its body as if it was carrying a backpack.

Sirens wailed in the background as she touched its head with a bloody hand. Its eyes changed, becoming life-like while her own eyes dulled.

The doll said, "You know what to do." Then it left, walking away into the yard, leaving behind the woman, who slowly raised the gun in her hands.

Forty-Eight

The banshee wail of sirens replaced the harsh sound of gunfire. It wasn't any less unsettling, and it unnerved me more than the gunfire. I headed back to the stairs and heard the tablet buzz. After a couple of buzzes, I realized it was an incoming call.

Picking up the tablet, I didn't recognize the number but accepted. I didn't know my neighbors, but some of them might be nice enough to check on me.

Especially given someone was shooting up the place right outside.

The voice that came through was pitched like a child. What it said threw me for a loop.

"Hello, Bret. Lucky, lucky, Bret. Why are you loved more than me?"

That freaked me out, so I hung up. I don't care who that is. I'm not going to listen to that — some damn freaky girl voice.

The voice didn't stop talking, which made me throw the tablet. It made a decided crack when it smashed against the fall, and the screen flickered out.

"Now, don't have a tantrum. Does your mind really not have space for something as odd as a voice talking to you out of nowhere?"

This was not the usual brand of nuts that I had just decided was not crazy but real, so I wasn't sure how or even if I should answer. The stairwell didn't seem like a suitable place to stay, so I went back to the room.

The voice went on.

"This is not how you treat a lady, idiot. It's probably why you are still single. Going back to your room isn't going to help, by the way. In fact, if you don't learn to walk out your front door, to break past your normal limits, you will forever be the prey, waiting for the hunter to come and harvest you. The next meal for the hunter's table."

The statement made me pause with the door open to the room and the stairs to the roof behind me. The voice had followed along, like it was right next to me, though I couldn't see it. I was creeped out but not panicking. Not sure why. Just felt that I didn't need to. That some of the majesties of On-Raze lingered, telling me it should be me, not the other way around. Plus, I might just be talking to myself.

"Who are you?" It was all I could think to say.

"Not a bad question to ask and completely fitting for the situation. Let's say I work with QVD and that she and I have a deal. A bargain."

QVD? Like the lady who made a good number of the art pieces that Alice collected? I couldn't decide what that meant, except I needed more information.

What did the two of them having a bargain means, and was it connected to the gunfire I had just experienced.

"Can you tell me what's going on? Was that you out there, lighting the streets up like you were playing a game of Grand Theft Auto?"

That got me a giggle. It sounded youthful, childish, like her voice. Creepy, too. Real fucking creepy. I could feel the goosebumps rising on my arms.

"You think I actually know everything and can just dish it up for you on a platter? Please. I have even less freedom to act and speak than you do. Though, you wouldn't be wrong in that I was the one with a gun tonight. Lucky you. Otherwise, it would be a cold ending for you."

"I don't understand what you mean, who you are, or even what's going on. I'm thankful that you didn't shoot at me, but I'm not sure why that makes me lucky other than for the obvious reason. I like my body without bullet holes, thanks."

"Poor Bret. You had better get smarter. Stronger. Better. Not getting shot at is the least of your problems. By the way, do you know how much I want to eat you up right now? You smell so good. Like the atypical virgin in the story with a bag full of gold. So yummy ... and so totally unprotected. You are not even a tiger in disguise. More like a kitty cat just wide open to anyone with a nose to find you. You need to fix that. Learn how to protect yourself."

I found her words both terrifying and annoying. Part of me wanted to run while the other part wanted to slap her. If I could see her. If she wasn't a disembodied voice talking to me. Who I was praying on one level wasn't a delusion of mine. Even if that meant some scary thing really existed instead. What burst out was what I was thinking versus what I should have said. Damn, this mouth was getting me in trouble.

"So, you are here to what, mock me? I'm lucky to not fall apart on any given day. Protect me? Against what? Also, why bother to taunt me with this shit, anyway? Are you supposed to be the calvary?"

"Were you expecting a sugar momma teacher to help you get stronger? Do I look like your mother? Also, what do you think I just did? So, yes, I am the cavalry. Not that I wanted to be. Allowed to act, I would have eaten you completely instead of fighting that cold bitch. I would have taken your authority for myself. Not like you have the slightest understanding of the valuable, amazing thing you hold. You fucked it up once. I suspect you will fuck it up again this time."

What did I mess up? "I haven't a clue to what you are talking about, Miss disembodied voice. Why don't you come here in person?"

"I wish I could. Instead, I have this chat with you with my last bits of energy. That's okay. I know what's on the other end. Unlike you, you poor, poor fool. Grow up before you become someone's dinner. That's the advice I'll leave behind for you. Consider it my only and most effective teaching. That and you really should learn the Eschatos Diagram."

Fearing that meant she was leaving, I couldn't help but explode out a lot of questions.

"Eschatos Diagram? What is that? What does it do? Who is QVD? Why does she see the same things I do? Are there more people? What's really going on? Is someone trying to kill me? What is —"

"Dear boy, shut up. I'm not going to answer any of those questions. Figure it out or die. Plus, allow a woman her frailties. Her mysteries. I don't have much time left, so allow me to leave you with this little mystery. After all, expectation and a sense of mystery are what gives a woman her charm. It would help if you thought about that, now and then. Maybe consider a visit to your sister's grave, even."

I shouted out more questions and waited, but no one answered. So finally, after expressing some frustration, I went back inside. Digging around, I found Immerlin and realized he had come back on at some point. I accessed his recordings and had him playback the last hour.

When I heard the voice again, it released a quivering tension inside me that I didn't realize I had. After muttering and laughing like an absolute crazy man for a few minutes, I called Howie. He had been trying to contact me, but Immerlin did not take non-emergency services calls when he was in low power mode like this. Something I planned to fix after this was said and done.

Howie was already on his way over. He was in his car the minute I told him the power was out, and someone was shooting in the neighborhood. I told him it would probably be crawling with police and emergency vehicles. While he drove, I played the recording Immerlin made. He was freaked out enough that he almost wrecked. Especially when I said I wanted to go to Alice's grave. He couldn't believe it.

"Some magical voice tells you to go there, and you are just going to do it? Really? You, Bret Byrne, are going to leave your house and go to a public place voluntarily? Did she cast a spell on you or something?"

"No, she didn't," I retorted. "But we don't know anything. Nothing! If this can let us figure out something more, then I think we should do it."

"I'm pulling up to the police barricades. You listen to me. Let's talk about it. No matter what, I'll support you. But you have to let me go first. Make sure it's safe. Then, if I can't find this magical thing that you don't know what it looks like or even is, we can talk about you going there. Promise me that."

"Okay." I didn't mind promising. I didn't love the idea, but it wasn't giving me giant surges of anxiety — like usual. Who knows, maybe something positive would come out of this ball of crap.

"Alright. I've got to get off the phone to convince the police to let me get to your house. Later."

"Yeah, Howie," I said, even though he had already killed the call. My mind was spinning in every direction possible. Maybe it was time to fall forward. Alice used to always talk about falling forward. She said I kept falling, but I just had to remember to fall forward. That way, even face planting moved me a bit closer to the goal. The problem was, I wasn't sure what the plan was now, except maybe not dying. This hadn't done anything to calm my mind, but it sure had it spinning.

Forty-Nine

My hands were shaking, but the nausea I expected hadn't returned. We only had to stop twice to let me vomit. Overall I considered it a win, given I was without all my regular soothing items and in a strange — Howie's, but still not mine — car, sitting at the cemetery.

Howie was gone. He made me wait while he went to check it out. I think Howie didn't believe me when I said I wanted to go in person. When I actually got in the car, even if I did vomit not long afterward, he was genuinely astonished. I'm glad it ended up being days later. I'm not sure I could have done it otherwise.

The discovery of the two bodies and their apparent battle spread across several blocks had the cops talking to everyone. That had been incredibly hard to do, even with Howie's support. The cops were not accommodating at all, or at least the one that came to the door wasn't. I struggled through it and said what I knew, which wasn't a damn thing. It took the police two days to clear the road to allow traffic. My poor neighbor down the street basically had her backyard completely ripped up and put into those little police bags that you see in the movies.

The tablet in my lap buzzed, signaling an incoming video call. It was Howie, and I accepted. His face came into view. I could see the sky behind his head.

"Bret, I've looked around but don't see anything that shouldn't be present. You want to look still?"

"Yeah. Pan your camera around."

Howie flipped the camera and slowly turned one way, then another, taking in the landscape in all directions before returning to focus on Alice's headstone. It was a nice one, in white and black. The Yin Yang symbol Alice loved was carved above her name and the dates that spelled out her time on this earth. Seeing the end date to her life made the tablet shake. I breathed in deeply, trying not to let it unsettle me. Howie realized I was trembling — probably because the video was all over the place for him because of it.

"You okay, Bret?"

"I'm good. It's good. That's a nice headstone. Thank you."

"I did my best," Howie said, returning the camera to his face. "I don't think there is any reason for you to come here. I don't see anything. Did you?"

I shook my head. "Probably not. I do like the flowers. That's a nice touch. I didn't see you bring them."

Howie paused, and I saw him look downward. Probably at the headstone. He looked back, face a little odd. Then, pursing his lips, he said, "Hold on." The camera flipped around again, focusing on the headstone. I heard Howie's voice ask, "What flower did you like the best?"

That struck me as odd since they were all white. But, of course, I'm not an idiot and realized that something was off. "You can't see them, can you?"

"Nope."

We both were silent when he said that. I stared through his camera for a minute, looking at the flowers lying in a bouquet on the grave.

"I need to go there. To see it directly."

Howie was understandably alarmed and switched the camera back to his face. "I don't know if that's wise. I mean, effectively, you are seeing something that I don't. I don't like that and feel it's unsafe."

That made me laugh. It eased some of the tension. "I know, I know. But, hell, who knows, the flowers might turn out to be something that eats both of us or chokes us on pollen. Who knows? I just don't think it's like that."

"Based on what?" Howie asked, incredulous. "Too much strange shit is happening for you to rule out anything."

"Hmmm, not really. Think about everything that's happened. The childish voice — that might have been some tech that you and I just can't detect. The two women and those people at Inverse Voices were shot, not eaten by some Lovecraftian beast. If we lay it at this unknown organization's feet, even my car accident was because another car forced us to collide. You know my suspicions, there."

The video paused, and I heard him taking a couple of pictures. "Look and see if you still see the flowers in these photos. I'm curious if there is a difference between the video and a still picture."

I looked. Still there.

"Yeah, I see the flowers."

Howie shook his head. "I don't see them, though. That's wrong, Bret. Very wrong. I might believe some sly technology is behind what you mentioned — the voice, the car, and so on. This, though, this — the flowers present that only you can see and I cannot — this ranks up there with the artwork that shows knowledge of your Flashes. Especially those that really hint that the artist was either present or had a scene described where you were also present, just in a Flash. That's not a co-incidence. I'm not going for causation yet, but I'm fast getting there. It's enough to correlate that you, and likely other people, experience other worlds together. At least to me. Add to that this mystery voice that said to come to Alice's grave and you seeing flowers where none look to exist — I'm weirded out. You can't tell me this is technology. It smacks of magic."

"Do I need to quote Arthur C. Clarke to you?"

"No," Howie said with obvious disgust. "I know it as well as you do. Any sufficiently advanced technology is indistinguishable from magic. Blah, blah. I get what you are saying, but are you listening to it? Put this in perspective — I mean, why not, since we are on the phone in a graveyard. Say this is technology, some type of technology well beyond what you and I know, at that. They — some unknown, definitely present something, possibly some deep state, shadowy group — god, this is going all kinds of Hollywood conspiracy shit — are pulling you and others, its reasonable to say into other worlds when you sleep. Not as a dream but as an actual transfer of consciousness. That's amazing and powerful and crazy. Let's put aside that no one asked for permission or that it's been happening since I've known you, which is pretty much, what, since you were four? Three years old? It's been destructive, dangerous, and harmful. Your family was ripped apart over it. You were consigned to a damn hole, drugged and incarcerated until I could dig you out. It's —"

"Howie, calm down. I'm the crazy one, not you. Take a breath, dude."

He took a couple of deep ones. It sounded labored, so I knew he was distraught. "Howie, something is going on. Yeah, it's been ugly and hard. I know it. Not just on me. I'm selfish but not blind. This mess that's my life has taken its toll on all of us. The idea that it is caused by someone or something drives me mad. Funny, huh. Being potentially made mad is driving me mad?"

Howie spit. "That's horrible, buddy. Horrible. Terrible, horrible, and if this were Reddit, I would upvote you right now. That's balls. But it's not Reddit. It's life. Maybe you walk over here, and nothing happens. Maybe that Lovecraftian beastie shows up. I don't know. I just know this is a bizarre situation, and there are many dead bodies piled up tangent to it. That alone is blowing my mind right along with elements of this connecting back all the time to Alice. I can't see the link. I don't understand the situation. As a lawyer, that's unconscionable. As your friend, no way I want you to be at risk."

"What, do I go home and sit in my house and wait? Wonder if this might be a clue? Choose to put my head in the ground and hope for the best?"

Like a good lawyer, Howie argued with logic. "No. You go home and work on understanding the information in the material that Alice left behind. Link it to her records and then cross-index that with what you know about all the murders. Analyze. It's what you best. Me, I go and buy the swankiest, badass security system I can for your place and mine. See what private security I can scrounge up that isn't a ripoff. Those kinds of things."

"I want to retort and say that's all a pile of crap, but you are not wrong. We need to do those things. We don't know enough, and because of that, we are losing. Failing. Falling short. Which is why I have to go over there. We can't afford to give up even the smallest clue."

I popped the door to vomit. Howie yelled at me from the tablet. Wiping my mouth, I told him I would see him in a minute and killed the video chat. Sliding my legs out of the car took a couple of tries. Moving them felt like moving giant trees, even if they were nothing but my normal toothpicks for legs.

A jacket, even though it was hot — pods for my ears and requisite calming music. A hat, for no reason other than it seemed to fit.

I made it a couple of steps before Howie showed up. He propped me up when I staggered. Like he always did.

Together we walked towards my sister's grave.

Then, finally, it was time to see what clue we would uncover.

Fifty

Distracted, my eyes darted over the sketch I had made of the flowers on the grave. It was on the wall next to my other pictures and sketches from the Flashes. It was the only one I had made in this world. It felt strange to say that, but it was true.

I pushed away from the desk and walked over to the wall of pictures, leaving behind the work I was doing to reach out to prospective clients. It had been a couple of days since the cemetery, and I had shivered under the blankets enough. More legal hassles had tied up any money I might take from the trust Alice set up. Dereck just wouldn't rest but had to live up to the devil image he portrayed.

My fingers touched the flowers on the grave in the sketch. I shivered because, under my fingers, I could feel the soft texture of flowers versus paper. It made me lift my fingers and flick them, trying to remove the disturbing sensation.

It made me recall what had happened when I arrived at the grave. The flowers that Howie couldn't see that I could. I sketched them so that he could see them. Then, after much debate between the two of us, I reached out to take them.

They withered at my touch.

I freaked out, and Howie dragged me away. No matter how much I urged him, he would not relent and let me return. Eventually, I gave up. And I gave in to Howie's insistence that I get a complete exam done. We settled on Malika and a full-body scan. Everything came back fine, thankfully.

What I didn't tell Howie when I touched the sketch or any sketch I made of the flowers: I could feel them. I didn't know what to make of it or what the child's voice meant with the flowers. I had listened to that recording over and over. Immerlin and I spent a lot of time digging on the Internet for anything linked to what she said. Not a lot of what came back made sense. At least, to me.

Only one thing came out of it that I latched on — the Eschatos Diagram. I found a sketched image of stars and pathways linking them after combing through reams of crap posted by people who played games and equal amounts of religious or philosophical equivalents. Some pictures from the Internet, but the real discovery was in the mass of art, papers, and manuscripts Alice left behind. The sketch had no clues other than the words Eschatos penciled on it. I put it on the wall with different pictures as potential associations, mainly some constellation maps and star landscapes that I thought might make sense.

Chasing down more of the artwork had led to a disturbing list of dead people who made fascinating art. Plenty of the creators were alive, and I had a long list of fake accounts talking to the few who would respond over the Internet. Not a lot of leads there yet, but I had hope. Same for the ones that were dead. Some of them died in various bizarre ways, too. I wasn't the only one who was watching this pattern, either, come to find out. I found a subreddit where a couple of profiles aggressively pieced together information linked to the artwork and the people who made it. I made a new account and joined and was mainly siphoning information they posted, with an occasional comment, so I didn't get kicked out.

QVD. If there was one person I wanted to find more than anyone else, it was her. Who was she? Of the information I knew, she and I had the most likely chance to be in the same boat, experiencing Flashes. Plus, she was connected to the child's voice, or at least the voice alleged that was true. It was another conundrum. She implied that she was the female serial killer who shot those people at Inverse Voices and other places. If so, she was the person who died a few blocks from my house.

Right next to Dr. Escarra. From what I could puzzle out, they had essentially killed one another. That didn't make sense to me — their deaths. No more than magical flowers invisible to everyone but me — ones that disappear at a touch — do either. All of it pointed to something sinister. It looked like house cleaning. A horrible way to say someone killed a lot of people that were linked to this company. Two of them died a very short distance away, too. So far, I had avoided the police on that topic, but I wouldn't be surprised to have another policeman at my door asking about it someday. Like me, they are not going to believe it was a coincidence.

Howie and I had strategized what to do. Howie had everything I had done for them, including all contacts, work, and information that I could provide. If it looked prudent, we would give that to the authorities. If it didn't, we would hold off. Neither of us wanted to invite a third party into this current mystery.

Perhaps most agonizing was I had not Flashed for days now. It bothered me though it shouldn't. Flashes weren't always back to back. I never figured out the rhythm of it.

I considered too many things, making my head hurt.

Immerlin's baritone broke into my thoughts. "Incoming call from Ron Desantos."

That pulled me back to the present and out of my thoughts. Then, figuring I should answer, I said, "Accept on speakers."

"Bret." Ron's voice was subdued.

"Ron," I said back.

"No video today?"

"Not today, Ron. I'm pretty wiped out from the last train of events running over me."

"I understand. I almost didn't call but decided to ring you anyway."

"I appreciate that, Ron. I'm fine, however, and doing well. I expect to be back to my old tricks in a few weeks."

"That's good to hear. I ... well, hell, feel bad about what happened at Inverse Voices."

"Me too, Ron." Yeah, I'm a lot more upset and disturbed than I can tell you about that serial killing.

Ron coughed. Then, he asked, "Bret, did you and Dr. Escarra become close while working for Inverse Voices?"

That was an odd question. "No, not especially. Dr. Escarra was a ... distant woman. I had a few interactions with her, all professional. So why do you ask?"

He coughed a few times. "I wasn't sure. But, you know, she was killed not too far from your house."

"I'm more than aware. I've told the police everything I know about it, which is zero, zilch, nada. I don't have the slightest idea what Dr. Escarra was doing here any more than the police do. She did not come and see me or indicate that she would be in the area. Ron, you have seen me. I'm 100% not a ladies' man or her type, I suspect, by any stretch of the imagination. While I know it's the trend for geeky guys to be considered sexy, I don't have the chops, money, or charisma to pull it off."

Ron laughed. It was strained but contained genuine mirth. "No offense, man, but I couldn't see it either, but I wanted to ask. Plus, I always suspected she was not interested in people in general. Or, at least, men."

"While I don't feel up to speculating why she was here, I'm not so sure I would put it at the feet of a lover's quarrel or anything like that."

"I guess." Ron didn't sound convinced, but I suspect he was just trying to put it in perspective to deal with it. "It's just a bit out of the way. You don't exactly live in a mainstream location."

"I like to feel I'm just far enough from the hustle and bustle of the city but close enough to dip my toes in if I needed to do so. That's why my neighborhood has a lot of Airbnb rentals. I suspect more than one person likes that feeling, or at least to experience it. Perhaps that was why she was here, or maybe she owns property out this way. I don't know."

"Good points. I hadn't thought of that," Ron said.

"Ron, I'm a bit tired. I'm sorry to run you off, but I think I will need to. If you need something from me, I will be around in a few weeks."

He hurriedly said, "No problem, no problem. But, really, I wanted to check on you. If you are open to work in a few weeks, I have a new project I would love your assistance on."

"Perfect."

We disconnected, and I made a few notes. Then, feeling a bit of fatigue, I laid down. Incomprehensible in the past, but a habit I was starting. I had a feeling my answer lay not just in this world but in the worlds that unfolded in the Flashes.

"Immerlin, time, 30 minutes. Standard wake up music."

His baritone responded. "Acknowledged."

I got comfortable. Let my eyes close, and the darkness enter. Starting to fade, I almost felt like I was part of something greater.

True or not, I looked forward to finding out instead of dreading what was to come.